100
YEARS
SIMON &
SCHUSTER

Also by Cebo Campbell

Violet in Some Places

SKY FULL OF ELEPHANTS

Cebo Campbell

SIMON & SCHUSTER

New York London Toronto Sydney New Delhi

Simon & Schuster
1230 Avenue of the Americas
New York, NY 10020

First Simon & Schuster hardcover edition September 2024

Simon & Schuster: Celebrating 100 Years of Publishing in 2024

For information about special discounts for bulk purchases, please contact Simon & Schuster Special Sales at 1-866-506-1949 or business@simonandschuster.com.

The Simon & Schuster Speakers Bureau can bring authors to your live event. For more information or to book an event, contact the Simon & Schuster Speakers Bureau at 1-866-248-3049 or visit our website at www.simonspeakers.com.

Interior design by Wendy Blum

Manufactured in the United States of America

1 3 5 7 9 10 8 6 4 2

Library of Congress Cataloging-in-Publication Data has been applied for.

ISBN 978-1-6680-3492-7
ISBN 978-1-6680-3494-1 (ebook)

For Riann

You can ask me a thousand times, in this lifetime or the next, and the answer will be the same: every day.

SKY FULL
OF
ELEPHANTS

1

THEY KILLED THEMSELVES.

All of them. All at once.

We unsealed the jails first.

Folks showed up swinging bolt cutters to liberate their lawless relatives into a world different from the society out of which they were exiled. Because no one stood guard any more. No longer could anyone be exiled from anywhere.

All banks closed down. Their silent, towering buildings became mausoleums, having been worshiped long enough.

Time slowed down too. Sauntered like hours did in places like Chattanooga and Charleston and Savannah. A notoriously southern phenomenon now spread like honey over everything. Ask the time and folks just looked up at the sky, mumbling, "Quarter 'til," because gone was the appraiser of hours into wages. Gone was the gaze evaluating for its resource every minute ticking inside a body.

They killed themselves. All of them. All at once. You could feel their absence in everything. On the subway. In the streets. In all the places the wild reclaimed. Where sunflowers grew through office buildings, over golf greens plagued red with ant mounds, where the earth crawled black up the sides of monuments, where all those Chihuahuas and cocker spaniels scavenged and begged in packs, their dog sweaters ragged, bedazzled collars dulled of sparkle.

They killed themselves. One morning, every white person in America walked into the nearest body of water and drowned.

Even now, on nearly every shore from southern gulf to northern sound, crosses stand like the skeletons of those old beach crowds. Water crushed in waves, lapped and babbled, unwilling to respect in silence what was otherwise a graveyard.

No one expected the event. No one was prepared.

Some people were angry, cursing God for doing the business of gods. Some were quietly contented, seeing the horror as penance. Some longed for the world before, settling into movie theaters to watch *Ferris Bueller's Day Off* and *Titanic*, sharing in the awe of misshapen memories.

Howbeit that we remained breathing on this earth at all, after such a thing, terrorized the conscience. Shame. Tortuously complex. Mornings came like a curse to be among those still waking up, even if rising to easy sunshine warm on the skin. Some nights were worse than others, some mornings better. A year later, Charlie couldn't say which emotion grabbed hold of him the morning he swiftly, and finally, pulled down all their photos.

He'd found himself a nice house out in the suburbs. Two stories tall with fat white columns and a skirt of porches. His front yard sparkled green except under the shadow of an oak where, innocently, a tire swing bolted to its arm whined on every breeze. His home, of course, added to the sum of thousands taken over as we hollowed out city tenements, spilling into the outlying neighborhoods of Germantown, Rockville, and Bethesda. To hear Al Green's voice drifting over aboveground pools out there wasn't uncommon anymore. Charlie, and he suspected many others, tried to keep the photos and memorabilia from the families who'd once owned the houses.

For his part, and for months stacked on months, Charlie kept the birthday cards and perfume bottles, jewelry, and golf clubs. He left portraits hung up on the walls and photobooth strips magnetized to refrigerators as a monument to their lives, hoping the solemn act might absolve him somehow. Maybe looking at all those blue and green eyes every day, those easy, easy smiles, might make him feel things he didn't.

But Charlie still felt what he always felt.

A husband in a suit, a blond wife, two children, and a yellow dog. Charlie did not want to know their names nor what became of their dog. When he finally took their pictures down, he did not cry. Wedged in a box, packed into the garage, Charlie put away every article in the house that made him feel as he did before all the oceans went from waving to wailing. Photos, of course, stuffed animals and unopened mail. He unstuck the souvenir magnets on the fridge making caricatures of Paris, London, and Rome. Even the small library of self-help and sci-fi books, which for him held together a watchful consciousness, he stowed deep in boxes. Anything that hovered and pulsed like memory got set aside. And when, at last, the house sat empty of character, quiet but for the crickets playing symphonies in the yard, Charlie could nearly convince himself he deserved that which he could never quite bring himself to accept.

Charlie had class that morning. The day would result in his third teaching lesson ever. And he wasn't awful at educating. His students eagerly arrived to his classroom and departed energized. Moreover, he did believe his lessons were deeply important offerings to this new world. The problem was, a year ago, the only books he read came from the prison library. Indeed, in his mind, under his cardigan and argyle socks, down naked as a hound puppy, he still wore prison's uniform. Couldn't shake it. The result, one so oddly unexpected, came when he looked around bewildered at his big house and green lawn and forward to all those students desirous to absorb what he had to teach. Him. Of all the good folks still living. One day he withered away in a cell, and the next he waltzed into a world without white people. From prisoner to professor. Bewildered. Bewildered and bewildered.

Charlie packed the last box into the garage, bit down on his emotions, and held them under his tongue the full commute to Howard's campus. Held his thoughts back until he stood at the door of his classroom, where they surfaced as a sudden anxiety. Afraid to go inside. Strangely, Charlie liked the fear. So often having to overcome that prick of terror, he'd learned to find nobility in enduring it. A sense of self, even.

From outside the classroom, he heard his students laughing so loud they melded together in the sound of joy. He took a deep breath, fought off the shadows of the world before, and resolved to give this new world as much of himself as he could—as noble an act as he could muster.

Halfway through his lecture, one of Charlie's students, Gerald, a tightly edged, stylish young man, raised a hand.

"Mr. Brunton," Gerald asked. "My question, I guess, is more of a philosophical one. Seems like the only difference between conventional electricity and solar is the source. Why can't we just put panels on every house one by one instead of trying to rebuild the whole grid to have solar foundations? Save ourselves a lot of work."

"Yeah, we agree on that. You might save some man-hours in the short term," Charlie answered. "But if we're speaking philosophically, then you're also selling yourself short." What Charlie aimed to say next weighed his shoulders down. "Right now, every city in this country is built on an electrical system created for two agendas: make natural power measurable and make money off those measurements. Priority in reverse order, of course. Yeah, sure, you can fit panels on top of every house in the city, but, philosophically now, you're just putting Band-Aids on bullet wounds. Might stop the bleeding, but damn sure ain't gonna do anything about why you got shot in the first place, follow me?" The class responded in the puzzled language of blinking and squinting, so

Charlie went on, careful not to let too much of his past slip out. "We have to strip out what existed before. We have to do it for the function and, I'd say, the freedom of it too. It's the electrical system and its sustainability, but it's also how we think about power in general, you follow? Our new power won't come from some faraway source that feels like magic, but from a source you can see every day right above you. Same power that powers everything. So, it makes sense why it'd be free. And the sun has all kinds of energy: heat, radioactive, vibrations—one day, one of you will figure out the ways to use all of it. And not just one house here, another house there, but the foundation itself. Better to understand *why* you do it, not just how."

"You almost make it sound righteous."

"I suppose anything sounds righteous when you pay it enough respect."

Gerald smiled big and looked coolly around to his classmates. "That's why I love this class. I told y'all, Mr. Brunton be preaching!"

Laughter popped and sparkled throughout the class like fireworks. Again, the weight in Charlie's chest sagged, his heart finding the reaction difficult not to conclude they were laughing at him. A moment had to pass, as it always did, for Charlie to recognize that feeling as his conflict. He understood, but could not reconcile, himself as both a man with little to offer and yet their teacher. Gently, nausea rocked him; too many thoughts that always swung back to the same place. Charlie centered himself, cleared his throat, and went on.

"All right, everybody, let's look more closely at these photovoltaic cell systems."

The small class gathered around him and the solar panel splayed before them like a cadaver. There, Charlie went on with the business of teaching his class everything he could.

Systems had always come naturally to Charlie. He understood their composition, necessity, and capacity. Even as a child, he excelled in math and science and kept, without great effort, the best marks among his peers. When his uncles made him do calculations in his head as a party trick, they called him "Baby Carver." That always made his mother smile and frown at the same time. By thirteen, everyone in his bitty Michigan town called him for repairs. Fixed their televisions, their sprinkler systems, even their cars' engines, which he had found easiest to diagnose. A few dollars to fix an air conditioner, a few more to fix a lawn mower, and by high school he thought maybe he'd have enough saved to send himself to college and apply that special mind of his to something more important than people's radios. But, by and by, he came to understand why his mother smiled and frowned in the manner with which she had, how she could be both proud and terrified of what was possible as a result of his talents.

Bells no longer rang in schools. Lessons started at a general *feeling* of time and continued until they found a good place to stop. By those measures, Charlie taught for another hour or so before letting his class out into the beloved Yard.

The Yard hummed of people and music. A thin fog of smoke from someone grilling something thickened the grassy square with the smell of barbecue. Speakers roared reggaeton as good as thunder. People laughed loud and broke out into little dances. They'd see a friend and shout them over all the way from one side of the Yard to the other. Greetings, here and there, collided in hand slaps and embraces that thudded chests and patted backs. Students flirted and smiled at each other as effortless as sunlight on a breeze. So much life and so much energy. Easy to forget that half the world died. But then again, Charlie noted, neither grief nor calamity had ever stopped the joy of black people. *We smiled through the worst the world had to offer,* he thought. *Smiled even when our lips bled.*

Charlie moved quickly through the Yard, nodding to all those who respectfully tilted their heads at him. He walked far out from the noisy crowds, out to the farthest tree still offering a bench under its shadow. He sat there and marveled.

After the event, all historically black colleges drew what remained of

America's crowds, looking for doctors, dentists, scientists, therapists, and other qualified individuals. D.C. and Howard University's surrounding neighborhoods now bustled with colorful energy filling restaurants, parks, and museums, and on campus, one would hardly think the world changed at all. When Charlie looked back at all those young people, he did so thinking of Harvard, Yale, and Penn State, schools whose halls, no doubt, sat haunted with vacancy.

He folded his arms and swallowed the conflict surging up in him, careful not to mistake Howard's smiling energy for indifference. Howard University, and especially its youth, cared about what happened to America a lot more than he did. Probably cared too much.

Indeed, in the aftermath of the event, some thought it had been the Rapture and prayed that God would come back and take them too. Some went wild in retaliation against feelings they could not name and went on boarding up police stations, burning down country clubs—one fella even ran naked into the old White House and pissed himself empty in the Oval Office on the oval rug. Sorrow to rage to resolution, everyone felt something every moment of every day and would for the rest of their lives. All because they cared so much. Cared beyond what they knew how to express.

Charlie, for his part, knew how he *should* feel and was made worse for not feeling it. So he focused his mind on the systems failing all around him. And fail they did. Too sudden did America fall into hands unprepared to hold its bounty. Too few knew how to fish. Too few could skin a buck. Too few understood how to run a farm, or the mechanics of a clock, or the variable shapes of government. Only a fragile structure remained, consequently, without the reinforcement of porcelain beams, ultimately punctuating precisely who'd made that system and kept charge of its maintenance.

Many of the large-scale infrastructural pillars of medicine, agriculture, economy, and technology sought new ways to function. Gas stations, big chain grocery stores, and even online shopping defected, all of it as a result of us having too little a say in the running of the before world. We were stabilized by our familiarity; as much as we could keep things as they were, the better we felt. Televisions still offered a version of the news; doctors, though from local clinics, still saw patients; and information still flowed through the sparsely available internet and libraries. People still got paychecks, although many of them in cash, and went duck-lipped when, slowly, small things disappeared, when stores stopped carrying their favorite snack cakes and potato chips, or in realizing that HBO series would never have a resolution. Different, but as much the same as we could manage. Brightly, though, amid the struggle for footing, black colleges offered a varied system, imperfect but assiduous. So when Charlie marveled at all those bright smiles, he understood that those smiles didn't directly amount to happiness. Those smiles, with all their luster and irony, were the same ones that carried their forefathers through centuries of horrors, teetering on a nearness to both jubilation and madness in equal measure. The only thing keeping Charlie from smiling along with them, pursing his lips just to stop himself, was the conflict—more specifically, what he'd come to know as the conflict of his own darkness.

Charlie stood up and wandered the edges of campus, watching without engaging. In this new world, he could figure neither where nor how he fit. Charlie had conflict in his heart long before the event. Before prison. All the way back to when he first learned to define himself by the language in the eyes of others, quick to articulate their bias. Ubiquitous enough for him to question the rationality of his very existence, the conflict of Charlie's darkness could only be resolved in the way any black man sees himself, that insoluble calculus. Does he see himself from within, as a divine composite of the joys, fears, hopes, and passions that make up any human being? Or does he see himself through the eyes of the world and how it reacted to him? His darkness was as elementary a question as it was existential: Who was he?

Charlie first read the dictionary definition of *black* in prison: "The absence of light. To be soiled. Hostile. Wicked. Devoid of the moral quality of goodness. Evil." He didn't believe these things about himself, yet the results of his life said otherwise. Indeed, he loved to laugh. Joy rumbled through him when he offered kindness to others. He relished the smells of his mother's stew and cut grass and the ocean. And on those nights when he stayed up late fixing people's broken things, he felt as bright as any star in the sky. Still, he had no answer for whether his darkness made him evil. Cruel? Wretched? Was he those things before he was even born? Or was it after he made the mistake of believing himself otherwise? The very question mutated his darkness into a deeply embedded self-hatred, a bitterness that too often steeped into fury. And he believed bitterness would have remained in him forever.

But then all those people killed themselves. And all Charlie felt was relief. Only a dark man could see such a horrible thing and feel what he felt. Too dark to be good. Too dark to be redeemed.

Charlie wandered until the sun cascaded from orange to pink to lilac. When evening arrived violet all around him, he felt that longing for tight walls of which his big house could not provide. Instead, Charlie ambled back across the campus to his office, a place small enough to confine the hum of his thoughts. He kept spare clothes and a cot under his desk. Wood paneling lined the walls, making any light at all flush gold. The office did have a large window looking out over the Yard, but he rarely disturbed the blinds from their dusty, shut lashes. Inside, he had a landline phone, shelves and shelves of books, a record player with a couple of LPs, and a few bottles of whiskey. He'd been trying to drink more scotch, if only to feel a bit more refined in his drunkenness, but kept a cheap Kentucky bourbon within reach. He shut the door behind him, locked it, and drank Wild Turkey straight from the bottle until the laughter and music died outside and all he could hear was the wind talk through the trees.

He lay on the floor of his office, silence as warm as a blanket, and drank, yawning and slipping in and out of sleep, in and out of the past, in and out of who he was and was becoming, in and out of rising to the potential of this new world and putting a bullet in his head. And he might've gone searching for a gun, but the phone rang.

"Hello," he answered as a matter of course. "Charlie Brunton's office."

Still adrift, the living silence on the other end sat Charlie up. A moment passed, giving him space to realize his own formality, the late hour, and the question as to who would even think to call him at all. He heard breathing on the other end, the fright of the old world tightening his etiquette.

"Hello. This is Charles Brunton. How can I help you?"

"Yeah." The voice paused. "How can you?" A woman's voice—young, cautious—seeming to reveal itself out of that dark silence as a mouse.

"Sorry? Who is this?"

Silence swelled into a weight Charlie couldn't see.

"Hello? Who is this?" he repeated.

"I'm . . ." The voice, he sensed, paused again not just for emphasis but to gather strength to speak at all. "I'm Elizabeth's daughter."

Elizabeth.

The name was a ghost against his skin. In his nose, inexplicably, he smelled lavender. And how his heart pounded when he realized what the voice had said.

"Daughter." He echoed the word absently, though purposely not as a question.

Only the breathing silence responded. Then: "I guess I could hang up right now, and maybe we'd be even."

He listened to her voice, the music of it. So familiar. So impossible. "Well, shit. I didn't believe this world had any surprises left to give."

Again, the breathing silence. "I think this was a mistake," she said, finally. "I don't know why I called you."

"Just wait." The darkness inside him appealed to keeping the voice on the line. Charlie had let go of so many things since before the event, so much of himself. In his office, shoved deep in the back of a filing cabinet, were the items he carried out of prison, specifically a letter written in Elizabeth's hand, still in its plastic bag, that told the story of her daughter. *Their* daughter. And he'd let that go too. "You called for a reason. To say something or to ask something. Whatever it is, ain't no sense in holding on to it."

"They all left. Just like you. They left me." Anger flared in her voice. More than anger. Sadness. Exhaustion. "I don't know why I called you. I guess . . . everyone's gone now. And I keep thinking I might as well go too."

He realized she'd lived through the event in a very different way.

"There's one place left that's a world for people like me. I'm calling you because I don't have anyone living that I mean something to. But you . . . you owe me. So I called to ask you to take me there."

Charlie hung in the vacancy after the ask, stuck on what exactly she meant by "people like me." His darkness, to his astonishment, reminded him that he was not cruel, or cold, or incapable of feeling something profound. "Where . . . where are you?"

"Wisconsin. Outside of Oshkosh. On Lake Winneconne."

"I'm in D.C. I can get to you in two days. Might take a little longer. Roads aren't as dependable as they used to be."

"Nothing is. But I need to get to the south."

"You want me to take you south?"

"Yeah."

"To what?"

"Are you gonna take me or not?"

"South ain't a place anyone should go these days. I hear it's dangerous."

"Then you're exactly what I thought you'd be: no help at all."

"Just wait a second. I'll help you. I will. Tell me your address."

"2580 Sunset Lane."

"What's your name?"

"It doesn't matter."

"It does to me."

"I know right now you probably think I'm your daughter. But I'm not. Your blood might be in me, but that doesn't make you my father."

The phone died.

Charlie lingered in the darkness of that silence, feeling shame like a fever.

He had forgotten so much of who he was he never once considered that the only child he had a hand in bringing half black into this world might still be alive and not at the bottom of the ocean. He had not even once thought to look back, but he could never forget the questions, now surrounding him like a storm. He didn't want to sleep. Not anymore. Not with so many things unanswered. He drank until the alcohol pulled him down, down. Into himself.

Down. Where the conflict was all there was.

Down into the yawning fathoms of deep, deep darkness.

2

THE EGGS BURNED.

From the upstairs bathroom Sidney smelled the smoke. The tang mingled with the singeing of her own curls tamed between the blades of a flattening iron.

Wrestling and laughing in the next room, her twin brothers thudded against the walls. And that distracted her too. Sidney imagined Adam, always the bully and only three minutes older than John, using those minutes to prove his superior strength and viciousness over his twin. Adam always liked to play the villain in their wrestling games, which empowered his finishing moves to be backbreakers, and neckbreakers, and facebreakers, when they fake-smashed chairs against each other. Indeed, the best way to tell the brothers apart was to look for bruises, and the one reddened or purpled was always John. Sidney used to listen to their wild roughhousing before flying in as last-minute hero, to save her youngest brother from defeat. But not today.

Summer was over, and soon she'd be filing into a dorm at U of W. First time away from home. First time away from her mother. She'd barely scored high enough on her SAT, her GPA had absolutely no twinkle, and she still didn't have a license to drive. She'd gotten into the school not by the weight of her own merits but by her stepfather's ability to move mountains. And, perhaps, by the relentless desire of all those around her to see her succeed. But Sidney wasn't ready for any of it, and for more reasons than just grades.

In the bathroom mirror, Sidney observed herself. How scarcely she resembled her mother. Even when she straightened out the curls in her hair, the effect, as she saw it, actually further articulated their differences, seeming to widen her nose and pronounce the plump in her lips. Her stepfather said straight hair made her look elegant. And though Sidney didn't accept herself as elegant, she liked the way the notion of elegant made her feel—deserving, maybe, of something she couldn't quite resolve. She accepted what he said as having something to do with an abiding sense of unreadiness, experiencing her life from a sort of waiting room—waiting to achieve the transcendence of becoming, suddenly, something more. More of what, exactly, she couldn't fully imagine. Nevertheless, she felt the gravity of everyone's patience. She saw patience in their eyes when, with a glimmer of pity, they regarded her, or heard patience in the lilt in their voices, subtly altruistic, as kind words came down to her from some higher, if not inaccessible, place. So she remained in her waiting room.

She sighed as she gripped the straightener to burn the last bit of vigor out of her hair.

But her hair wasn't the only thing burning.

Her brothers had stopped thrashing. A quiet bloomed in the house.

"John? Adam?" Even as she called out to them, the quiet seemed to absorb her voice. She set the iron down on the edge of the sink and stepped out into the hallway. The burning smell sharpened in her nose as heat crisped closer to fire. From the window at the end of the hall, Sidney saw her stepfather out back wading ankle-deep into the lake. He hadn't gone for a lake swim in years, and never had he done so fully clothed.

"Mom!" she shouted down the stairs. "What's Rick doing out in the lake?"

No response followed, only the souring smell of smoke.

She saw her brothers first, as she skipped down the stairs, standing shoulder to shoulder at the base. They both stared out at the lake. John was red under his neck, but they looked more twinned than ever, the same mindless glare washed across their faces. Not really mindless, she saw, but closer to curious—listening even. All four of their blue eyes tilted upward by a small degree, which pulled their noses and their eyebrows and chins, as though they could hear music far away and somehow smell it too.

"What are you guys doing?"

But they just kept looking. Listening. She asked again, and still nothing changed in their eyes. They both kept looking out, beyond her, beyond the house.

The fire alarm went off.

In the kitchen, over the stove, smoke billowing from the pan of burned eggs, she found her mother washed in the same listening stare, still gripping the spatula, frozen in mid-scramble. Smoke curled around her mother's chin, creating a halo above her head. In her serenity she did nearly look angelic, if the stillness of the moment weren't so frightening. On she went, listening, smelling. Sidney turned off the stove.

"Mom, what's going on?"

Sidney's eyes bounced between her mother and her brothers, then off toward the lake where they all gazed. She couldn't see, hear, or smell anything beyond the smoke. But they did. They did, and she didn't. They could, and she couldn't.

And then, suddenly, her mother started to walk, her eyes still gazing out to that beyond. John and Adam were already outside. Her mother walked onto the deck, never once taking her eyes off the lake. One after the other, they went—listening, staring, walking.

Sidney followed them down into the garden where her mother had planted lavender bushes in rows. Her mother had told her, countless times, how her grandmother had planted lavender too, and her grandmother before, going all the way back to the first Irishwoman to boat to American shores. The first of their line brought lavender, planted it, and sold it in bushels as her only source of income. And it was all she needed to get by, to build a family, a home, and a future. Her mother made that garden as a reminder to never take for granted the struggle their forebearers endured to be here.

She watched her mother march through the garden, unfazed, her brothers joining her at the shore. The three of them advancing like penguins toward a body of water.

Ripples, she saw, shuddering in the lake. Bubbles too. Rick had gone in and he hadn't come up. All was silent—death silent, terrifying her down deeper than reason. Deeper than her ability to reconcile what was happening beyond the fact that it wasn't happening to her. And so she tried to stop them.

Her mother powered right through her hold. Sidney screamed and ripped at clothes and arms. She even tried to tackle Adam, in the same manner she had so many times in their wrestling matches, but, pinned down, the boy convulsed, seizing and foaming until she released him. He got back up as if nothing had happened and went on walking into the water. Sidney followed them into the cold brown lake, up to her knees. Then up to her waist. Up to her chest. Followed until the blond tips of her mother's hair drifted soundlessly across the lake's surface. Until her brothers submerged. Until the lake floor disappeared beneath her feet.

She went underwater with them, pulling at their arms and legs, but the weight of their bodies, walking across the lake floor, felt like stone. Felt like the ocean floor itself, in that she'd have to lift the whole of it to bring her family back to the surface.

She followed them underwater until she could no longer breathe and swam back for air. Until she could no longer see anything in those depths. Until she no longer had strength to keep diving down. And she tried. Swimming, screaming, fighting. She tried her very best. To drown herself along with them. To feel what they felt. As she had been trying to all her life.

Sidney floated face up in the water, her family somewhere below, the air smelling sweetly of lavender, but also of smoke.

3

CHARLIE DREAMT OF LAVENDER.

Not so much a dream as a sort of melancholy ferrying him from one side of the night to the other. He'd lain with his back on the floor, his heart beating faster than it had in years, waiting out the whiskey to clear his picture of the voice through his phone. Not even in his thoughts would he dare call her *his* or *daughter*. A voice in the dark—detachment enough to keep him from changing his mind about seeing her.

He spent the early-morning hours mapping his route to Wisconsin. Nearly everyone drove electric cars and kept travel close to major cities. Charlie had first pitched developing an electric rail system as an easier way to get people where they needed to go. He even invested time in building a prototype system to show how they could establish charged tracks while still using the current D.C. infrastructure. But, by default, the school board managed the city, and any considerations of a new grid bypassed both its understanding and desire for the endeavor. So Charlie proposed dedicating manpower to maintaining, building, and mapping the charging stations for their cars, but the school board responded to his enthusiasm with an offer to teach, keeping his plan in a lingering state of infancy.

The fastest route to Wisconsin offered few known functioning charging stations. And only some sections of freeway had been cleared of all the cars emptied of their drivers. When he mapped the distance by what was known, the effort would take him mostly off the freeway, heading north, then south, then north again in a switchback pattern up into Pennsylvania and Toronto, then across to Detroit and around Lake Michigan. Nearly thirty extra hours of driving. Faster ways existed. Blind, but faster. Charlie understood, in a way, that was just how the world now felt: blind, or all vision warped by having worn someone else's glasses.

He still wished for stability, which surprised him. Prison, for all its horrors, offered certainty as indisputable as the stone and metal. Hate it or love it, government had been there, giving structure, consequence, and a framework for living that one could either jibe with or not. This new world lacked such certainty. Indeed, even the event's calculation determining who lived and who didn't wasn't so distinctly black and white. Best Charlie could deduce, the judgment, more or less, had something to do with identity in America. Didn't matter what race box a person checked on a voting form. While not everyone checked white, none of them aspired to check black. Not in America. Not in a courtroom or a country club. Not on a back road or in a bank. Not in any of America's serene places, sparkling and forbidden. No one else *wanted* to be a black person in America. And *everyone* knew that fact, however cruelly the result played itself out. No matter the worry in their lives, they could all but count on a voice, redemptive and default, whispering as a comfort to their hearts: *At least I'm not them*. And so they carried on, the injustice of it as natural and inconvenient to their lives as a bit of rain.

Seemed to Charlie the event had something to do with the fact of that.

So people made their own rules. Even local news devolved into what felt less like reporting than sermonizing, talking heads too quick to thrust opinion without substance, emphasizing that no one runs the country anymore. No one rose to make a new president, no Democrats, no Republicans, no halls filled with representatives. No unity at all.

The event shattered many, many things, but none more than the *United* in United States. Physically and philosophically, all governing deteriorated. Titles evaporated, as did sovereign formalities; even the language of government would be gone entirely in a generation, as one no longer needed to *declare* one's independence or stand atop a bill of rights. Aside from the Registry of Those Remaining, an online index of all the people still alive in the country, nothing felt united at all. Already, authority passed down to local leaders and activists whose tenacity to make a difference was matched only by the imprecision of their management. No real union or clarity, a reality in existence long before all the white folks marched into the sea.

Absently, Charlie pondered unity as he mapped his journey, deciding to brave at least some unaccounted areas through Toledo, Fort Wayne, and Gary. Unity, he supposed, began with knowing, and knowing dulled all risk in the grind of a purpose. In truth, he wasn't afraid of those unknown roads, but he wrung his hands at the thought of where the roads led. To a place where a voice in the dark became a person looking back at him. He feared seeing his daughter's face. Feared recognizing their differences as much as their similarities. Feared experiencing the impact of his absence. But, as fear had all his life, the difficulty again presented an opportunity for that quiet dignity. Dignity he'd need if he planned to look his daughter in her eyes. So Charlie chewed on the inside of his cheek, packed a small bag, left notes for his students and colleagues, and went on with the business of getting on the road. All but ready to leave, he got back out of the car. He returned to his office for the letter addressed to him, tucked in his filing cabinet, still in the plastic bag branded SUSSEX STATE PRISON. The only letter he'd ever kept. The only proof that he and Elizabeth made anything worth salvaging.

Charlie took in the city on his way out. Even at the early hour, D.C. pulsed. Gospel music spilled out of barbershops. Electric scooters zoomed down sidewalks and bike lanes. A line of people wrapped around a McDonald's with its arches torn down, where somebody's grandma captained the kitchen making enough cheese grits and biscuits to feed the neighborhood. The city almost resembled life before the event—with subtle differences. There were no more homeless people. Less trash littered the shoulders, because no one mass-produced single-use plastics and containers anymore. The biggest difference, he determined, was better felt than seen. The only word he could think to describe life was *easier*. On the rare occasion that he spoke to someone about the event, most of them would lower their eyes, say how big a shame it all was, but go on to soberly acknowledge how free they felt. Free to walk alone at night. Free to climb a tree. Free to fall asleep somewhere in the sun. Freedom that inspired them to change their names, calling themselves after plants and animals, looking, Charlie suspected, to reclaim something true about themselves that now they could.

Charlie drove an hour to get out of downtown and didn't feel the quiet of the open road until well past Germantown. Charlie had seen other ethnicities after the event, but rarely and in too few numbers to not have been diminished in some way by whatever took the others. No, the rules weren't so black and white. Only then did that fact sting Charlie. Because if it was identity that killed all those people, who then was his daughter? Charlie had contributed nothing to her identity, wasn't so sure he ever had anything worth being offered, yet on this earth she remained, same as him.

He let the window down in his Prius so he could hear the wind hum. The sky's blue hem frayed into treetops on either side, and a single, bloated cloud dallied in the distance. The open road looked like a great black ribbon stitching the world together.

Charlie didn't stop until he reached far into Pennsylvania's deep lush. A known functioning charging station blinked its lights high up on a lookout. As he pulled over and plugged in, a realization arrived on him that he hadn't truly left the city and seen America after the event. In truth, he hadn't done much of anything after spending twenty years in prison, like those bars dulled in him any sense of adventure. He hadn't thought much about other towns and had not witnessed the stalled engines of the country with his own eyes.

He gazed from the lookout at wide-open land, cascading down and out seemingly without end. The Pennsylvania forest mangled together in a great wrestling match, trees clawing up on top of one another to make false mountains, all of it scarred and bleeding in autumnal colors. From there, Charlie could see America's backyards, the tender places highways sped past. Where deer and bears grazed craggy slopes that chawed into the scalps of neighborhoods. Humble houses popped up like cowlicks, and Charlie could imagine how silently their chimneys used to smoke. At one time, that land busied with kids at play behind fenced-in yards, televisions running behind bolted doors, all the sticky diners with staff who knew too well when somebody walked in whom they didn't know.

In those hollows of American life, its best version played itself out like a movie in the mind. Cheerful towns impaled with the familiarity of some man's name: Philipsburg, Williamsport, Johnsonburg, Lewistown—names carried through the years like the law of the land itself. Like another essential element of nature, definitive as the Appalachian Mountains, true as the Mississippi River—and equally a dare to cross. For, at the far edges of these vast stretches, black folks squeezed themselves into ghettos, hung like beads on the necklace of every Martin Luther King Boulevard. In the ghettos, the sun didn't quite shine like it did out here, nor the land open up with all its plenty. Just looking at all that light made Charlie's eyes ache for it to be dimmed under the height of buildings. The vastness made his skin crave the proximity of something solid. A wall. A ceiling. A choice already made. He took a deep breath. He needn't fear that land. Not anymore.

Within three hours, he reached Virginia, where the hills rose up to cradle the sun. There were empty houses in those hills too. Empty neighborhoods with empty schools and empty Walmarts. Those hills, where once it felt like no one else was welcome, no one now resided. Not empty exactly, but vacant, an impression nearer to longing. Like ambling through a graveyard, but it was the whole country bereaved.

Through Virginia, reverence shut Charlie's windows, and the silence that followed brought his thoughts back to where he was going and why. He became aware of the letter he'd sat like a passenger in the seat next to him. Not once had he opened that envelope since the day he received the letter all those years ago. Still, within the silence of the wide road, in more than literal ways, he understood that he carried the letter's message as good as any passenger. Carried the scribblings in his heart and his mind for enough years that what the letter was created to do, it no longer did. Even if he did open it, right then and there, he wasn't sure he would still hear the written words in her voice.

Elizabeth.

He nearly pulled the car over, if only to steady himself in the after-shock of her name. Instead he let the windows back down. Better to endure the ghosts outside than those in the heart.

Ohio sat empty. Where abandoned cars had lined the roadsides closer to the city, the open road turned sparse and thunderously silent. There were broad distances between open gas stations, and trees leaned fearlessly over untended freeways. Deer roamed in nonchalance, and Charlie swerved from lane to lane dodging white-tails, fox, and skunk. His map offered no known functioning gas or charging stations until near Chicago. And there were no lights on in the houses he passed. No movement at all. Only the vastness of the road, the treasure of America's immensity abandoned by its keeper. Nearly an entire nation seemed, suddenly, discoverable. He wondered if this was what Columbus felt: to look upon something already there with nothing to stop you from claiming every mile as yours.

Charlie watched the land go on like that, empty, rolling hills through Toledo and Fort Wayne, until the landscape changed with such sudden drama that he stopped the car in the middle of the highway. The battery meter flashed red: only 20 percent power remaining. He knew he didn't have enough charge to make the distance to Chicago, but a more worrisome reality spread out before him.

Everything was burned.

As far as he could see.

Blackness like tar. Everything burned to flakes. Trees shriveled up black, grass charred up the roadside, and the height of nature felled low for miles under the clear midwestern sky. There was no smoke, but the charred, sooty smell radiated off everything in every direction. Charlie drove through that scorched landscape until his charge meter dropped to 15 percent. Mile after mile of burned earth. Not some freak forest fire, he saw, but a burn with intention. Someone meant to do this. As Charlie had come to expect in this new world, what he saw wasn't just scorched earth alone, but somebody's absolution.

He reached Warsaw, just outside of Fort Wayne, when the charge light held red enough to put real fear in him. He'd thought by then he'd have already found another car to take or an abandoned house that still had power to plug in. And though he cringed at staying over in the remains of someone else's home with their half-eaten dinners still rotting on the table and the once glittering blue pool fallen to the toads, he'd assumed he had that as a last option. The problem was the burned earth. No houses stood. Not one. Everything, everywhere, coated in blackness. He wanted to kick himself for not pushing harder to map the charging stations with greater detail, but it didn't much matter this far out of the city. Whether he decided to go back where he came from or keep moving forward, either way he'd eventually run out of power before he found a place to recharge.

His charge dropped down to 1 percent, and his heart in concert. No sign showed the char giving way. One percent and an afternoon sun. That's all Charlie had left.

Then, in the distance, and like a raft in open sea, a house poked up on the horizon. The 1 percent charge held on like the car knew Charlie's life clung to it as the house neared and Charlie saw the burning stop like a line in the sand. There was a lawn, proving his theory that the burn had indeed not been wild but managed. Rage in a blister. And, at the edge of that contrast, a yellow house on a slope not far beyond. Charlie didn't believe in God, but seeing that house, amid all that lifelessness, his relief sprung to the edge of spiritual.

A driveway, well swept next to a tended lawn, welcomed him just as every function in his car shut down all at once. The little yellow house rose much bigger up close. Empty. Dark. Three stories high with large, unshuttered windows and a wraparound porch, the house looked every bit like the type of country home Charlie might've cautioned himself approaching. But no one living, certainly no one he should fear, occupied that house. Not anymore. Still, he felt the phantoms of alarm in his chest, alarms he knew he would never be able to fully quiet. Just around the back of the house, sheets of light reflected off three rows of solar panels. Good panels too, well-tended and south-facing. Two covered power outlets were coupled at the base of the porch. That those panels, adjacent scorched wasteland, remained clean and those outlets functional called to the guile in his mind for a closer look, but he went on quietly with the business of getting his car wired up and charging. And, to his delight, the charge fired right up. He figured he'd just spend the night in this house, or in the car if the night and its empty whispers became unnerving, and that should be enough power to get him to Wisconsin. Then he noticed her: an old woman sitting on the porch. Silently, she'd watched him go through the motions.

"Oh, sorry, ma'am, I didn't see you."

"No, you didn't," she said. She sat back in the shadows, not moving at all in her rocking chair. The shadows pronounced her wrinkles, and her repose suggested a fragility the strength in her voice defied. "Seems to be you got more problems than worrying about me."

Charlie squinted his eyes to see her—southern accent, southern mannerisms, skin like the shell of a pecan. Her presence seemed to offer Charlie contentment; *safe* was the word that came to mind. He felt safe. His own mother died while he stared at prison walls. On that porch, under those shadows, he felt some part of her ghost looking out at him. To not walk up on that porch and hug her took a powerful resolve. Whoever she was.

"I'm sorry." Charlie wiped his feet. "I haven't lost my manners. My name is Charles . . . Charles Brunton. And you are?"

"Ethel."

No, she wasn't rocking her chair, but her presence swayed with the gentleness of highway grass. "Ethel, would you mind me using your power to charge my car?"

She said, looking up at the sun, "Ain't mine to give. Come on up here on the porch, Charles, and let me have a look at you."

Nervously, Charlie climbed up the short steps to meet her, the last rays of sun trapped under the porch overhang. Seeing Ethel up close, the way her eyes studied him as though skimming the volumes of his life, Charlie folded his arms and shuffled nervously, pondering the ground.

"Who is your peoples?" she asked. "And where're they from?"

"Michigan, just outside of Detroit. We're from around that area. My mother's maiden name was Smith."

"And her mother before that?"

"Can't say. Don't know what name came before that."

She smiled a row of lovely white teeth. "Ain't that about the whole of it?"

"How do you mean?"

"We finally inherited the earth and can't remember who we was back when it was promised to us to begin with." She chuckled through a sly huff of breath. "Come on in, Charles, and I'll make you some dinner. I suspect that car gonna at least need the night to finish doing what it's doing."

Charlie followed her inside the house where the air smelled sweet and warm, like hard candy melted down. The radiator hissed throughout the house. Charlie noted the flower-patterned couches and the wood complaining under his steps. He followed Ethel down a hall lined with family photos. The photos made up *her* family, not someone else's like those in the home he'd claimed. School portraits, group photos on that same porch out front, generations going back to the grainy film photos of the fifties and sixties. This house was Ethel's home long before the event.

Ethel led him into the kitchen, where she gestured for him to sit at a fully dressed table set for eight, complete with doily placemats, candles, and cutlery. Seemed strange to Charlie that such a table would be set for just the two of them.

"Are you expecting company?"

"You're here, ain't you?"

"You saying you expected me?"

"These days you can't really say no more what somebody should or shouldn't be expecting. You get me? It's just logical. You're here because everything else out there is burned up. All there is to it. Somebody's always arriving, and I'm always expecting."

She didn't speak another word and went on making dinner. In the fridge, she had stored leftover beans and rice, and filets of fish already cleaned and ready. She even had a roll of dough enough to bake a few biscuits. While the fish fried and the sides warmed, she soaked collards in a pot and cut up peppers to make something new. His dinner was somewhere in between leftovers from the person before him and new dishes that would become leftovers for the next person to arrive. Ethel said nothing at all until his food steamed on a plate in front of him.

"Been a while since I had fish."

"Well, I got more than I know what to do with. Put a net down in the lake out yonder and the walleye jump in like they're trying to escape."

"Well, thank you either way."

"No need to thank me. We have to do for others more now than ever. That's what we had before, that's what we got left," she said.

Charlie nodded, suddenly ravenous. He barely took a breath while scarfing through Ethel's food.

"You headed to Chicago?" she asked, handing him a cup of water just as all that good food started to clog in his throat.

"No, I'm on my way to Wisconsin."

"Wisconsin? Fine place to start fresh. All those lakes and trees. Fine place."

"Oh, I'm not starting fresh. I'm just going to help . . ." Charlie swallowed more than a bite of food. "Going to help somebody in need."

"That so?"

Charlie experienced the same sensation he'd felt looking up at Ethel from the driveway. She wasn't just another person left over, but something more akin to the surface of a well. One that went deep enough to hold the aspirations of his mother and all mothers.

"That land out there," Charlie asked, "did you set fire to it?"

"I did."

"But it's burned for miles. You couldn't have done that all by yourself."

"You don't know what I can and can't do. And more than that, who does anything all by themselves? I started the fire, see? But the wind took some. One tree handed some to the next. Clouds held back the rain until their bellies turned purple just so. So, no, I wasn't by myself. I started what needed to be done."

"You make it sound like something magical."

"Ain't it?"

"So why? Why burn all of that?"

"Don't play fool, Charles. You already know. How anybody supposed to build a new life on top of so much cruelty and pain? If I could've, I would have burned it down to the bones of the world. Down to the foundation. You understand me?"

Charlie's conflict shuddered inside him. "I think I do."

"They did everything they could to stop our sun from shining. But I'm still here. A sun that just kept on rising."

"What do you think happened to all of them, Ethel? Why did they do that to themselves?"

"I don't know. Don't make much sense trying to figure it out neither."

"I don't think we'll ever really know the truth. But I guess I'm wondering . . . what do you feel about it?"

She stared at him long enough to make him uncomfortable. "Well, I feel like you've got the jewel of the world in your hands now. And how long've you begged somebody else's god to have even a piece of it? People done sacrificed everything for it, just hoping, and now you have it. The whole thing from shining sea to sea. And damned if you don't have a clue what to do with it, except keep wondering if you deserve to have it in the first place. I think you shouldn't be worried about the truth of what *happened* to them and busy yourself with the truth of what's *done happened* and what's *going to happen* to you." With those relentless studying eyes, she watched Charlie. She could read his shame. "Charles, it's okay to be two things at once. Every day that a tree is growing, it's dying at the same time. If it can do that, then a very sad thing can also give you release. This is my house. My family left the south and claimed this land. I raised my kids here and my kids raised theirs. It's my land and I still burned it. Limit how you feel about any of it and you are *limited*. Get me?"

"I just don't know what I'm supposed to feel."

"I suspect that's what you'll figure out in Wisconsin."

Charlie remembered his daughter. Ethel stood up and took his plate to the sink.

"Go on and get yourself some rest. Spare bedroom's upstairs, and there's hot water to shower. The wind gets cold and loud at night, so I'd keep your windows closed."

Charlie took that as his cue to leave, started toward the end of the kitchen before turning back, suddenly aching to remain connected to Ethel as a child would a mother. "You're not scared to be out here in this house all by yourself?"

"What I need to be scared of? Ain't but one reason anybody comes to this house and it ain't to do a thing to me. People come through that door to heal. That's all. To heal."

"Is that why you think I'm here?"

"Why else would you? They're gone. Now you got no excuses for who you can be. So who you gonna be? Same as you were? Or everything you would've been otherwise?"

She turned away, putting the leftovers into containers, and Charlie carried on up the stairs, aware that something had shifted inside him.

Through the night, he stared up at the still ceiling fan, windows open, welcoming the chill in the air to remind him he could feel. There, finally, he allowed his thoughts to consider his daughter as more than a voice in the dark. He wondered what she looked like, about the life that she lived, and if she enjoyed her every morning in the effervescence of happiness. He wondered how much she knew about him and if that knowledge taught her to fear and despise him as her mother did. He remembered how his daughter said "people like me," and he couldn't decide the meaning of such a thing. He fell asleep imagining what really separated *us* from *them*. The seemingly insurmountable emptiness between. The science of it. The spirit of it. The quality. The cratering impact of something to which we can react but never see. Destructive emptiness. Like a dent in the earth.

4

VIVIAN STOOD WITH *her husband at the corner of Government and Royal Streets.*

That corner, to her amusement, also made the cross streets for the energetically opposed History Museum of Mobile and Mardi Gras Park. Only the day before, she stood in the same spot with a lump in her throat she couldn't swallow. At her own protest, the opposition outnumbered her group ten to one. They'd arrived like their very own Mardi Gras parade, shouting with spittle on their lips, the slick red of their Confederate flags whipping sunlight in every billow. And still their holstered AR-15s seemed to darken the day. Hundreds of them gathered to stop the removal of a statue. A monument. One she'd been fighting for thirty years of her life, twenty years of her mother's life, to have finally taken out of their sight line. Raphael Semmes, officer in the Confederate navy, still stood as tall and as cold as ever. The monument reminded everyone in the city that some of its residents used to be somebody's property. A threat, Vivian understood, packaged as heritage.

Five years ago, Vivian would have filled the square with thousands of eager protesters by her side. People committed to making change. But she'd been gone for so long, she allowed herself to believe their absence simply meant they were just as tired as she was. Can't fight forever. Still, the few dozen who came wore their most intense expressions, hoping after all these years her voice would still be big enough to drown out the opposition's mania, and inspire them as it had for so long. What her comrades didn't understand was that the size of her voice didn't matter. Never did. Truthfully, she never even looked at an opposing crowd. She just closed her eyes, reached out with her heart and mind, and tried to tune in to their energy. Sure, they were angry, staunch, pitiless, but she could always find the right frequency and reach them. Because, beneath all the entitlement they'd kill to protect, they still knew what she knew, the feeling of which lived in their bones same as hers. They knew. *They sat in the break rooms when their friends said "nigger" categorically. They shopped in the same stores where the staff let them be while they followed someone darker. They saw police officers choke a man to death in broad daylight for something that they'd never even known was a crime. They knew how easily a contrast could make them feel threatened. They were not the* other. *They knew that too. A fact made clear by what their ancestors did to ours. So, for most of her life, Vivian could tap into that knowing and change their hearts. But no longer. No matter how loud she spoke, they'd stopped listening. They couldn't hear her anymore.*

Vivian didn't speak that day. She didn't have to. Everything changed the next day anyway.

The square sat empty. No more shouting. No more stars crossing a flag. Birds sang over leaves rustling over breezes over the cooing of deep gulf waters. She listened, but she couldn't hear them anymore either.

Next to her, her husband, Hosea, breathed heavily and looked down at his hands.

"The fight's over, love," she said.

5

IN THE MORNING, Ethel made Charlie breakfast, another fresh biscuit with scrambled eggs and coffee. He told her the truth. He was headed to Wisconsin to see his daughter, whose name he did not know. He told her his daughter's mother was white, and the fact that he hadn't questioned whether his own daughter had lived through the event shamed and scared him. Ethel just smiled warmly, said nothing, and passed him a cup of orange juice.

With 90 percent charge—more than enough to get him to his daughter's front door—he drove through the silence of Indiana. Occasionally cars passed him on the road, loaded with people en route from one part of the country to another. He supposed they were off to find what Ethel called "a good place to start fresh," leaving the cities and their monochromatic suburbs for something richer. More natural. Charlie imagined them all suddenly aware of all the rules no longer enforced. Who will stop them from taking a house on the Hampton beaches or building themselves a cabin at the edge of the Grand Canyon? Who will tell them what they can and can't afford or where they are and are not welcome? They could take over any farm in Kansas or bourbon and horse land in Kentucky, or be the only person on a shore somewhere taking up an entire yacht club. No one would stop them from anything they wanted anywhere. Shamefully, just how little of America Charlie had ever thought of wanting dawned on him. He couldn't begin to picture the Rocky Mountains or the California redwoods. He'd never seen a desert or where the ocean crashes against cliffs in places like Malibu. For once, he considered all that was now possible and, in so doing, crystallized, spitefully, all that didn't seem possible before.

He finally hit traffic around Chicago, whose energy resembled D.C., then to Milwaukee, where again everything dipped back into silence. He didn't slow down until he reached Lake Winnebago outside of Oshkosh. Slowly he drove through Fond du Lac's downtown. Not a single person walked the main streets of what otherwise might've been a charming place, with its colorful buildings and overgrown flower beds. Antique stores resembled something akin to memorials, as did the empty bakeries and the movie theater, with its unlit marquee inviting patrons who would never return to see some romantic comedy unlikely to ever again play. Even the welcome center, which stood over the town like a cathedral, idled as if haunted. The front doors of every home remained open, wailing mouths, they seemed, lamenting the loss of their lords.

The way the wind moved through so freely, tilting signs and bending tree branches, chilled Charlie to the point of speeding up. Fond du Lac wasn't just empty. Charlie could manage empty. Fond du Lac's wanting felt ravenous.

Charlie sped into Oshkosh. His mouth fell open as he arrived at the address he'd been given, 2580 Sunset Lane. A florid wrought-iron gate protected all entry into the sprawling estate. Beyond the gate, the imposing house, hulkish in the distance, stood at a size that seemed intentionally just smaller than a mansion, if only to extend that modicum of humility. Inscribed in the iron across the gate: WAGGONER. Yes, that was her name. Charlie swiped the awe from his face and closed his mouth.

Elizabeth Waggoner.

How little, he realized, he'd known about that woman. Theirs had been a romance short and powerful, far from his home and far from hers. So far and so long ago that standing at the gates of her family home, he felt he was meeting Elizabeth for the first time. Again, he quelled the impulse to turn back. Pride kept his feet from moving. Pride, bitterness, and something else for which he did not yet have a name.

"I didn't think you would come." The voice cracked through the gate speakers. Same voice, youthful, brooding, that stunned him back on his office phone.

"I'm here," he answered. "I keep my word the best I can."

"Do you?" Tension in her voice pushed through the speakers. "Stay where you are. I'll come to you."

"The car needs to be charged before we get on the road."

"Charged? Can't you just get gas?"

"You don't get out of the house much, do you? You can't depend on gas. I don't even think there is much gas left."

"Why? You people stole it all? Like everything else?"

"Gas is gone because the people who liked to drill into the ground to get it killed themselves, that's why." He heard her suck in air, and he knew his tone plucked on something painful. "Look, I promised you I'd take you where you wanted to go, and I will. I don't mean you no harm. But this car needs to be plugged in for a few hours before we leave. There's a station down in Milwaukee. Once we get on the road, we can get a full charge there."

"An hour, max," she said, "and then we go."

The gate clicked and churned open. Charlie stuffed himself back in the car and followed the quarter-mile-long dirt driveway, canopied under the menacing arms of leafless trees up to the house. Through the treetop fingers the house rose up like a minor mountain. It was three stories high and, though set in the midwest, built in the distinctive architecture of traditional southern plantation homes. Six white columns held the structure in place and created wraparound porches and balconies on each floor. Every one of the rounded, cartoonishly large windows sat shuttered closed.

At the base of the house, Charlie got out and took it all in. A gas generator broke the quiet, grunting and sputtering like a bull. She'd already stretched a cord from the back of the machine across the driveway for Charlie to charge. That, he understood, was the most welcome he would receive.

With the car plugged in, he waited for a moment for her to come out and meet him. He hoped she would at the very least be curious enough to draw out toward the man whose blood pulsed in her veins. And he, for his part, filled up with anxiety waiting for the door to open. A man meeting his daughter should feel triumphant. But that meeting should have also happened much, much sooner. In the end, she didn't come out to meet him, but the door opened just barely, a black sliver into an all-white house. Not an invitation as much as an armistice: come forth, but find no welcome here.

The smell of lavender met Charlie on the porch and thrust him briefly back in time. What returned him stark to the moment was pushing the door open to find, standing in the foyer, his only daughter pointing a long rifle at his face.

Instinctively, he raised both hands and pinned himself back against the door.

She'd used a gun before, that much was easily discerned. Her focus on him held steady, no wavering or shivering. She gripped the rifle as comfortably as she walked on solid ground.

"Is that what you called me here for? To shoot me?"

She exhaled slowly. "We both know if that was the case, you'd deserve it."

Two thoughts settled on him: those were the first words he'd heard unfiltered in his daughter's voice, and, unnervingly, he wasn't exactly certain what he deserved.

She lowered her gun and set her eyes on him, chin up and proud.

Her gold-black hair, curly at the top, straightened in the front, and matted in the back, burst in different directions. In her face, behind the sallow constellation of red freckles, he regarded elements of his own. His nose. His lips. The shape of his eyes. There was more to consider as well. In the way she stood, in the manner she looked at him, he was bombarded by a collage of elements he'd forgotten about her mother.

"I expected you to be . . . wilder." Her eyes rolled over him.

"I expected you to be more welcoming."

"I was nine the first time my mother told me about you. She said you were proof God was real."

"And how is that, exactly?"

"The worst sin of her life gave her the biggest blessing. Me." She strapped the gun over her shoulder with the familiarity of putting on a pair of glasses, then walked deeper into the house. "Do you want something to eat or drink? There's clean water and beans . . . lots of beans."

Charlie followed her. Staircases with iron balusters spiraled up to the second floor. Paintings hung on every wall, most of them depicting American landscapes except for one large portrait of a pale Jesus hung at the top of the stairs. They walked into an open kitchen where the floor stepped down just beyond to a gaping living space, corralling a couch, a television, and a fireplace. Bedding and pillows took up the area where a coffee table might've sat to make his daughter's camp, the whole place packed thick with a stale smell. She'd not left this house since the event, Charlie gathered. She'd not seen the outside world in the year since the majority of its population ceased to exist.

She poured him a glass of water from a clear pitcher and set the glass on the kitchen bar, careful not to move close enough that her hand might touch his. Charlie drank the water slowly, watching her through every sip.

"What's your name?" he asked.

"Why does my name matter to you?"

"Can't really tell you why. But I'm standing here right now looking at you, sure that I really am your father. All I want is to be able to call you by your name."

"Don't get sentimental."

Nineteen. Charlie quickly did the math in his head. She was only nineteen, although she seemed older. Age showed especially in her eyebrows, which furrowed emulously against her youth.

"I found you in the college directory. The class you taught must mean you're a math man, right? So tell me, how much power do you need to get me where I'm going?"

"Charge, you mean? Depends on the plan. You said you wanted to go south. Based on what I've heard, I still wouldn't recommend going south. But even if we did, you'd have to keep charging as you go, and as far as I know, there are no charging stations. There may not even be much else down there."

"I want to go to Kenosha first, then Alabama."

"Kenosha's fine, but as I said, the south isn't a place anyone wants to go. It's bad enough in the midwest. I can't imagine what anything's like south of Virginia."

"I'm sure they probably destroyed most of it by now."

"They?"

"The world got left to the heathens. That's why everything is going to hell outside these walls. You know the sky was smoking for months? Like everything was on fire. I wouldn't be surprised if most of the country is already burned to the ground."

He regarded her differently, suddenly alert to what she said and the manner in which she said *they*. A word used with a certain, distinguishable distance, as though explaining an infestation not even God could exterminate. And if *they* made up all the people left, he wondered, what exactly did she think that made her?

"You haven't left this house, have you?"

"Why would I? This was my grandmother's house and land, which she gave to my mother. Now it's mine to protect. Besides, I have everything I need right here."

"So why leave now? Why call me all the way up here just to take you through what you're calling hell?" Charlie watched her chew down on purposeful words and swallow them.

"Because I never learned to drive. I tried. And I'm running out of time. You're the only person left who owes me anything."

Charlie paused for a moment, suddenly aware that she grew up in this house, with this family, and he might very well be the only non-white person to whom she felt any real connection. And she didn't know him at all. "If all you need is a ride, anybody could help you. All you have to do is leave these walls and ask the first person you see."

"I did ask an *anybody*. You." The muscles in her jaw flexed, but she kept talking. "I'll let the generator run for another hour. Then we leave. Got it?"

"Sure."

"Good. You can wait outside."

Charlie nodded and started to turn, but stopped and said, "You know, it's not the way you think it is." He sensed her rifle lift. "Outside, I mean. It's not hell beyond these walls the way you describe it. People are thriving in a lot of places. They're happy too. Finding themselves. Finding more than they had before."

"You mean before the world died."

"Sure, yeah. Before that. A lot of the world died, but not all of it. You're locked up here in your castle thinking we are all damned. But we're the lucky ones."

"Lucky how?"

"Lucky because the world has tried to destroy me in every kind of way, but I am still here. So are you. So are a lot of good people. Ain't no other people in the history of the world ever had so little of a serving of living as us. And now, we got all of it."

She stared at him long enough to keep herself from crying. "*We?* There is no *we*. I said this is my grandmother's house. My mother raised me in it. Nowhere else would take me and my mother in after you left. Now my family's dead and I am stuck here with you. If it wasn't for them I wouldn't be living at all. No thanks to you."

"Child, where do you think I've been all this time?"

"Don't know. Don't care. You left. The only reason you're even here now is because you're guilty. All the good in the world is gone and nothing's left but the guilty."

"I didn't leave you."

"My mother never told me why you didn't come back. But now's your chance. Why did you leave? Where were you all of my life?"

Charlie couldn't speak. He didn't have the words to tell her about all those years of being nameless and in shackles, and what all those years taught him to believe about himself.

"Didn't think you'd have much to say. I don't want to hear your excuses anyway. Outside. Now. I'll be ready in an hour."

Numbly, silently, Charlie followed her command and carried himself back through the front door, his mind blank but his heart racing. Outside, the day felt electrified with aggressive light. Confrontational. Her mother never told her the truth about what happened to him, not where he'd gone, nor the unforgivable things she'd done to send him there. She didn't tell her what so many years in a prison spoils in the spirit of a man. His daughter knew nothing of him. *Nothing*. Not him as the aggressor. Not as the felon. Not as the rapist. Not the fullness of his darkness. Indeed, the entirety of her association with his name made up only a vacancy and a bit of anger sprinkled into the void. Moreover, she represented something from inside him now out. His own darkness, imbued with life and lips and looking, capable of making a case upon him. Judgment. Judgment, he understood, was the chief function in the life of any man's daughter. To declare her father, in the simple courage of living her way through this world, as a man of value. Or not.

In the harsh daylight, his conflict reorganized itself. He could never fully answer the equation of who he was or could be. But all he was to his daughter was an emptiness he could fill up with any version of himself he wanted.

That's what the daylight revealed.

Within his daughter's innocence, a chance to reclaim his own.

6

THEY RESEMBLED EACH OTHER.

That fact annoyed Sidney most of all, the undeniable clarity of that resemblance. The nose she'd fretted over was his. The lips the boys at school teased as too big to kiss were his. And the eyes, shaped like they were created solely to be mad at the world—sloping, scrutinous, and weary—they were his too. But more than seeing their similarities, she felt them, as shudders to the chill of coming rain. That her mother loved her as much as she did implied that there was something in his features that maybe her mother once loved too. Maybe those eyes or that nose. Perhaps a mysterious element of his nature that met her mother at the peak of a youthful rebellion.

Sidney sat down her rifle and slumped her body on the pallet of pillows turned bed in the living room. More practical than comfortable, she told herself that taking residence in the living room over her bedroom meant she'd see possible intruders and escape them if needed. But the truth was that in the living room she didn't have to be who she was in her bedroom. She wasn't that girl anymore. Not the one with a mother who loved her, little brothers who pined for her attention, and—none of it mattered to even think about. In the end, her room lacked the necessary abstraction. Too uninterpretable to be a proper monument. Much too tangible to be a ghost. Every time she opened her bedroom door, the breath of air recalled that certain *something* within her not brave enough to stay underwater and drown with the rest of her family. That *something* too weak to walk through the gates of heaven before they closed. And she believed—was certain—those gates had closed. Heaven took all the good people, and she was not among them.

She got up, restless, and checked her bag once more. She'd stuffed the insides with more of her mother's things than her own: jewelry, scarves, diary pages she was afraid to read, dresses she hoped an occasion might inspire wearing. Death made everything her mother ever touched sentimental. Worse were her mother's things she couldn't take. The kindness, the safety. Sidney hoped to carry enough of who the woman was to retain something familiar where she was going. The last place on Earth that still mattered. She dug down to the bottom of her bag to read the note again. She'd found it taped to the entry gate, written on cardboard in a handwriting she couldn't mistake.

If anyone is alive, I am leaving to go be with the other survivors in Orange Beach, Alabama. We are not all gone. We are not all gone.
—A.W.

"A.W." stood for Agnes Waggoner. Her blond-haired, green-eyed aunt, still living. They weren't close before the event. Agnes was her aunt by marriage, so they rarely talked without her uncle near, and when they did, the conversation regularly turned awkward, short and rashed of sighs. But none of that mattered. *We are not all gone,* the note said. And that message meant, even in the smallest way, she still had family. She scanned the note a dozen times before she started to believe what the letter said. A few more dozen times and then crashing Rick's truck led to her calling on the last man she ever believed she'd need.

She stuffed the cardboard note back down into her bag. *Just get south,* she thought.

Then the house alarms went off, and she jumped to her feet.

She'd forgotten to close the gate.

She sprinted for the door, rifle high just as Rick taught her, the words thumping in her heart: *We are not all gone.*

We are not all gone.

7

CHARLIE SAW THEM coming before he heard the alarms.

A figure, as dark as a shadow, ran up the driveway. The figure moved fast, arms flailing, too spirited to be a man. Charlie squinted to see the jubilant little dreadlocks leaping up.

A child, no more than ten years old, running, laughing, leaping toward the Waggoners' home as if toward his own. When the child froze, mid-leap, all the excitement in his face shocked to white-eyed fear, Charlie finally heard the alarms.

The rifle barrel appeared in Charlie's periphery like a sharp cut through the sky.

What happened next happened fast.

"Get off my property!" His daughter deepened her voice to give weight to her command. "Turn around or I will shoot you."

Charlie watched his own child hold the gun with a concentration he'd witnessed many times before, a focus that did not see a life in its scope, only threats, deserving—all of them, regardless of offense—equal penance. She held the rifle butt against her cheek, her breath sharp but controlled. The sun made gauzy her skin's indoor paleness, and up close her hair looked like a complete failure to care. *Wild,* Charlie thought, as he watched his daughter aim a rifle at a boy.

Out of the trees, to the left, another figure appeared, running into the fray.

"Please don't shoot! That's my son!"

A man. A father. Charlie saw his eyes before he could make out his face. Big, terrified white eyes, poking out like the two last eggs in a carton.

The child, with both hands up, never looked back at his father, only the gun now withdrawing away from him. Charlie watched his daughter's aim go from son to father.

"Stop, or I will shoot you," she repeated. "Both of you."

She spoke those words as though she'd heard them before, believed them, and made them her own. But the man didn't stop, and wouldn't.

She squeezed the rifle butt closer to her cheek, adjusted her grip, and focused through the scope. She clutched the trigger to shoot him. Charlie knew she would, the man and his child knew she would, and Charlie suspected his daughter knew she would shoot two people dead on her mother's lawn. So he put his own body in front of the barrel.

"No. I can't let you do this." Charlie kept his hands down and sought out the similarity between them in the shape of her eyes. More than blood bound them together. She endured the same darkness that tied both of their hands and feet to questions they could never answer. "Put the gun down. You gonna shoot that man and his kid? You gonna live with a death on your hands for the rest of your life?"

She said nothing as she looked past him. He put his hands together like a prayer over the barrel and slowly guided the weapon down. "I know you want to protect this house. And you can, but not like this. We don't live in that kind of world anymore. We gotta be better than this."

We. He heard it in his own voice as though outside of his body. *We*. Like a ripple through time. Her tension gave, the gun dropped, and her brow ruffled at him in mild astonishment.

"That's a child, understand me? You can't go killing a child. Ain't a thing in this house worth that."

Charlie turned to the man, shielding his son, and showed him the palms of both his hands. "It's all right, friend," Charlie said. "We're sorry to scare your son like that. I promise you, we mean you no harm."

The man sent his son running back into the trees, where, Charlie saw, two more figures waited. A mother and a daughter. Less jubilant than relieved, the boy ran back into his mother's arms. Charlie glanced at his daughter watching the scene unfold.

"I swear, we was just passing through," the man said, his voice still shaking. "On our way west. We've been stopping where we can, that's all. My son likes the big houses."

Charlie smiled. "I bet he likes sleeping in the big ones."

"He does. That's all. I promise you."

"This big house right here belongs to my daughter. But there are plenty of mansions all over this neighborhood. I'd say be careful, though. They're gone but they're still in the air, y'know." Charlie looked over at his daughter, who stared down at her feet, unwilling to make eye contact, then back at the man. "You said you're headed west? Where?"

"Don't know. We just going until it feels right to stop. Like explorers," the man said. "There's a lot of country out there to be had. Never even knew someone who's seen the Grand Canyon with their own eyes. Heard people talk about it, learned about it, but ain't never seen it, y'know?" The man glanced over his shoulder to see his daughter chewing on an immature apple. "Appreciate you stepping in front of that barrel. If we can't protect them from bullets in this world, ain't a world out there where we can, feel me?"

"I feel you."

Charlie sensed his daughter's eyes slip away as he dapped the man and embraced him.

"We'll be on our way. Sorry about this. Best of luck to you all."

The man turned and jogged back down to his family. They were gone as fast as they came. Charlie watched them until they disappeared in the shadows of trees. When his eyes went back to his daughter, she had vanished, her rifle lying in the grass like a dead snake. He followed her trail into the house, through the kitchen and the living space, and out a sliding door into the backyard, where the breeze smelled richly of lavender. He stepped out onto a wooden patio complete with a hot tub and a metal firepit, and beyond that, a long slope of stiff brown grass spiking down to a lake. The air skimming the lake's surface offered a chill that reached all the way to Charlie's backbone. And there she was, knees to chest, sitting at the shore and staring out. Still, but searching. Searching for answers, he imagined, quietly seeking the therapy of calm waters. Then Charlie understood. His daughter looked out at much more than a lake, more than just beautiful scenery.

The lake was a graveyard.

8

HER MOTHER HAD always called her special. And no matter how often her mother made the claim, nor even the sincerity with which *special* was uttered, she always heard *special* as *different*.

Sidney knew she didn't look like her mother. She had no attributes at all of the stepfather her mother married and moved into their family home. Her two brothers were many things to her, but her mother never called them special. Only her. And she felt *special* at school in the locker room shower, when her hair curled at the mouths of drains unlike the other girls'. She felt *special* at her baptism in the white basin and the white gown and the clear water she hoped might wash away her skin's explicit contrast. She felt *special* in the questions whispered between words to her mother, her father, her brothers. Family walks drew stares. Friendly outings mutated into interrogations. When she put her name on paper or her face on camera, examination, however subtle, often followed. Because she was special. And she never stopped being special. Not even as her entire family walked themselves into oblivion.

Special showed itself in a new way after Charlie stood in front of her rifle's barrel. She felt a certain specialness in the way he regarded the intruder on her mother's land as a *we*. As an *us*. Acutely she felt that alliance didn't include her. She'd heard *we/us* many times before. "*We* have to work harder than everyone else," a black teacher would say. "There ain't no quit in *us*," said the black janitor at her first job. They'd said these words with the same glimmer, same certainty, as Charlie had when he embraced the intruder. Same as when, stunningly, Charlie looked at her like a father would a daughter and said, "*We* gotta do better." But she felt no *WE*-ness. No *US*-ness. Just the walls of her glass house and the lonely reflection staring back at her.

Lost in those thoughts, she'd run back down to the lake. She kicked off her shoes to sink dry toes into the shore's supple red sand. The lake was still, afternoon sunlight coating the surface in a soft copper glaze, all of it wrapped by trees dying their way through fall hues. All was silent except the hush of ghosts.

Sidney knew she would have shot that man and his child. The shame of that knowing called her to the waters. A place to be reminded of the fragility of life, death as the ultimate erasure, and all the mindless decisions too easily made in between.

"I understand why you did it, why you pulled a gun out on that family."

She hadn't heard Charlie walk up. She didn't even know how long he'd been standing beside her. Sharply though, she felt his voice disrespectful, spoken aloud in such a sacred place, yet glad to have something other than the ghosts for once.

Without her contest, he gazed out at the dull water and said, "This is where it happened, isn't it? Where they did it?"

"I felt it, y'know? That morning. It was in the air, like music you could feel . . . like somebody switched on a radio. Mom was in the kitchen and the eggs were burning. When I saw her, she was looking up like she heard something far away. Real far. Then they just started walking. Rick was already underwater. Then Mom walked right in behind him. John and Adam, they went in too. I tried to stop them, I did—I tried so hard. They drowned in that lake anyway. There'll never be a day when I don't hate myself for not going with them." She sighed but did not turn to him. "Whenever my mother would sit out here and stare at the water, she used to say, 'A shore knows. A shore always knows.' I didn't know what it meant then. I don't even know what it means now."

They looked out to the lake together. The water's stillness made the surface a mirror for the sky, hell's eerie mimic of heaven.

"It's not fair," Charlie said. "Death never is. Neither is life. So you have to come to understand that you weren't left behind. You were saved."

She caught herself staring at him hard enough to see herself in his chin. From what shores did he hail? she wondered. African, Caribbean, Indian? She couldn't be sure but saw in his face how little she'd ever thought of the Nile. How little she thought of the Congo. Or the Serengeti. He existed to her like a sealed gateway to some other point of origin, leaving but broken lines destined to encode the lineage of malformed fathers and angry, puzzled daughters.

For the first time, she considered how she must look to him. Half of him and half of someone he hadn't seen since before she was born. Quickly, she combed through her hair with her fingers, only clawing it an inch before getting tangled in the matting. She should've straightened the curls. She should've made herself more elegant. But then she remembered who he was and that the only reason he was next to her was because her world came to an end. To keep herself from crying, she said, "My name is Sidney. My mother named me Sidney."

She watched shock spread through him like a wave, from his raised eyebrows to his shifting feet. She had only ever known his full name: Sidney Charles Brunton. Her mother had named her after him, and that name was the only thing that led her to believe that her mother had any feelings for him other than regret. Speaking his name worked like magic on his ear.

"She named you Sidney?" He rubbed his hands over his face and head. The complexity of his thoughts, the conflict of being happy and troubled, radiated off him like a warmth.

"That's how I found you in the registry."

"And now, it seems, I finally know something about you. It's a start, ain't it, Sidney?"

Hearing the sound of her name spoken in his voice, she realized she would never hear that name spoken in her mother's voice again. "It's a start and it's a finish too. It's all you need to know to get us where we're going."

"And where exactly are we going?"

"I told you, Kenosha. Then Alabama."

He got down in the damp red earth with her. "Sidney, I'm not here to do anything but help you. I ain't gonna pretend that I mean anything at all to you other than that. I ain't so sure I'd even be here now if the world didn't break. But the fact is I am here. You don't have to like me, but I need your trust. If you want me to help for real, I need you to put it all on the table. What are we doing here?"

Sidney realized her arms were folded up tight, muscles tense. She didn't want to speak to him, but when she tilted her head a little, the sun dipping behind him made him as dark as a silhouette, so speaking didn't feel like talking to a person but to something more like an emptiness waiting for anything to be poured into it. "You wouldn't believe me anyway."

"I promise you, if I've learned a thing at all in this life, it's that anything's possible."

She adjusted herself to face him and considered telling him about the note, but the man before her was no man she could trust. However much she looked like him, she wasn't made of the same stock. What version of the truth she could say, she paused just long enough to make more dramatic than she wanted. "White people aren't gone. They are alive and thriving down south."

He rubbed the short hairs across his chin, then sighed like something large and heavy had been discarded. "On my way here, coming through Indiana, I met a woman who set the land on fire and let it burn for miles."

"Why?"

"Trauma is my guess, but I don't know. What I do know is that the farther you go south, the worse people's traumas are. I don't know what we would be going into, but I don't suspect it's going to be a lot of white folks just hanging out."

"I knew you wouldn't believe me."

"It's not about belief. You have to understand, right now the south is a black hole. No communications are coming out and none are going in. Long before the event, the south for a lot of people was already hell, you understand? Hell for centuries, where statues got put up for the monsters who terrorized folks their whole lives. If that woman burned miles of land to dust for her trauma in Indiana, I'd guess folks in the south are not rolling out the red carpet for anybody thinking they white."

"You're wrong!" Sidney shot to her feet, his words having pulled tighter a knot already in her chest. The nonchalance with which he talked about *them* and earlier *us*, neither of which included her, burned her bright on the inside. Tears blurred her vision as she tried to run, but something strong grabbed ahold of her. A grip stronger than anything she'd ever felt. Strong enough to keep her from running back to her own loneliness. Her father spun her around to face him.

"Listen to what I have to say. I don't have any idea what it's like to be you. I'm sure you've been to your own hell and back and did it all by yourself. You're clearly damned strong, Sidney. Strong and stubborn. Which is exactly why you can't stay here like this, suffering and punishing yourself over something you didn't have a thing to do with."

"But they left me. They all left me," she said. "Forever."

"And they loved you. And the way love works is that it is and . . . it goes on." He turned her hand over in his and shook it. "Look, I promise you I'll take you where you want to go, whether it makes sense to me or not. I won't leave you until you're where you want to be."

"Why should I believe anything you say?"

"I'm here. Right here, right now. That has to count for something."

"But you said the south was dangerous. And now you're saying you'll take me?"

"I'll try to keep you safe and take you as far south as you want to go. I ain't saying it's gonna be easy. Hell, I don't even know how we'll make it that far, but I won't stop until you tell me to. That's my word."

It was the grip. His were hands conditioned. Hands that had learned to defend themselves and protect others. Hands that loved things by making them, shaping, fixing, forming broken things into admirable ones. Hands that could grip time itself, holding on to every tether to the past and to every hope for the future.

She shook his hand, and his grip felt like the beginning of climbing a tree.

"Say your goodbyes, go in the house, and get your things," he said. "If we leave now, we can make it to Kenosha before dark."

9

THREE WEEKS AFTER *it happened, Vivian hid in the shadow of her daughter's doorway, listening. Nearly a dozen teenagers wedged themselves into Nona's bedroom, all of them circling a manbo conjure woman.*

"Papa Legba," *Vivian listened to the conjure woman pray, and then,* "Marasa, Èzili Freda," *followed by the musical hum of her daughter and her friends rapt in the ritual prayer. Prayer that typically came before a spiritual reading*

Remodeling her room was the first thing Nona did when they returned from five years in Haiti. Her clothes and dolls, of course—those years aged her out of any lingering adoration. But then she took down all the celebrity posters, along with all the school honor roll certificates and various superlatives. She minimized her furniture and replaced her guest bed with a lounge of couches and soft chairs, intent to host her own salons, poetry readings, drum circles, and spiritual ceremonies. Vivian marveled at how seriously her daughter took all they'd learned back in Haiti, mostly because her daughter fought her from the moment they decided to leave and fumed all the way through those first three years. Fought like Vivian was the enemy. Fourteen years old then, Nona made sure her mother knew leaving America meant she would be abandoning her friends, meant never donning a ball gown and attending prom or ever strutting proudly and in single file across her graduation stage. All reasons failed to measure up to what Nona felt she'd sacrificed to obey her mother. Didn't matter that her father's father had been beaten bloody in a sundown town and then served five years for battery. Didn't matter that her mother's mother walked with King after a church was bombed with little black girls inside. Didn't matter just how long Vivian, as a result, had fought for space in America, which was as long as she could remember. Community organizer. Stump speeches. Sit-ins. Stand-ins. Street marches. Appeals to police. Appeals to judges. Appeals to school boards. Vivian's voice rallied the masses. And she was known across the south as the one to call when your plight didn't warrant Jesse or Al. But none of that mattered to her daughter. Not back then. And if Vivian was honest with herself, by then those things didn't matter to her either. She was tired. All that fighting and too little change. Too many hopes dashed. Too many funerals. Tired leaned into spent when she became the mother of black boys, three of them; first Tau, then Herald, then Fela. But when she mothered a black girl, feeling spent dropped into outright surrender. Her fighting spirit focused itself on protecting her daughter. Hosea helped with the boys, but protecting her little girl made Vivian less a sword than a shield. How could she possibly keep her daughter safe from all that being black in this country weaponized against her? Protect her life, of course, but proportionally protect her mind and heart? Did any place exist where the path to her daughter finding herself wasn't obstructed? Was there ever any room in this country for little black girls to fully self-actualize?

The conjure woman asked, "Whose name shall be prayed over the cards?"

"Nona."

Vivian listened to the shuffling of cards along with the shuffling of feet as a specific energy filled the room. Vivian barely knew the family she had back in Haiti. But there was land on the island with her name in soil that grew mangoes and tamarind. She had to take her family and leave, if only to show them roots that went down to the center of the earth. Roots that were theirs forever. And she did. She showed them proof there was more to this life than what U.S. borders could ever offer. Showed them that if they could not change the country, they could still change themselves.

"Ancestors spread," Vivian heard the conjure woman say. "Five cards to hear the guidance of those who came before."

Easy, Vivian mused, to hear the ancestors now.

10

CHARLIE WENT TO prison charged with raping his daughter's mother.

The lucidity of that fact smothered the last gleam of light in the depth of his darkness. He glanced over at his daughter, sitting in the passenger seat as they sped toward Kenosha, her face against the cold window looking out. Between the flashes of trees and houses, she shivered every time the still, blue Lake Michigan winked back at her. He would never tell her what sent him to prison, nor what he went through as a consequence. And, if not him, no one would tell her his truth, because everyone who knew had water stopping up their mouths from telling. Truth, Charlie learned, could be whatever he decided. Because if truth really mattered, the truth was he didn't rape Elizabeth at all. He loved her. And he believed she loved him. But like the bulk of a mountain broken down by wind and water, truth devolves. With enough lies, one cannot defend himself with his own truth no more than stone can stop a river. So, what is a truth when fact is no longer accepted as true? Charlie's courtroom verdict made its own facts about him, facts prison eagerly endorsed. The years to follow meant he no longer had to think about truth or lies anymore. What happened happened. And there wasn't enough truth in all the world to change it.

"So, you're what . . . just graduating high school?" She kept silent. "We've got a lot of hard miles to travel. I don't like talking any more than you do, but it'll make the miles move faster."

She didn't turn away from the window. "Fine. Ask one question."

"All right, but it goes both ways. I ask you one, you ask me one."

"I graduated high school right before it happened. I was supposed to go to college. U of W. But that's so far, far gone now. When I found you I was surprised colleges even still existed."

"They do. The best that they're able. What's your question?"

"You're a teacher—professor. I guess that's my one question then. How did you . . . When did you—were you teaching before everything happened?"

"No. I became a teacher out of necessity. When I was your age, I thought I would go to a college like Howard. I didn't, of course, but after the event I went there because I figured it would be the only place still on any sort of functioning axis. That hunch was right."

"What do you mean?"

"Well, black people've been activating and organizing since before America became America. As I thought they would be, the people at Howard were figuring out a way forward. But they didn't have all the minds to get them where they wanted to go. When I came, I filled a hole that needed to be filled, because I understand systems."

"Systems?"

"Yep. Systems. Any kind, really, but especially electrical. And that's what was mostly needed. They didn't have enough people who understood solar power grids and maintenance. So, now, I teach it. Wasn't hard for me. When I was younger than you I was already building my own radios, computers, power capacitors, and fixing every kind of appliance. Even used to make solar lanterns for people who didn't have light at all. End of the day, I fix things. Always have."

"Guess you don't need a degree anymore. Or even certified training," she said, not trying to mask her disdain.

"As long as you have something worth learning, you teach. That's the way of the world now."

"You're a repairman. We used to have standards. You don't have any business teaching anybody anything." Accusation in the tone of her voice spiced the air between them. "I wish every day that things could somehow go back to the way they were."

"Is that what you think you're gonna find in Alabama?"

She turned to him, flashing a familiar rage he often saw in the mirror. "You're glad it happened, aren't you?"

He'd resolved to keep his secrets from her, but seeing the fury in her eyes, he couldn't bear to lie to her face. Some part of him felt she'd experienced just as many lies as he had. And pain, whether sugared in falsities or tart with truth, was still pain.

"Yes," he said, but offered no softening context.

When she asked why, he realized he hadn't expected her to respond, for he hadn't at all considered what the answer might be.

"Because I'm tired. I'm so tired. And for the first time in my life, and every life of everybody I know, we finally have a break. As much as it pains me to say it, I'm glad to not feel the way I used to."

"You don't sound pained." The rage cooled enough for her to look away from him and back out the window.

"Don't you understand, to even begin to relish this feeling automatically makes me the villain they always thought I was?"

"There you go with that *they* talk."

A sudden, intractable annoyance added heat to Charlie's voice. "When I turned thirteen I begged my mother to take me to this fancy restaurant. It was outside of a country club, and I would watch all the nicest cars go in and come out. I wanted to see what they were doing. Didn't even know what kind of food they served, I just wanted to see it. For months on end, I asked my mother and she told me that I couldn't go. She wouldn't say why, but every time I brought it up, she'd look at me like I was mad and tell me to hush up. 'Out of your mind,' she'd say. But I just kept insisting. I had made my own money by then and wanted to spend it. For both of us. Eventually she gave in and we went. Damned if the whole place didn't go quiet the moment we walked in, and it was the first time I realized that there was a *they* and an *us*. I felt my blackness, and that blackness wasn't supposed to be in that restaurant. It was like we'd broken a spell just by being there. Everyone stared at me and my mother. Cutting their looks. Here I was, a child, and I could pain the eyes of other people by just being. Make them angry—make them feel invaded—for doing nothing at all but breathing the same air through a different-looking nose. We sat. We ordered. And then I saw what they delivered wasn't anything like what I was used to eating at home. It was all small plates you couldn't share, and all these rules for which fork when, which spoon when. I couldn't even tell you what the food tasted like because all I remember is feeling people's eyes on me. The whole time I could feel the question in their throats, wondering who let *them* in. So, yeah, there is a *they*. I didn't make it that way. But you can blame me for it if it makes you feel more like one of them."

She didn't turn back and he didn't take his eyes off the road. The silence between them stiffened and chilled. Charlie's mind drifted back to that night. After that dinner, his mother told him being black is being the villain in someone else's story. She went on repeating that conviction until it came true.

Charlie heard his mother's voice in his own as he told that story to Sidney. He remembered his mother as sweet, but in the expression recalled the grimness of her gestures. She didn't smile often but pursed her lips, seeming to almost protect herself from even the curl of a smirk. His memory felt her warmth but visualized the heat as an alertness, eyes watching, darting, questioning, on guard for something a young Charlie hadn't endured enough yet to see. The truth of her fears revealed themselves in the way she gripped his arm when they crossed a street, in the hard honesty that would not allow him to be naive, in even the way she stuck kisses on his forehead that felt like punctuations. His recollection of childhood was blushed red with love, but understood that red as more a terror in focus. She feared everything because everything seemed coiled up to injure her son while in the simple activity of living life. Feared like he just dangled out there, naked, blind, and alone, prey to something he couldn't stop no matter how hard he tried. And Charlie, glancing at his daughter, appreciated why his mother carried on protecting him the way she did. A lack of protection against invisible forces was the reason his daughter gripped her rifle the way she did. So Charlie allowed the stiffness of that silence its necessary space until they reached the edges of Kenosha.

Anytown, America. Tire repair shops, Burger Kings, Dollar Generals—nothing at all proved particularly special about Kenosha until they passed through its version of a downtown and out into the residential neighborhood, where the street opened wide, empty, and butchered. Every window on every building had been busted, walls scarred up, doors torn off their hinges. Hollowed breezes and little animals scurried in and out of homes shocked into a state of paralysis. Worse than all those houses and their startled expressions, every wall, the trees, the grass, the sidewalks, even the black asphalt, was wildly graffitied in white spray paint. Panic rose up tall in Charlie.

"This can't be good."

With two hands, Sidney gripped her rifle. "Who would do this?"

"I don't know, but whoever did can't be in their right mind. A lot of that has happened since the event, people losing their heads. We have to be careful."

Sidney rolled down the window to look more closely at the graffiti. "It's words. Bible quotes, I think. Quotes on everything."

"Tell me again why you wanted to come to Kenosha?"

"We won't be long. A few blocks up on the right."

They drove slowly, and Sidney pointed out where to turn. Even as they moved down the street, the graffiti and open houses continued.

"There." She pointed with one hand still on her rifle. "Number 105."

That house looked no different from the others: front door torn off, every window smashed, white words painted over the exterior.

"Sidney, I ain't so sure we should go in there. I just got a bad feeling."

"How long have you been following your feelings? And how far did that get you?" She opened the car door, slung her rifle over her shoulder, and stepped out toward the house. Charlie shifted the car into park and followed her, the confidence in her actions almost commanding him along.

A ranch-style house, wide and featureless, only a swipe of front yard to separate the house's entrance from the road. Charlie trailed Sidney down the stone pathway marching up to the porch. There, the graffiti read: I SEEK YOU WITH ALL MY HEART; DO NOT LET ME STRAY FROM YOUR COMMANDS.

Walking into a home without a door didn't feel like someone's home but anyone's. Charlie stepped inside and walked straight into a hallway lined with photos, which led to a kitchen that looked out on a living room of equal size. Sidney, familiar with the house, scanned the space quickly, then rushed down another hallway. Charlie kept behind her, enduring a sensation that struck him with the same intensity of being caught in a trap.

That feeling froze him in the hallway, where he caught a glimpse of a face scarred like a red-hot brand into his memory. Memories in a wave staggered him back just as Sidney breezed past.

"Whose house is this?" Charlie asked.

"Why?"

"Tell me, Sidney, who lived in this house?"

"My aunt Agnes and my uncle Thomas. Why, you knew him from before?"

He did. Nothing teaches knowing more than hate. And so he knew

Thomas as well as he knew any man. Charlie's stomach soured. He braced himself against the wall, his skin tingling with fury, his mind adrift in a sea of confusion, flashback, and anger.

"Hey. Are you all right?"

"I'm fine."

"You don't look fine. Just find a seat somewhere or something. I won't be long."

"Okay." He didn't say the word as much as toss it out in surrender.

Sidney slid past and left him drowning in that hallway.

Charlie stumbled into the nearest bedroom and sat down on the bed. Dizzy in his present state, the puzzle of his past pieced together into a stunningly clear picture.

Three nights. That's how long the love between him and Elizabeth lasted. Three nights of whispering sweet things, kissing, laughing with their hands over their mouths. Three nights for his life to both peak and unravel.

On their last night together, the moon hung as fat and as yellow as a grapefruit. They danced together at a honky-tonk college party where no one knew either of them. No one knew Elizabeth was only visiting her brother for a long weekend any more than they knew Charlie couldn't afford to go to the college on the other side of town. The secret couple danced and kissed until the night whisked them to a bed somewhere in someone's dorm and made no effort to keep the clothes on their bodies. With the lights off, they were both dark, and in the warmth of their embrace, the exchange of their breathing, they were entwined. Two lovers in the dark. Until the light came on.

Blinding white. Thomas calling rape. Screaming rape like a siren. Thomas pulled Charlie naked out of that sweet darkness. Off his sister. Into a blur of fists and elbows and kicks mixed with screams that felt like punches. And the light was so, so bright.

When the gun went off, Charlie expected to see his own blood. Naked. Cold from the drying sweat. His blood stained the dull dorm furniture. He remembered how his blood looked plum-colored against the drabness. How his blood matched the tone of his naked body. And then a crowd of young white men pinned him to the ground until more white men came in uniforms and suits. Charlie was still bleeding when he heard Thomas say, "I caught him raping my sister. That's why I shot him." Charlie couldn't see Elizabeth. But he felt the whole room leaned toward her when an officer asked, "Is that what happened?" Charlie didn't hear what she said. But no one came to tend his wound. No one came to hear his side. The only thing to come out of that darkness still dark was Charlie.

The next thing he knew he sat in a courtroom and his mother was crying, and he watched Thomas tell a lie that solidified into conviction. He remembered looking at Thomas on the stand and thinking how much he resembled Elizabeth. He had those same geometric cheekbones, those same near-smiling lips, and he always looked right at Charlie. Right into his eyes, so hard and piercing that it was Charlie who looked away, Charlie who felt ashamed. When Elizabeth finally took the stand, Charlie couldn't look at her either.

"Did Thomas shoot Mr. Brunton?"

"Yes," Elizabeth had said.

"And was Mr. Brunton imposing himself on you? Without your consent?"

It took all Charlie's strength not to look up and meet her eyes. He remembered how strange the feeling was to love the eyes condemning him.

"Yes," Elizabeth said.

And she had exploded into tears. A gasp sucked the air out of the courtroom, leaving people to hold their chests and shake their heads. Trauma tears. That's what everyone thought Elizabeth experienced. But Charlie understood the truth of it in ways the people in that courtroom could not imagine. There were sides. And the maintenance of that division was, to her and everyone in that room, more important than any one man's life. More important than love. More important than the truth. She sacrificed Charlie to save that line of division, to save her brother. She sacrificed Charlie's body, his dreams, his potential, and gave his soul to the division. What astounded him most was how natural that moment felt. How expected. Everyone including him saw the inevitability of the outcome as if they were watching a film. He'd seen that story, and the ending never failed to properly deal out righteousness so visibly black and white. He watched Elizabeth cry and fill the courtroom with the smell of salt and lavender. Charlie never saw her again.

In time, he had forgotten Thomas's face. The inhuman pressure of prison days grinded all those lies into stone-cold truth. Charlie became the villain in Thomas's story, just as his mother feared. And he would've fallen completely to the darkness, believing the lies along with everyone else, if, but one year later, a letter hadn't arrived that he had the strength to read only once.

From the kitchen, Charlie heard what sounded like a muffled scream, but was unsure if he'd dreamt the sound. He scanned the room quickly, idly aware that he sat on the bed where Thomas had made love and slept soundly each night.

"Sidney," Charlie called out into a silence that didn't budge.

The air soured wrong. Just wrong. That feeling confirmed itself when Charlie reached the kitchen and found Sidney's rifle still snake-like on the floor. He picked up the gun and, as fast as he could, checked every room and opened every door, finding no sign of Sidney. Terror whipped across his back. He raised Sidney's rifle and raced outside. He'd never held a gun before. Never even aimed one. But what he found outside forced his hand. He raised the gun with every intention to shoot.

A figure, cloaked in white, had his daughter by the neck, covering her mouth and dragging her across the spray-painted grass. A Ku Klux Klan uniform. That's what the figure wore. White pointed hood. White gloves. White robe. And behind all that white, a black-faced man and his black eyes looked back at Charlie.

"You ain't welcome here, nigger!" the figure screamed. "Y'hear me? Get! Get, goddamn it. She's one of us and you ain't gonna make a nigger out of her! Get!"

"Let her go." Charlie adjusted the gun, then cocked the rifle as he had seen others do.

Sidney, screams stifled under the man's grip, reached out to Charlie. The sight of her steeled him.

"I said, release my daughter."

Like a snake, the man hissed at Charlie, then shook his head violently. "Nigger! Nigger! Nigger!"

"I don't want to shoot. Let my daughter go. Now. Or I swear I'll shoot you dead where you stand."

And then the man's eyes widened and he fell to his knees, weeping. Sidney broke free and sprinted into Charlie's arms. He guided her behind his back and kept the gun's aim steady on the sobbing hooded figure. And then, suddenly, the man's tears stopped. His eyes seemed, disturbingly, to be smiling as they focused on Charlie. When he spoke again, his voice shifted, softened, like a second person suffered inside him.

"Brother, brother man. Be easy, why don'tcha? Ain't nothing to it but to do it. C'mon, now, you know what it is." A weariness added syllables to his every word, dragging *A*s, pulling *O*s, and stomping *T*s into *D*s.

Charlie, confused, watched the man crack open a light inside himself, returning to something nearer to civil. Behind Charlie, Sidney whispered "shoot him" over and over.

"What's your name?" Charlie asked.

"Little. My daddy called me Little. Too little. Always too little."

"Little, why did you do all of this?"

"Little don't want to go backward. Only forward. Away, away . . .

away." His whimpering stopped abruptly. Tears turned to spittle flying from his mouth in a rage, whipping him back to the other person inside him. "Motherfucker! You hear me, motherfucker. This world ain't meant to be. Ain't meant to be. This hell. This hell, you hear me? You ain't welcome here, nigger! This here a segregated town, coon. Don't be here after sundown. Your ass gonna be swinging from a tree."

"Shoot him!" Sidney gripped tightly to Charlie's back.

"Please." Instantly the second person inside him resurfaced and the man's whimpering returned. "Please let me go. Little ain't done nothing to nobody."

Charlie observed the man, his oscillation between grief and rage, between the powerlessness of being Little and draping himself in the only real power he'd ever seen. A man cracked in half under the pressure of being.

Charlie whispered back to Sidney, "He's insane, but harmless." He relieved the gun's aim. "Go on, Little. Get as far away from here as you can."

Little sprang to his feet and ran, flinging back over his shoulder, "Coming back with the whole Klan, nigger! Gonna roast you like the pig you is."

Little ran until he reached the end of the street, cut to his right, and disappeared behind the spray-painted houses.

When Charlie turned, Sidney hugged him tight, her body shivering with tears.

"I got you," he told her. "I got you."

Charlie wrapped his arms around his daughter, who felt like a small child against his chest. He held her until her tears stopped, until her only movement became a burrowing, snuggling up close to a safety he had no idea he could provide. In the fray, she seemed to have forgotten who Charlie was to her, filling that void with a father. Suddenly, powerfully, Charlie imagined himself so much more than he ever thought he could be.

With difficulty, Sidney pulled herself back. "I'm sorry . . . I didn't mean to . . ."

"It's all right. I'm with you."

"I can't be here anymore."

"I'm gonna take you where you want to go."

"You don't understand." She stepped back, steadying herself to reveal a truth. "A month or so after it happened, I was down at the lake behind my house paying respects. I didn't hear anything, didn't see anything. And when I went back in the house, the alarm was going off, so I figured it was somebody trying to steal something. When I went to the gate there was just a note written on a piece of cardboard. I couldn't believe what it said. Read it over and over again just to be sure. It said that not everyone had died. And, to prove it, the note was signed by my uncle's wife, Agnes. You understand? She's white and she's still alive. She said there is a colony in Orange Beach, Alabama. What I know is that if Agnes wrote that note, it means she has to be alive. And if she's alive, there has to be others too," she said.

"I just don't understand the rush."

"It's been a year! I have to see what's out there. She's the only person I have left from my old life."

"All right, all right." He nodded, scanning the silent street, trying not to imagine how many times his daughter tried to leave this world. "Seeing this now, I don't think it's a good idea to drive the full way."

"How else are we going to get there?"

"You think she left any cash in the house?"

"We're not stealing from my aunt."

"We are if you want to get to Orange Beach. We're going to have to get a flight."

"Fly?"

"Yep. Airports are still functioning. They're different from what you remember, but I suspect it'll be safer than driving. Hopefully I have enough on me to get us both a ticket."

She folded her arms, scoffing. "I've never even seen a black pilot before."

"That don't mean they don't exist. We're lucky the closest airport to us is sure to have plenty of them that can get us where we want to go."

She looked at him, confused. "What airport is the closest?"

"O'Hare, Sid. Chicago O'Hare," he said. "Leave the rifle."

11

THANK YOU.

For Sidney, *thank you* made up the only words worth speaking on the drive from Kenosha down to Chicago. Charlie had saved her life, saved her from that demon of a man.

From the passenger seat, Sidney observed Charlie. His eyes did more than drive. They scanned the road, the woods, even the sky, for the possibility of danger. Something had turned on inside him back in Kenosha and was now fully activated. She'd felt the ignition in his chest when she burrowed herself up close. Heard the start of something like a second heartbeat pumping from some other place, some other time, some other world, here to confirm for her a truth. But what she felt in Charlie she experienced as a contradiction, exposed by a man calling himself Little. He was wild, fearsome, destructive—mad with bitterness and ferocious with lust—everything she'd been taught of black men. Their eyes, she'd gleaned, often gave them away. Seeking eyes. Hunting eyes. Wide and dark, attached to granite forms, bodies as strong as oxen, minds feral as cats. Little had confirmed those lessons as truths, his arms so powerful, intentions so dark. The contradiction came as a shock when Charlie arrived to her rescue like a hero from a movie she'd never seen. Protective. Still as bedrock. With a voice like its own god, he'd commanded, "Release my daughter." In his arms, she imagined one of those children lost in the woods and raised by wolves. Charlie came out of the dark to save her life. And she knew he would have done so at the expense of his own. Safe. That's what she felt. Not comforted or understood. Just safe. But wasn't Charlie also a black man, same as Little?

She watched him, keeping the car on a slower and not particularly scenic route off the coastline just so she didn't have to see the water. Driving with his bright eyes. Not hunting, securing. Not wild, alert. Sidney's heart had no preparation for the feeling that stirred within: protected, by a force the world and everything in it taught her to fear.

As the car toured around the knob of Lake Michigan, she could smell the frightful waters she couldn't see. Only then did she even question everything that ever made her imagine this man as a wolf to begin with.

"Thank you."

She said the words once more, unaware how deeply those words connected them. Deeper than language. Deeper than skin, bone, or blood. Down all the way to the foundations of time and lineage itself. Where all the true things are.

12

THEY ARRIVED IN Chicago just as the sun set. Charlie watched Sidney marvel at the speed and energy of the city. Crowded with cars and bodies flowing up and down throughways, cold gusts of air conquered by the heat of black and brown faces.

"So many people," she whispered. "All the lights and cars. It's like nothing ever happened."

"No. It's not. It looks busy because people're working hard trying to get back to some kind of normal. Figuring what we can and can't do."

Outside, billboards flashed upcoming comedy shows, people bundled up around barrel fires, drinking and laughing steam into the air; Charlie could even see the Centennial Ferris wheel, still lit, still turning.

Thick lines of paint slashed across the signs near O'Hare, except for Terminal 1, marking it the only possible exit. If that wasn't enough, military vehicles blocked lanes with Humvees and muscular SUVs tinted with the dark shapes of people inside.

"I didn't realize America still had a military."

"No, just everything anybody needs to start one."

Charlie followed the implied demands until he reached the exit for Terminal 1's outdoor parking lot.

"Are you sure this is safer than driving?"

Charlie had flown only once in all his life, a short flight over two decades ago. "Only one way to find out."

When Charlie parked the car, the airport terminal system illuminated into making sense. A key box stood at the end of every row of car spaces, and every car space had a number.

"We have to leave this car," Charlie said. "It's part of keeping the transience."

"The what?"

"Keeping things moving. You leave your car when you depart, so when new people arrive, they have a car waiting for them."

"Like rental cars . . . but for free?"

"Yeah. Like that."

The lot was three-quarters full, with groups of people walking toward the terminal. He grabbed his bag as well as offered, though Sidney refused, to carry hers. He hung his keys on the hook with the corresponding number in the key box at the end of the row.

"So you're just going to leave your car for anyone?"

"Wasn't really mine to begin with."

Together, they marched the distance to Terminal 1. The crowd grew in that space, coming together to feel, by previous standards, exactly how airports used to feel: buzzing with the activity of individuals intent to go somewhere else. Inside, though, truth clarified just how new this airport experience would render.

One long service counter stretched the terminal's full length, making one grand check-in. No Deltas, no Uniteds, no Southwests. No brands or companies at all. No priority lanes, classes, or special lounges. Just a long counter, dotted with well-dressed representatives ready to assist. Charlie slid into the shortest line and scanned the terminal. The counter reps wore cloud-blue button-down shirts with navy-blue berets, their posture and smiles resolute in keeping decorum. Charlie observed similarly dressed people, distinguished by different-colored berets. Yellow. A few greens. Dozens of reds. The red berets, he noted, positioned themselves like trees, though their eyes darted back and forth, alert. Military, he considered, remembering the Humvees outside the terminal, or at least some type of police force. Sidney squeezed close enough to him to be an inch from touching, her eyes looking out, skipping from face to face, in as much fear as curiosity. And then Charlie saw something he'd not seen since the earliest days after the event. A face bobbed about that was not black, but Asian. He saw a man first, moving quickly beyond the check-in counter, followed by a woman and two teenage boys.

Sidney nudged him. "Did you see that?"

"Yes."

"They were Asian. If there's Asian people, then there's gotta be people like me."

"There's certain to be people like you, Sidney. But I haven't seen a single person that looks like the other half of your family."

She flashed angry eyes at him.

"Next!" One of the reps, a muscular young woman with a smile like a light bulb, waved Charlie and Sidney forward in line.

"Welcome to the new Chicago Airport. How may I be of service to you today?"

Sidney cut in front of Charlie before he could speak. "How does all this work now? I don't see anyone with tickets, no actual airlines or security. How do we even pay? I can't imagine that any of this is safe."

The woman beamed again as if she'd been turned on. "Yes, as I am also sure you can imagine, many things have changed. Still, the simple fact that I am here with you right now proves that some things haven't changed at all. You're right, there are no more airlines because, well, why would there need to be? We are one airport now. We have regular flights to all the major airports across the country, but the smaller airports require permission."

"From who?"

"The pilot, of course. And there is security, but not like it used to be. All passengers need only a stamped pass to enter the gate, and you can remain in the terminals for up to seven days to get your flight."

"Why would anyone want to stay at an airport for that long?"

"Because, as you pointed out, some things are different. Throughout your stay you'll note that the blue berets like myself are customer service. Green is property maintenance, yellow is flight crew, and red is security. This is meant to be a transient space. After your pass has expired, you will not be allowed back for thirty days. After that, the red berets will usher you out."

"What if we want to go somewhere else during those thirty days?"

"Then I'd say you're doing too much. Now, where are you looking to fly?"

Charlie stepped in front of Sidney as much to speak as to stall her interrogation. "We're trying to get as close to the Gulf Coast as possible, or anywhere in Alabama ideally."

The woman, still smiling, shook her head. "I'm sorry, but Alabama is a no-fly zone."

"Well, I'll be damned." Charlie cut *I told you so* eyes at Sidney. "Why would Alabama be a no-fly zone?"

"As far as I understand it, Alabama is now a monarchy. Alabama has a king."

"A what? That's absurd. How is that even possible?"

"Sir, I stopped asking what is and what isn't possible a little over a year ago, if you catch my aim. It is what it is. In fact, not many pilots are willing to fly south at all. Something about their navigation messing up. Best we've got is a flight to Houston in two days and Atlanta on Friday, but both flights are full and the Atlanta flight has a wait list. We used to have one to New Orleans, but they stopped welcoming flights at all. Outside of that, you'd have to petition for permission." She looked down at her computer, sighed, then leaned forward, her voice as low as a whisper. "Only one pilot I know is willing to go anywhere near Alabama, and that's Sailor. He's a right grumpy old man too, so I can't promise he'll take you. You'd have to convince him somehow. The problem is that if I give you this passport and he says no, after your seven days expire you'll have to wait another thirty days to try again. Up to you, of course, but those are the options. That or driving. There's talk about a train being built next year maybe, but, again, I make no promises. So what will it be?"

Charlie looked at Sidney, who seemed to be biting on the inside of her mouth. "We'll take our chances asking permission. How much for a ticket?"

"Oh, tickets are free. People gotta get places, y'know? But you'll need money to buy anything in the market."

"All right. We'll take it."

"Wonderful. You'll find Sailor and his crew at gate sixteen." She stamped two yellow cards with a blue date, giving one to Charlie and one to Sidney. "You'll need these passes every time you use the facilities, so don't lose them. I wish you luck with Sailor. And a word of advice: he loves to fly. They all do. That's why they do it. That's always the best bargaining chip. Enjoy your time at the new Chicago Airport."

At that, Charlie and Sidney followed the slow-moving crowds through security, except there wasn't much security. No bag scanners or body scanners, but the sound of the concourse was on them before they reached the corridor, a thunder of music and voices blasting them as soon as they made the turn. Sidney drew closer to Charlie, and when the corridor opened into the vast hall, she gripped his arm, confronted by chaotic energy.

"This is wild."

The airport terminal vibed more like a night market, buzzing with the chatter of people, the clatter of forks and spoons on plates, grills hissing, vendors clamoring, horns barking music through the clutter of color, noise, and confusion. So many smells, spicy, sweet, and charred.

Every numbered gate now resembled living rooms, rows of plastic chairs replaced with cushiony love seats, tables, and bean bags. People by the dozens lounged about their gate, laughed, ate, played dominoes, listened to music. Charlie's heart thudded and his mouth fell open; it felt like walking into the rawest, most exhilarating form of human nature.

Sidney's grip loosened, slipped, and before Charlie could stop her, she ran off to the farthest, emptiest corner in the crowded space.

Charlie pursued, but could only watch her slide down against the wall, tucking her tear-glistened face between her knees.

"Hey, it's all right," he said, unsure if he should touch her.

"It's not all right. It's all wrong. It's all wrong!" She looked up at him, her eyes strained and red, and Charlie's heart sank to a depth previously undiscovered. "It's not yours! Don't you understand? This isn't yours—none of it is!"

Finally, with a hand on her shoulder, Charlie tried to calm Sidney. "It's all right. Take a breath."

"You people haven't changed anything. It's like you just moved into somebody else's house—kept the couch and the drapes and just claimed it. But it's not yours. None of it. Same as that man who tried to take me—I look at all of this—you're all just wearing masks. Just trying to be something you aren't meant to be."

Her tears ran more confused than angry. And still, Charlie heard something true in what she said. That same feeling he experienced every time he walked through the Yard or woke up in a bed that wasn't his. In the absence of white people, the American identity moved forward, but with a handicap, limping under the weight of old ways and a crippled sense of self. Even the airport, different as it was, retained a tether to before. People still came to work on time and wore uniforms, still got paid by the hour, even valued the quality of their work as if quarterly reviews and raises awaited. Water in a cup, Charlie thought, with no memory of being the ocean.

"You're right, Sidney. You're right about all of it." Charlie sat back against the wall next to her. He searched for other things to say and settled on, "I imagine to you I'm no different than the people in this airport. But it isn't the world we have to remake, it's how we see ourselves in it. I've no idea how to do that."

Sidney's tension released in a sigh, and she leaned her head on his shoulder. Charlie felt like he did when fear curled her up into his chest. Felt like a father.

"When I was young, I used to fix everyone's electronics," he went on. "I'd sit out in my mother's front yard next to a tree from day to night, just tinkering away. I think that's the only time I ever felt like I was who I was supposed to be—born to be. I used to imagine I was a wavelength, like a radio frequency, moving free but still attached, y'know. Any problem in front of me, I knew I could fix it. Didn't matter if it was a washing machine or a car or an air conditioner. I could fix it because I was connected to the whole world, past and present. All the ideas, lessons, learnings—my radio wave could just plug in and know things. Like I pulled it out of thin air. That's the only time I felt like this world and all its ways made sense to me. Only time I felt like I was a part of it. Getting something and giving something back."

"That's great and all, but I don't feel connected to anything."

"You're my blood, Sidney. You're connected to me."

"This is a nightmare that won't end."

"And we'll navigate it the best way we know how. Come on, up on your feet, we have to find a ride to Alabama."

He took Sidney's hand, stood her up, and, together, they waded into the scramble of people. Charlie searched over and around bodies for gate 16, working hard not to be distracted by the smells of chicken frying and corn bread warming in a nearby oven. When he found the gate, the activity around it was much quieter than the others. Minimal in its design, it offered only a few places to sit, most of them messed with tools and plane parts tucked under tarps, all of it resembling an auto repair shop. A rep in a yellow beret waited happily at the desk. The closer Charlie came, the less and less he could determine the rep as a man or a woman. Long, ponytailed hair; smooth, teak-colored skin; and a soft brush of hair mustached over the top lip. What tilted Charlie's head wasn't simply androgyny, but how flamboyantly unassigned the rep seemed to be.

"Hello, welcome to gate sixteen." The shape of the rep's voice only furthered the indistinction. "My name is Zu, spelled *Z-U*, not like *zoo*, y'know, with all the animals in cages. What can I do for you?"

Charlie fought the urge to look at Sidney to see if she was as confused as he was. "I'm looking for Sailor."

"Oh, I'm sorry, Sailor is out at the moment. Working on the plane. Maybe there is something I can help you with?"

"Maybe. We want to get to south Alabama—"

"Alabama?"

"Yes."

"No. You don't want to go to Alabama. Nobody wants to go to Alabama. In fact, I'm not so sure anybody can even *get to* Alabama. Sailor says flying over it is dangerous, so I can't imagine what it's like on the ground."

"Why do you call it dangerous?"

"You'd have to ask him to explain . . . but, yeah, sorry, he's not available."

"When will he be available?"

"You all in a hurry?"

"Yes," Sidney injected. "We are. Can you help us?"

"And here I thought this world wasn't in a hurry anymore." Zu shot a narrowed stare at Sidney that softened nearly as quickly as the glare had arrived upon seeing the tears, as did Charlie, still glassing his daughter's eyes. "Hold on a second, little one, let me see what I can do."

Zu stepped back near the jet bridge door and picked up a phone. Words were mumbled that neither Charlie nor Sidney could hear, but Charlie gripped his daughter's hand tighter, hoping enough for the both of them. Zu hung up the phone and waited. After a moment, the jet bridge door swung open and in came a graying, but sprightly, man. He was small, nearly a head shorter than Zu, with wrinkles and a scowl to suggest he knew no other emotions than anger. He wore a work jumper splotched in grease stains, and Charlie considered the faraway possibility that a man who worked on planes could also fly one.

The man reached the rep desk, his every breath on the verge of a growl, and said, "I hear y'all want to go to Alabama?"

"That's right," Charlie said.

"Why?"

"All due respect, how is that any of your business?"

"You want me to fly into a place where more than a couple of planes've disappeared without even a broadcast, don't ya? Then it's in my best interest to know why. Go on and speak the truth. I ain't here to judge you."

"We're going to Orange Beach," Charlie said, shivering at his next words before they crawled out of his mouth. "We believe white people started a colony there."

Charlie half expected the man to laugh in his face. But Sailor just sucked at the back of his teeth, staring. "White ain't a people. White is a spell they put on themselves. Losing they minds in it too much is probably what killed 'em. So there can't be a white colony, because *white* ain't an idea no more. You follow?"

"That said, we still need to get there. Can you help us?"

"You've heard that Alabama has a king now, haven't you?"

"Yes."

"Then you've also heard that planes can't even fly over it without going haywire?"

"I have."

"And you still come here asking?"

"I was thinking that, well, as much as I want to go, all these people who don't know what's really happening down south would maybe want to know. The truth, I mean. Ain't you curious to know?"

Sailor stared at Charlie for a long time, cut eyes at Sidney, then back to Charlie. "Come, follow me, let's talk privately. You can leave her here. Your child is in good hands with mine."

Charlie then saw Sailor's resemblance to Zu just as he felt the panic of him leaving spike up inside Sidney.

"It's all right, Sidney. I'll only be gone a minute." He turned his tone to Zu, but kept his eyes on Sidney. "You keep safe watch on my daughter here. She is the only family I have left."

Charlie watched his daughter blush, then nodded to Sailor before following him out on the jet bridge, keeping pace with him all the way out to the plane and into the cockpit.

Charlie had never seen a cockpit before, awestruck at all the lights and switches and dials. Sailor sat down in the captain's seat and looked up at Charlie. A seriousness dimmed his eyes.

"What were you in for?"

The question stunned Charlie. He shifted his feet but did not look away and did not answer. Sailor held his gaze long enough to make the moment uncomfortable for the both of them before finally smiling to relieve Charlie of the standoff.

"I always wanted to be a pilot," he said. "The first time I ever saw one of these birds soaring above me, I wanted to soar too. I went into the air force as soon as I graduated high school. 157th Fighter Squadron, Swamp Fox. And we were goddamn demons in the sky, man. I loved it. The force taught me how to fly just about every plane there is, over every terrain. Taught me a lot more too. How to take no shit. How to fight. How to kill. So if ever I had a drink or two in me and the wrong motherfucker said the wrong thing, sure as shit they got the right answer. Damn near beat a man to death once. Fucking off-duty cop. That got me put in a cell for so many years I stopped counting the days. That shit took my whole future just like that. Violent is how they branded me, so I couldn't fly planes no more. Closest I could get was working on birds at whatever airport was paying. And even that had to come with a recommendation from my old commanding officer. I tell you all that so you understand: I know what it feels like to be a prisoner walking in a free world. More than that, I know what it looks like when I see it."

Charlie could see that look then too. He'd mistaken Sailor's gruff, stoic demeanor purely as anger. The man was angry, but an anger stomped down, pummeled flat, heat hardened, but stirring. Charlie said aloud what he hadn't said in years.

"They said I raped a woman."

"Did you?"

"Of course I didn't. But it's hard to prove yourself right when it's already decided that you're wrong."

"Then say it. Say, 'I am not wrong and I am not a rapist.'"

The words were strange in Charlie's mouth before he ever spoke them. "I . . . I am not wrong. I am not a rapist."

"Good. I'm not violent. Words are magic, you see? You say anything enough and you believe it. Belief is the first step on the path of being. Now that we know each other, let's talk business. There is something in Alabama I want, but I'm not ready to risk my freedom again to get it."

"What is it?"

"I work at this airport because I want to be up there in the sky. But, see, these planes run on fuel, and the airports have a monopoly on almost all of what's left. And I ain't heard no plans to dig in the ground to get more, so eventually gas will run short. I give it maybe two years or so, and we'll have to start figuring out a new way. Until then, I want to keep flying. Free as I want to. I don't want to be tethered to this airport. There's plenty of little ports I can take. Live in. Keep flying. But I need fuel, understand? Alabama's got plenty."

"You want me to get you gas?"

"That's right."

"How am I supposed to do that?"

"I expect you to be able to figure it out. If Alabama has a king, you could just ask him, assuming he is a polite enough man to give it to you. But in my estimation, ain't ever been a man in power that's a man polite. So I'd guess you need to steal it."

"How does a person steal gas?"

"Damn, I thought prison would've taught you at least a little cunning. Steal a gas truck, drive it across the border back to me."

"You gonna fly a truck all the way to Chicago?"

"No, fool. I have my own plans. And those plans ain't none of your business. What I need to know is if we have a deal. I will fly you down and get you across the border; you come back with the truck, and I'll get you back here. That's it."

"But I have to take my daughter—"

"Yeah, yeah . . . to the people who think they're white. But you don't strike me as a man who thinks he's white. So, you planning on staying in some wannabe white town with her?"

"No, I guess not."

"All right then."

Charlie thought of his daughter as he shook a hand that felt like stone, specifically how much of himself he put out for her and how, for once, it felt good to sacrifice himself. "Deal."

Sailor nodded and sat back in his captain's chair, seeming more like a captain than ever. "Now that that's settled, you'll have to wait a few days while I get this damned plane fixed. Keep getting an error and can't seem to solve it. Directional gyro won't point north. You don't want to be in the air without that working. I done replaced it twice and still getting the error."

"Maybe I can help."

"You ever worked on a plane?"

"No."

"Then what good are you helping me?"

"Well, by the looks of the error, the issue isn't your hardware, it's your software. My guess is the software needs new drivers."

"I'll be damned. Looks like you might be plenty good. Plenty good help, I see."

"It'll take me a bit of time. Like I said, never worked on a plane before. But I haven't met a system I couldn't fix."

"Good. Then, damn it, let's get going."

Sidney was laughing with Zu when Charlie stepped back into the gate lounge. Laughing with a full belly. He had yet to see his daughter happy, and just how much her happiness reminded him of her mother surprised him. Zu quickly stood to their feet and straightened up upon seeing Sailor. Sidney's smile evaporated when she saw Charlie.

"I think we have a deal," Charlie said. "He'll take us to the Alabama border, then we have to find our way down to Orange."

"When do we leave?"

"Might be a day or so. We have to fix the plane."

"A day!" Sidney nearly collapsed. "You want to spend the night? Here?"

"I've spent nights in worse places."

"Well, I haven't. I can't stay here. I'll sleep in the car."

"We can't leave, Sidney. You heard the attendant. We step out and we can't take another flight for thirty days. That's the rule."

"Then I'll walk."

"You can't walk all the way to Alabama."

"You don't know what I can and can't do!"

"Do y'all always fight like this?" Zu stepped between Charlie and Sidney. "They don't let passengers leave, but staff can, as long as they come back. I have to make a run. Sidney, maybe you can go with me. At least get yourself some fresh air."

Charlie watched as a leap of panic sprang through Sidney. "It's all right, Sidney." Suddenly tired, he said, "Go on and see the city," before shooting a look at Zu. "My daughter will be safe, won't she?"

"Yes, sir. Ain't nothing out there but space and opportunity."

Sidney's eyes dug a hole through Charlie. "Don't call me 'daughter.'"

Sidney didn't hug Charlie or say goodbye. When she turned her back, Charlie experienced a combination of feelings he never imagined could exist together. Anger, pride, sadness, respect, all rolling up into a word that again draped itself over his shoulders: *father*.

As a uniform, father slid under teacher. Under prisoner. Under, even, man. His heart raced as Sidney disappeared into the crowd. Father. Once on, that uniform would be impossible to take off whether or not Charlie had any business wearing it. Of all the things a man could be, this was different.

Father. Charlie, for certain and without any sign of letting up, felt like a father.

13

TOO ANGRY NOW to be afraid, Sidney trailed Zu through the terminal with a yellow beret fixed atop her head, making her an airport employee. Together, exhilaratingly, they strolled right past the stiff guards in red berets toward terminal parking.

Not until the open road, the arrival of Chicago's glittering skyline rising like tidal waves before them, did the exhilaration of escape settle into fear and fact: she rode alone with a stranger, racing toward a city she'd been taught all her life was crime infested. A war zone, her stepfather called Chicago, and people like Zu, freaks.

An etiquette tightened her body and her breaths drew short. She knew better. When Rick took her and her brothers deer hunting, that was his very first lesson: don't let fear draw you out of a safe place. "Animals aren't smart," he'd say, "but they aren't stupid." Anger, fright, and pride walked her into a more vulnerable position.

"You're safe," Zu said, sensing her panic. "If it helps, you can even drive."

"I don't know how to drive." Sidney adjusted upright in her seat. "I don't even know where we're going."

"The truth is, I didn't really need to do a pickup, but it seemed to me that you needed a bit of fresh air. So I thought maybe we could get some food. Chicago's famous for hot dogs, and I know a place that's just magic. But if you prefer, I'm happy to take you back too."

"It doesn't matter. I'm realizing there aren't any safe places left in the world. Not for people like me."

"Except Orange Beach, right?"

"That's right."

The curl of Zu's smile made heat next to her, a heat that turned her suddenly childlike and silly.

"Look," Zu said. "Don't you worry your pretty little head not one bit. My job as a flight attendant is to get you to your destination safely and comfortably. And I am very good at my job, you hear me? Five-star ratings only."

"Five stars before or after?"

"Since the day I was born, darling. Since day damn one."

A certain joy in Zu's energy reduced the hardness in the air. That joy carried them into downtown Chicago, which, even at a distance, radiated with more light than she imagined any city shining anymore. The great skyscrapers and broad freeways lit up like a night from another time. Sidney could hear the churn of the city, still grinding, flowing and alive: the breathing of cars speeding past, the whirring of light against buildings, and all the echoes of life in motion. Music pumped out of building windows. People strolled sidewalks and crosswalks, moving and talking fast.

"Not everywhere is like this, y'know," Zu said. "Actually, outside of Atlanta and Detroit and maybe New York—*Brooklyn, anyway*—really nowhere else is like this. That's why we came."

"How is all this still so full?"

"Oh, honey. You really thought the world ended, didn't you? Poor thang. For some of us it's just beginning."

As they passed a bar filled with people and a theater with its marquee aglow for *Gem of the Ocean*, Sidney thought how different Chicago felt from Wisconsin. Emptied. Broken. That's what Wisconsin felt like. Nearer to sheltering in a carcass. But Chicago, in comparison, felt like nothing changed. Like nothing changed but the day of the week. Only the gentle sloshing of an immense Lake Michigan offered a lone reminder.

They drove in silence through the heart of downtown, where Zu bought them each a hot dog with mustard, peppers, and pickles, and found a spot at the top of a staircase looking down on Daley Center Plaza.

Down in the plaza, a Latin ball fluttered in full swing. Black and brown people, impeccably dressed in glitzy ball gowns and tailored suits, twirled and dipped in a vibrant formal. Everything from salsa to hip-hop to merengue to country music flushed the plaza with sound. Young boys held the young girls as they stepped choreographed ballroom dances. Circular white tables, arranged in little pods, were framed by long tables of catered food. The ceremony of the ball, that distinctly nervous but excited formal energy, lulled Sidney with its familiar sense of order.

"You want to go down there and dance?" Zu asked.

"I don't dance."

"You don't drive, you don't dance. What do you do other than don't do things?"

"Entertain you, as far as I can tell. What kind of party is that, anyway?"

"It's a quinceañera," Zu said. "They're celebrating one of those girls down there turning fifteen. I used to want to have one so bad."

"You didn't?"

"Nah. My mother was half Mexican, so we got to attend a lot of them growing up. After going to my very first one, I started begging my mom to throw one for me. I begged and begged. She died of cancer before I turned fifteen, but she never once even entertained me dressing up and dancing the night away."

"Why not?" she asked, aware suddenly that Zu experienced struggles with identity she'd never considered.

"She said boys don't have a quinceañera. Didn't matter what I said or how much I cried. She went to her deathbed keeping me from something that would've made me so happy, just because some faraway white fella shining in a white outfit told her what God expected of us."

"You can have all the quinceañeras you want now."

"I don't want one now. Hell, I'm ashamed that I wanted one to begin with." Zu stood up, looking down at all the boys in their tight jackets and all the girls in heavy skirts. "I look out there now and just think, *Is that it? Is that the best we can do?* We finally got the world to ourselves, and we still just continuing on with the program they made for us. I expected us to make something new. Something nobody's ever seen before. But all we do is become the best version of what they wanted us to be. The patriarchy didn't walk into that water, but I sometimes wish it did too. Don't matter, though. I'm Zu. Was before and damn sure am now." Zu, exasperated, sighed and sat back down. "Maybe you feel me, maybe you don't. But that's our struggle: identity. Who we are, and when we can finally be anything we want to be."

Sidney considered correcting Zu's mistake of saying *we* and *us*, but thought better of creating unnecessary tension. "I'm sorry about your mother. About what she did and, well, her passing too."

"Not a worry, darling. The parts of her I need to live on live on. And Sailor makes up the rest."

"You two are the oddest family I have ever seen."

"That's all a family is: space to be odd. We aren't perfect, but we are probably a lot more alike than we are different. That makes it a little easier to try and take care of each other. What about you and your daddy? Y'all always at the edge of a fight, or was all that arguing just being . . . odd?"

"My dad drowned in the lake behind my house. Charlie's my biological father, but he isn't my dad. I only just met him."

"Damn, girl. And he's still taking you where you want to go and trying to keep you safe?"

"I guess."

"That's about all any parent could do for their child. Especially ones like us."

"What do you mean, 'ones like us'?"

"Remarkable ones, darling. We are the remarkable ones."

They watched the quinceañera for a few more dances, chuckling but not speaking, finished their hot dogs and drove back to the airport. Sidney allowed herself, for once, to be free to talk, laugh, and make a friend in Zu, an expectation she'd not intended but enjoyed having.

By the time they returned to the airport, cots had been laid out in the gate lobby and most everyone in the airport slept, including Charlie. Sidney slid down quietly into the cot next to his. Behind her she felt the dark shape of his body and the gentle vibration of his snore cruising over deep, powerful breaths. He smelled of leather and the busyness of masculinity. A smell, she imagined, that all fathers are meant to carry. Only he wasn't her father. Not really. So she did her best not to let him hear her cry. Not him. Clenched her jaw to stop the swell in her throat, sniffled into the fold of her arm. All so he wouldn't hear. All so he wouldn't know how badly, even in the range of his safety, she still wished she was dead.

14

THREE MONTHS AFTER *it happened, Hosea stood at the port watching the ships come and go. And come and go they had. Over the last month, ships arrived from Haiti, Cuba, and the Dominican Republic. Reefer ships came carrying all sorts of perishables, ranging from tobacco and bananas to cane sugar and beer. The islands sent livestock carriers, as well as heavy lifts ferrying textiles and building materials. Ships went out too; Hosea made sure they were loaded up with equipment those islands severely needed, like medical wares, plastics, cotton, machinery, and all the gas they could handle. Good exchange. Good partnerships. That was key, Hosea and Vivian determined, to building a new society.*

Hosea nudged his son Herald, who looked so much like Vivian but had both his parents' intellect twice over. Just brilliant.

"Son, tell me again how it works."

"Well, you need silicon, gallium arsenide, and cadmium telluride, and together—"

"Explain like I don't know what you're talking about."

"Normal solar cells convert sunlight into electricity, right?"

"Right."

"Same thing, just made into a coating, like paint or stucco, in any color you want. I'm saying we should put that on everything. And everything will be able to retain a charge. Coat the buildings, roads, driveways, even cars. Make the whole city one big battery to use and store power so we never run out. Won't be strong enough to boost no rocket ship, but it's enough power to keep life moving."

Hosea and Vivian's eldest son, Tau, appeared next to them carrying, like a toy, a massive barrel over his equally massive shoulders. "And I guess you think I'm the one gonna be doing all that painting and shit, huh? Man, you crazy."

"Set that barrel down, son, and hush," Hosea said. "Ten thousand men and women standing back there looking for ways to help. You should be glad to be helping alongside them."

"I am, Pop, chill. You know I'm just playing."

"This ain't the time to play. We got enough work in front of us, understand?"

"Understood."

And there was plenty to do. Plenty to solve that Hosea still stood at the shores of disentangling. Hosea had gone to college to be an engineer. Wanted to be a city planner like his father. He had a good mind for it. But in his first year of school, he found himself spending less time in his books than he did standing in the courtyard listening to a tiny woman with a big voice tell anyone who would listen what needed to change for all people to be equal. That year, Hosea followed Vivian everywhere she spoke: he went to her rallies, attended her sit-ins, and gathered in the streets to march if only to keep in range of the most impressive woman he'd ever seen. He even went to the pop-up lounges where she sometimes used that great big voice to sing. Sing beautifully too. He'd played a little trumpet in high school and figured asking to be her player might be a way into having all that light she gave off shine, for once, directly on him. What happened next he would have never imagined. As soon as he was standing in front of her, she looked right at him and kissed him. Blew his mind. She said she knew right then she'd marry him. Like magic. She later told him that while he was a smart man and a solid trumpet, and in the right light he could be blood warming to look at, she kissed him because his values, she told him, were legible. She married him because she knew he could be trusted. That was Vivian's gift. Intuition. You couldn't lie to her or cheat her, certainly couldn't best her in a game of chess. She could always see a little further than everyone else. A little deeper too. So after all the years together, when she came to him saying they had to move to Haiti, he started packing.

He didn't know a thing about the little island except stories about the poverty and just how bad it was. But he would come to revere Haiti as a blessed place. Indeed, in the five years they lived as islanders, he'd be taught things that would change everything he believed possible. Taught so, so much. Vivian saw that coming too. Like magic.

Hosea watched their youngest son, Fela, start up a tugboat down at the base of the dock to pull platforms along the coast for distribution. That boy'll drive anything, *Hosea thought, thinking back when Fela was only a child and kick-started a motorcycle in Cap Haitien. The bike bucked him five feet in the air. He hit the ground and just laughed and laughed. Laughed as free as anything Hosea had ever seen.*

Hosea breathed deep. As he looked around at the world being remade before him, how intuitively everything came together, it seemed at times like magic too. But when you've been in a cave, chiseling for so long to get out, he mused, it will always feel a bit like magic when the light finally comes through. But there it was. Visible and bright. All that good light, finally coming through.

15

CHARLIE WOKE WITH the sun and found himself staring at his sleeping child. To be so near to something so fragile squeezed his movements tight with nerves. So rather than wake her, Charlie spent the day on the tarmac with Sailor, installing and testing the new directional gyro.

"All right, I'm logged in and running tests. Will be a little while, but we'll get a sense of what the issue is."

"Good." Sailor kept tinkering, deliberately not looking at Charlie. "A little space from their parent always helps. Lets lessons soak in."

"I hear you. But can't much of anything soak into stone."

"She always been that . . . tough?"

"Don't know. I only picked her up yesterday."

"That's your daughter, ain't it?"

"I was in prison when she was born. Wouldn't even be out now if what happened in the country didn't take her mother into the sea. So now I'm the only family Sidney has, though I can't say for sure she sees me as family."

"It's rough now, but it'll settle in just like everything does." Sailor sat down his wrench and leaned against the engine. "So you were in prison when it happened? What was that like?"

"Harrowing. I was at Sussex, out in the middle of nowhere. When it happened, just looked like all the staff had a meeting or something. Breakfast was due, and we were all still in lockdown. Then all the guards, the warden, even the clerks, they just walked out. Took a long time for us all to start to get antsy and the hunger to kick in. Honestly, we had all prepared to die in there and would have if people's families didn't show up in tractors, knocking down walls, and with bolt cutters for the locks. Our people freed us. First thing we did was go to the nearest steak house and cook up everything they had. Drank more cold beer than my body knew how to deal with. We laid up for a few days, and that's when I realized what really had happened."

"You mean all the dying?"

"I mean that what was left was all this negative, important space that black people didn't take up before. At least not enough of it anyway. So I went to work trying to figure out how I could help." Charlie thought about Gerald, from his class, and that maybe he wasn't just teaching mechanics after all. "Where were you when it happened?"

"Me? I was flying a crop duster in Mississippi. I saw it happening from the sky. Thought I was losing my damn mind. Hundreds of people—thousands—just walking. I watched them walk into the water so deep you couldn't see them no more. And they never came back out. Like they was being erased."

"That had to be terrifying."

"Yeah, but I was lucky to be up in the air. Had a cousin die on the operating table. Doc had just put her to sleep and cut her wide open before he walked out with the rest of 'em, left her bleeding."

"I'm sorry, Sailor. That sounds just terrible."

"Told her ass not to move to no damn Idaho. Ain't got no business in no place like Idaho."

Charlie's mind swept across America and all the places he didn't have any business being as Sailor continued: "Wouldn't call myself a godly man, but after that, you best believe I prayed like hell that what happened to them wouldn't happen to me. When I landed, well, I guess I understood the same thing you did. Everything was different."

"What did you do?"

"First thing was get my child. Then we both went to where we knew other black folks would be. Atlanta first, of course. Then Memphis, St. Louis, and we settled here in Chicago. Zu likes it here, and I want to make sure they have what they want in this world."

Charlie paused a moment before he asked, "Got any other tidbits on parenting you could share with me?"

"Well, I ain't some master parent. Zu's mother died when Zu was twelve. I made all the mistakes a parent can make since then, but learned from them too. Parenting isn't as much about them as it is about you. Don't matter who they are or who they want to be, you love and support them. Make space for it, understand? Not just raising them, but changing ourselves in the process. We spend too much time trying to wedge our children into something we think is right rather than following their lead. I don't want my child to carry what I carry, to feel what I feel. I want Zu to be free. And the only way to be free is to set them free. 'Go on,' I say. 'Go on and be,' and I make the space for them to be. That means moving my own shit—baggage, fears, worries—out of their way. Our children won't be like us, they will be better. So we can't put our insecurities on them. Space and time. For you and for them."

"Just not sure I should be doing this."

"You're smart enough to fix things, you're helping where you can, you're present here with your child. Go easy on yourself. The world needs as many Charlies as it can handle."

"The world was all too happy to put all the Charlies in jail."

"That was a problem, wasn't it? Ain't a problem no more. So what you gonna do?"

Charlie's computer dinged, its testing complete. "Good news. Just like I thought, you only need new drivers to be installed. Take about thirty minutes. Bad news is that you will need to take the gyro out and put it back in after the drivers are installed."

"Damn. Pain in the ass to take out. You a whiskey man?"

"Trying to be."

Sailor laughed. "Stop trying. Start being. Most things around here're cheap, but good whiskey ain't. You got money, don'tcha?"

"A little." A bit of regret spun through Charlie as he watched Sailor shake his head.

"So you planned your way south without cash on hand in case you get in a bind?"

"Hadn't really thought that far. What's the quickest way to get cash around here?"

"You mean aside from finding an ATM that ain't been cracked open already?" Sailor scratched his chin. "You play spades?"

Sailor took Charlie upstairs where once exclusive lounges were converted into entertainment spaces, complete with a small movie theater, an arcade, and a spread of gaming tables. With Sidney off with Zu, Charlie welcomed a moment for the tension to let up.

Sailor spotted Charlie a twenty to join a table. Dozens of games went on at other tables around them: spades, dominoes, dice, and others—a dim but raucous version of a casino.

Charlie and Sailor matched up against two women who, as best Charlie could gather, had been a couple that long broke up romantically yet maintained their spades partnership. A far stronger bond, seemed to Charlie. One of them—Boot, she went by, a short, round woman whose laugh made Charlie imagine an oak tree being shaken—talked relentless shit the first few hands. "Bag boy," she called Charlie when he bid four and booked seven. "Oh, you the weak one," she labeled Charlie when he short his books and Sailor had to win two extra hands for them to hit their bid. But Charlie had been watching the shuffles, reading the hands, and on the fifth deal did the last thing any of them expected. Charlie asked to run a blind dime. Sailor nearly fell out of his seat trying to take back the call, but Boot just shook her leaves. "Either a genius or a fool," she said of Charlie, "and I'm betting a fool."

But then the call worked, thrusting Charlie and Sailor into an insurmountable lead. At last, Boot's partner, Faye, poured herself a neat gin and finally spoke, each word revealing a mouthful of gold teeth. "Not a fool at all, I see."

Charlie won that game, so they played and bet a few more. As the more games went on, and the gin continued to pour, Boot spoke less and less, and Faye more. She seemed to want to talk about only one thing.

"I think we do it for nostalgia," she said, holding up a one hundred dollar bill. "How else could something mean nothing and everything at the same time? Y'all don't know the shit I used to do to get this kind of money. Didn't matter how many times my daddy said, 'I taught you better than that.' I wanted the car, the clothes, the jewelry—the freedom. Now I have it. All of it. And I'm still chasing something but can't call it, you feel me?" She laid the bill flat on the table. "Everything we know done changed, and I'm still staring at the same faces on these stacks. I don't know about the other cities, but in the Chi, it's still *cash rules everything around me*. Probably always will be."

As she spoke, Charlie cut the hand with a jack of spades and hit his bid. Over the course of their games, Charlie and Sailor had made over a thousand dollars. Could've made more, but Charlie had enough games for one night.

16

TIME AND SPACE. That's what Sailor said. So Charlie set a simple breakfast of fruit, toast, and tea at Sidney's side and resolved himself to avoid speaking until he had something worth saying.

Back out on the tarmac with Sailor, Charlie went about installing and testing the new directional gyro. Sailor tried to start up different conversations, and Charlie did his best to engage in them, but each time he'd drift off, gazing into the terminal window at Sidney. She stayed to herself mostly, sitting alone, people watching or observing planes arrive and depart. The only time she spoke at all was when Zu would come by and make her laugh. Otherwise, she seemed to exist in her own confined world. That she looked so much like her mother agitated him, forcing him to recognize a collection of features he'd all but forgotten. Worse was that she looked even more like him. Nose. Eyes. Chin. How strange he felt, the coding in his veins telling him most certainly he'd die to protect a daughter he barely knew. That code articulated, indeed, that his protection was aimed not at a person but at a possibility. All the possibility of his life, distilled in a face resembling the same one that took so much.

"Are you listening, or you gone dumb?"

"Sorry, Sailor." Charlie shook the darkness starting to cover his eyes. "What did you say?"

"I said the gyro is in, man. Run the test. If it works, we'll be out of here before nightfall."

Charlie clicked away on his computer, initiating the test. Within seconds, the test greenlit. "Looks like we're good to go."

"Damn, boy. If you ever need a job that don't pay much, I'll keep a spot open for you."

"I'll keep that in mind, just need to get in and out of Alabama with my head still on."

"Both of ours."

"You're going?"

"I said I'd get you to the border and that's what I plan to do."

"What do you think we'll find when we get there?"

"Trouble. Plenty trouble. But your child ain't likely to find what she's looking for. Seem to me she's looking for identity. That means she searching in the wrong place."

Charlie and Sailor spent the rest of the afternoon running through the preflight checklist and were able to get a scheduled outbound flight right at sunset. Charlie took his time going to Sidney to tell her the plan. When he found her, she sat alone in the empty, adjacent gate. Her eyes were different when she looked up to greet him. Not as angry. Not as expectant.

"We got the plane fixed," Charlie said.

"When do we leave?"

"In a few hours."

Sidney said nothing as she hugged Charlie. And as he put his arms around her, he felt the weight of her form. He experienced the embrace like time given back to him. Not linear time measured in minutes, but time in moments, measured in impact. He'd not been there to teach her to ride a bike, or read her to sleep, or help her with homework. He'd missed so many things in prison he couldn't imagine ever getting back. But then he received his daughter's hug, and, seemingly, experiencing such a thing just one time stirred in him the belief he'd lost no time at all.

Charlie and Sidney walked together in silence to tell Zu the news, and as if they'd been tickled, Zu squealed and picked up the telecom.

"Hello, Chicago Airport, this is Zu, your favorite representative, here to welcome you to gate sixteen. We will be boarding in a few hours for a six p.m. southbound flight into Vicksburg, Mississippi. Please have your passes ready to be stamped. We look forward to having you on board." Zu hung up and slipped back over to Charlie and Sidney. "It's protocol that we invite anyone onto the flights that we take. I am going to step in, clean the plane, and get it all ready. I suggest you both grab a bite to eat. You can bring it on the plane, as long as you don't make a mess."

"You're going with us?"

"Of course. You wouldn't want grumpy, old Sailor serving you gin and tonics, would you? He's my father and I don't want him serving me a drink. It's bound to have grease in it. Go on. I'll start boarding when you get back, that way you can sit in the first-class cabin. It's all first come, first serve now."

Charlie spent the next half hour sitting across from Sidney. They shared a roasted chicken with mac and cheese, and over the course of eating hardly spoke a word. Charlie sensed the tension between them had eased nevertheless. Something had changed. Something small and nameless, but important.

They walked back together to Zu, who performed the duties of getting them boarded and seated as if the world hadn't changed at all. Two rows of seats made the spacious first class less awkward in seat selection, Charlie choosing a window seat on the left side of the aisle, Sidney on the right. Only one other person boarded the plane, a Native man, tall and smiling as he passed.

"Brother," the man said, nodding.

"Brother," Charlie responded, enjoying the word in his mouth. The image of the man's smile burned in Charlie's mind long after he passed, and Charlie imagined that man feeling redeemed in the new world: dispossessed of his own land, now free to reclaim. Reclaim himself in the process. *We are kin,* Charlie thought.

Zu, ever the host, offered drinks and peanuts, and Sailor, on the plane speakers, simply said, "Welcome aboard."

The plane took off, rising up high into the night. Charlie watched the ascent from his window. At the cruising height, Charlie could see how little light still burned in the country below. So much of the land cloaked in darkness. All the space between cities and towns, connecting mountains to rivers, shore to shore. The darkness held America together. Looking down at a black immensity, Charlie saw the darkness as its own kind of beauty, experiencing for once the full shape of it, its beginning endless, its end ceaselessly moving. A form that held all the power of the universe and, without sound or grievance, gave every bit of that power all away. For once, Charlie admired the darkness down there and in himself until that deep black reached out, swallowed his eyes, and carried him off to sleep.

Darkness beyond dimension. Darkness beyond beautiful.

17

FIVE MONTHS AFTER *it happened, they showed up at Vivian's front door dressed in white, demanding land of their own. Maybe two dozen of them. Maybe more. Some of them, she had heard, had already started what they called "walking," and she dared not think what would need to break in the mind to choose that path.*

Vivian expected dissent. The way of life they'd built was not perfect, nor would it ever be, so she welcomed wisdom in any form wisdom took. Hers was not a philosophy of living in perfect harmony but living together, and harmony could come and go to the degree togetherness required. Still, what those folks showed up at her door to establish, dressed in the manner they were, was the other, *or better—prove* other *was anyone not wearing white along with them.*

Hosea wanted them gone. Banished. The advice of her council suggested banishment too. Indeed, most of the town wanted them gone entirely, taking with them all the talk of how things used to be. Vivian had seen enough of what other *could do. She wondered what Africans thought the day the Dutch landed in Cape Town or the Natives did as they watched Pilgrims carve a date into Plymouth Rock.*

Vivian could appreciate the irony of wanting to be heard. She knew well the desire for space to discover and fulfill oneself. That the power to even give such a thing fell on her shoulders did so as an ill-fitting coat. She'd fought all those years to have *those things, not to* give *them, and stranger still, she couldn't conjure enough anger in her heart to take them either.*

When Nona and her sons appeared on the porch, those dressed in white at the point of shouting through bared teeth, Vivian understood. These choices she had no business making.

She'd fought for the world. But it wasn't hers. Not then. Not now.

One among those dressed in white stepped forward to lead their call, mouth full of all the things they believed they deserved.

She touched Hosea just as he started to reject it all. By then, their four children had gathered around her. Hosea understood too. Wasn't the world they'd been fighting for, but to clear the lens through which their children saw it. And her children could see clearly.

Let them inherit the earth.

18

CHARLIE WOKE TO sunlight yellow-bright inside the plane. The harsh transition from deep-black sleep to day thrust him upright in his seat.

"It's all right." He heard Elizabeth's voice, but Sidney stood over him, concern steeling her expression. "You looked like you really needed the sleep, so we all decided to let you."

"Where are we?"

"Somewhere in Mississippi. Still on the tarmac. Sailor and Zu are outside, waiting to take us to the Alabama border."

"Thank you. For letting me sleep."

She handed him a juice box and a pack of airplane crackers, the concern on her face seeming to sag into concession. "Honestly, I should be thanking you. My mother taught me better manners than I've shown you. You helped me to get this far. And, well, I appreciate it. Thank you."

He still heard flecks of Elizabeth in her voice. "You're welcome. But my job ain't over yet."

Charlie watched her struggle through a smile, then gaze out the window, the depth of her concern nearing despair.

"You okay?"

"Yeah . . . fine."

"There ain't a lot of 'fine' in our current state. So, talk to me."

She held her words a moment before they surfaced. "I'm scared. I don't even know what I'm scared of, really—everything, I guess. Scared that Alabama is full of savages—a whole state of people who'll hate me. I'm scared that we might somehow actually make it to Orange Beach and it's not what I need it to be."

"You can't deny the truth of it: it's scary and it's unknown. That's a fact. But it's also a fact that scary and unknown is how everything has always been."

"That doesn't make me any less terrified," she said, sighing away her fears for the moment. "Zu made a pot of coffee that's still hot. I'll get you a cup, then we'll get on the road. Into the scary and the unknown."

Outside, the Mississippi sun burned with so much intensity Charlie had to shield his eyes. From what he could see, where they landed didn't much look like an airport. Flat grass stretched out in every direction, a flatness broken only by an oversized barn and house and a grove of orange trees in three rows. Dust hovered in the air. The dust didn't dull or settle, but made everything sort of sparkle. No, if not for the paved runway, Charlie might've thought he'd crash-landed on a farm.

"Sleeping like you don't have somewhere to be." Sailor stood at the base of the boarding stairs. "We've got a drive ahead of us. Gonna stop in Jackson to pick up supplies before heading to the border."

"What is this place?"

"My retirement plan."

On the ground, Charlie saw the scale of it, the massive sprawl of dirt and farmland that held a long, perfect landing strip at least half a mile in length, if not longer. And the barn, he saw, was not a barn at all but a hangar.

"I've got an F-16 Falcon in there. A Cessna and a Gulfstream too. On the lookout for a Stealth or a F-35, if you know where to find one. Been dreaming of flying a Stealth for years."

"This . . . is your own personal airport," Charlie said, realizing a number of things at once. "That's why you need the fuel."

"Gas is the only reason you're here."

If Ethel wanted to burn the earth to rid herself of something, Sailor, Charlie guessed, aimed to rid himself by getting above the earth and its troubles all for as long as he could.

Doors shut behind Charlie and he turned to see a van, Zu and Sidney squeezed into the back, on the opposite side of the plane.

"Now that you've indulged in a good night's sleep, we best get to it."

Charlie fought the urge to open up the hangar to get a look at all Sailor's planes and followed the old man out to the van, where Sailor got in the driver's side and Charlie sat in the passenger seat.

"Never been to Mississippi before. What's here?" Charlie asked.

"History. History everywhere you look," Sailor replied. "Hell, even right here in Vicksburg is where the Civil War was actually won. Lincoln himself said winning here was what split up the south. Wouldn't be no abolition without Vicksburg." Sailor pointed south. "Down the river a ways is Natchez—the Devil's Punchbowl—where they built a concentration camp for freed slaves. Killed a hundred thousand people. Men, women, and children. More black people've been lynched in Mississippi than anywhere. Seen everything from riots to shootings to segregation—they even voted once to send all the black folks back to Africa. Right here. Even God tried to flood the darkness outta Mississippi but couldn't do it. History gotta go somewhere." Sailor pumped the brake and sparked the ignition. "Now, I told you we have a quick stop in Jackson. Let some folks tell it, Jackson's where the civil rights movement started and damn near died when the Klan killed Medgar."

"Who is Medgar? And how do you know so much?" Charlie asked.

"Fool, I grew up here. And the fact that you don't know who Medgar Evers is is a damn tragedy."

Sidney watched Sailor more curiously than Charlie expected. "In school they never taught us any of that kind of stuff. Did all that really happen?"

"All that and a lot more. Mississippi is the shadow, the soul, and the skeleton closet of the nation. If America had ruins, Mississippi would be it. Every step you take got blood in the soil."

"And this is your home?"

"Was. My grandfather used to fly crop planes here. Worked for the man who owned this land. That's the reason I became a pilot." Sailor hit the gas, kicking up dust as the van sped off.

"So, this farm isn't your farm? You just took it?" Sidney asked.

"Look, for all my grandfather's hard work, that man promised him the crop plane as compensation when he retired. Of course the man didn't keep his word, and my father never stopped talking about it. He owed our family a lot more than a plane. So I figure his land is reparations. Everything else is interest."

The silence that followed made its own agreement. With so many cars still littering the main throughways, Sailor spun away from the freeway and took small-town back roads en route to Jackson.

Mississippi was green-brown lush in every direction, with no wildflowers to color life into the land. No chirping birds or happy dogs, just stray cats and too many damp places for cottonmouths to hide. Buildings stood no longer in use: shattered windows across the schoolhouse, roofs sagging in on repair shops, rubber tires stacked rotting outside gas stations. Run-down barns in overrun fields. Wild woods and muddy banks moaning for a city hunched over. Cowering.

Time itself, Charlie observed, lazed across this land.

They kept on those back roads witnessing town after town beaten down to the point of becoming almost beautiful to behold. Like photographs from a sophisticated editorial magazine. Such despair wasn't unfamiliar to Charlie, but in Mississippi the marring seemed to just go on and on, like everything America wanted to forget flowed down all the nation's rivers to get tangled up in the Mississippi Delta. And though the infrastructure in these towns appeared discarded and empty, people busied the ruin with activity: people walking foot-treaded paths in and out of towns, people aside their houses drying sheets on clotheslines, people sitting on porches just looking out at nothing. But Sidney noticed the odd nature of that busyness same as Charlie. The expressions.

"What's wrong with all these people?" Sidney asked. "Their faces—it's like they're all . . ."

"Lost," Sailor answered.

Their expressions, Charlie saw, were without emotion. No joy, no anger, no struggle, no determination. Dead-eyed, they seemed, plodding along as they always had, using no mind, only the memory coded into their nervous systems.

"What happened?"

"You know what happened."

At that, Sidney sat upright and still. Charlie wanted to shield her from the truths making themselves known all around her. She asked, "Why don't they just move into better houses or move away from this place?"

"Something broke in the minds of the people here after it happened," Zu explained, putting a calming hand on Sidney's shoulder.

"Most people's minds was already broke." Sailor didn't even look out at them as he drove on. "You been beat down enough, you learn to survive on crumbs. The things white folks put people through—my god, cruel in ways I just can't even reconcile. Should be ashamed for a thousand years for all the lynching and raping, using people like god-damn animals."

"Not all white people," Sidney added. "My mother wouldn't have been a part of this. She shouldn't've had to feel shame for something she didn't do."

"Shouldn't she?" Sailor cut eyes at Charlie and then in the rearview mirror at Sidney. "Feeling what deserves to be felt is the only pathway to understanding. Let's get it straight: white folks did rape and steal and kill, and black folks died by the thousands—was dying all the way up 'til a year ago. Never feeling shame for that, and not allowing us to feel anger over it, means we don't evolve. We just go on repeating evil we can't understand. I'm sure your momma was a nice lady with a good heart, but her not feeling ashamed about all that happened is the same as not feeling anything at all."

Charlie's pocket warmed where, at some point he couldn't remember, he'd tucked Elizabeth's letter. He clenched his jaw, understanding Sailor's sentiment, and kept his eyes forward, on the road, and not on the very different kind of empty infecting Mississippi.

"I pity these people," Charlie whispered, finally.

Sailor spit out, "Fool, you *are* these people."

They drove through more towns and more back roads, until, finally, street signage for Jackson led them to a freeway speckled in leftover vehicles. Sailor pushed the van to its top speed.

As Jackson came into view, Charlie could see smoke in the air. Damage had maimed nearly all the buildings, windows smashed in and more structures ruined by fire than Charlie could count. Along with the overturned police cars, Jackson looked like a war zone.

"Something broke in people's minds," Sailor repeated.

Just before downtown, they wandered off the freeway, turning down a maze of streets until a paved road gave way to dirt clay and, eventually, a sparsely grassy clearing. A dozen mobile homes together made a loose circle in the open field, surrounding picnic tables and gazebos. Grass grew up the sides of sporadically parked big-wheeled pickup trucks, a few of them with their doors open, one painted to look like a Confederate flag. The hair on Charlie's skin stood up, trained to recognize a place he shouldn't be.

"Sailor, why are we here?"

"Supplies, waiting to be picked up."

In the distance, Charlie saw a stretch of field and human-shaped paper targets at the end dotted in bullet holes. He realized what the place was just as Sidney spoke it.

"This is a gun range."

"Gun club," Sailor clarified. "Being military got me an invite here once to watch white boys drink and shoot and talk about heritage. I knew better than to ever come back. Else I might end up one of those targets." Sailor pulled the van up to the nearest trailer, put it in park, and got out. "Come on, they got every kind of gun you could want in there. Hell, they even got bazookas."

Charlie stiffened, afraid to look back at his daughter. "You want us to take a bunch of guns into Alabama?"

"Hell yeah. You think I'm gonna run up on somebody's land with nothing to protect myself with?"

"Sailor, anybody we find in Alabama most likely gonna look like you. Like me. You just gonna start shooting your own people?"

"I'm shooting anybody deserve to get shot. You need to drop all that righteous shit and come get you some of this heat."

Finally, Charlie glanced in the mirror back at Sidney. "No. We aren't here to do that. Not us."

Sailor sighed, more bored than annoyed. "What I've learned is that when them bullets start flying and you ain't got none to fly back, you lose. And I ain't the losing type. Now, c'mon, Zu, it's just like I taught you."

"Sailor—Dad. Mr. Charlie's right." Zu stared out the window, unwilling to look back at Sailor. "You taught me all that before everything changed. If we can't stop shooting each other now, when will we?"

Sailor said nothing and slammed the door, charging into the nearest trailer. The van, in his absence, fell silent, the sky wounded with storm and the distinct quiet it demanded. Charlie thought of his only daughter on the verge of shooting a child, then looked into the mirror at those same eyes holding his stare.

After only a few minutes, Sailor returned holding the biggest gun Charlie had ever seen, as well as a handgun tucked into a holster on his hip. He got back in the van, started it up, and said nothing just as the sky offered its first signs of rain.

Silence held the van, disturbed only by the intermittent, though bulbous, raindrops exploding against the windshield as they came off the road back onto the highway. Sailor took care to drive through the downtown, forcing everyone in the van to absorb the ruins. Devastation folded buildings, nature cracked pavement and invaded the streets; somebody even thought to climb up on billboards and set the advertisements afire.

"Everything's destroyed." Sidney rolled the window down to splashes of rain just to get a closer look.

"Not everything," Charlie answered, nodding toward the white domed capitol building fully, if not perfectly, intact. Dozens of people stood on the capitol steps, all of them dressed in white, barefoot, with dozens more walking through the grassy courtyard to be among the crowd. At the top of the steps, a woman held a Bible and recited nearly indecipherable Scripture loudly through a megaphone. The sight of it, again, raised the hairs on Charlie's arms.

"Walkers," Sailor said. "Believe they can get into heaven if they follow white folks into the sea."

"They gonna walk until they find courage enough to drown themselves," Zu added. "Or their legs give out and they just die thinking they ain't worthy. Madness, that walking is."

Sailor swerved through a cluster of cars, all of them with at least one door wide open, and one SUV with all its doors and hatch open like an animal displaying itself. "I talked to a walker once, in New Orleans a while back. Man said that when the event happened, felt like a bomb went off. Bomb in his mind and his heart. He told me he could either start walking toward that bomb or away from it. He chose away. Now he can't seem to stop walking. Walking away until he walks himself right into hell, I say."

Then, above the walkers, the sky finally cracked open with rain, going from drizzle to downpour in seconds. Charlie expected the crowds to scatter, but they started to shout with delight, throwing their heads back like the rain invigorated them—purified them—of the sin of still being here.

Sailor drove on. No one spoke, allowing space for what they'd heard to settle on their minds. Charlie shivered at the thought of being overcome with whatever ailed these people to walk himself into death. He feared that's what Sidney felt too, having experienced too little of life to actually warrant keeping herself here. As far as he knew, she didn't know how to drive, she never talked about a boyfriend, and there was no sign she'd ever even left Wisconsin. So little life lived between the both of them. So few chances to spread themselves out across the canvas of just being. As he looked out at the road before them, he felt hope for all the life yet to be lived.

Sailor took a winding exit just as the storm dissipated all at once, giving the land right back to the southern sun.

"This is I-10. Artery road, takes you all the way across the country and back." Sailor pointed as they merged onto the freeway, slowly snaking around the dead cars. "The Mississippi-Alabama border is east of here, but this is where I want you to bring the gas if we get split up, as I suspect we will. Right here at this exit. Understand?"

"Understood. How close are we?"

"Less than an hour out on this road. But anyone with a mind won't take the highway. We gonna go a bit south, take a different route, maybe make our lives a little easier going into the king's territory."

"Is it really true, Sailor, that Alabama has a king?" Sidney asked.

"The south has always been a monarchy in some form or another. Everybody thinks they're the king of something here. People, land, business. That's why you'd hear them talk about their manors and their birthrights and societies, all of them, carrying on like royals in court, having balls and cotillions while people was going off to war. Wouldn't be the first time some fool in Alabama claimed themselves lord of everything."

"Sidney, girl, you sure you wanna find out where this ends?" Zu asked.

"She probably already knows where it's gonna end up. For the rest of y'all, I suspect you gonna wish you took a gun when you had the chance."

The road turned south, then ran along the coastline. Sidney's breathing stopped sharp at the sight of all the water that absconded out before them, funeral silence filling the van to witness, just outside, a supremely beautiful beach. Sugar-white sand, blue water, wide-open sky, and a kingdom of clouds. Charlie watched the ocean shimmer in gold and indigo and silver, then roll toward him into white dunes. He might've felt joy in his nose along with the salted air, but there were more crosses punched into the sand than he could count. Markers for the dead littering the shore for miles. A tomb, he saw. A supremely beautiful tomb.

They toured in silence along the shoreline. Weary of hearing the wailing of the sea, Charlie turned away from the beach and into the barrel of Americana. McDonald's arches, Waffle Houses, CVS signs, billboards for cell phone plans—all the same elements of every small American town, just bunched a little tighter on the beach strip.

Again, Charlie considered Sidney. She'd pined for the world before with such intensity she'd shoot a child. Even entertained killing herself to keep the *way it was* remaining *as it is*. What power. Stronger than one's own reason and instinct, driving one to the malformation of the mind, body, and even to the forfeiture of the colors of the soul. Less a desire for one's own survival than the survival of that which none could say they fully understood.

They drove on, curving north toward the highway to the interstate, the van heavy with somber emotion. Charlie wafted in the dark of his thoughts when Sailor slammed hard on the brakes.

"What the hell?"

The road before them rolled on, completely cleared of leftover cars.

"What is it?" Zu leaned forward between the front seats and looked out. Open freeways were usually speckled in cars with their doors open, more markers for the dead. But someone had driven all the cars one by one off to the roadside shoulders.

"Somebody cleared the road," Sailor said.

"Is that a good thing?" Zu asked.

"I don't know. But it's a big undertaking," Charlie mused.

"It means the people here are expecting traffic," Sailor said. "Could be a trap."

"Or . . ." Charlie shifted with an idea, then leapt out of the van. "It's an opportunity."

"Man, what the hell you doing?"

"Hold on a sec."

Charlie skipped over to the first car he saw along the road, a little Nissan, keys still hanging in the ignition. He slid in, and the engine took only one turn to fire up.

Survival, he thought. *My daughter needs to be more capable of surviving beyond what she'd been taught.*

He went back to the van and opened the back seat.

"Sidney, I need you to come with me."

"What is it?"

"I'm going to teach you how to drive."

"You're gonna do that right now? Don't you see what's out there?"

"Just an open road. Come on."

Charlie suspected the same desire for survival taking new shape overrode her fear and drew her out of the van to follow him to the small car.

"Get in the driver's seat," he told her, feeling the familiar stirring in his chest. The same that inspired him to teach at Howard.

"Why are you showing me this?"

"No better time than the present."

She looked at him, confused. When Charlie learned to drive, his mother had put him at the wheel of her Oldsmobile and told him that driving wasn't just a joyride, but a tool for self-reliance. Meant you could keep moving. Until you find where you're meant to be.

He thought of survival as he talked her through the functions of the car: the mirrors, the gas and brake, the gear shift, the speedometer, the lights, and the wheel.

"Best way to make it do something is to make it do something. Just shift it into drive and let's move."

"I . . . I can't do this. I can't."

"You can. Don't think about it. Just start moving in the direction you want to go."

"But then what?"

"Let your instincts kick in. You got this. You do."

She stuffed her fear into a stiff nod, shifted into drive, and bucked them forward.

"Easy on the gas . . . a light touch. Let the wheels set you free."

Her hands shook as, slowly, she put pressure on the gas and eased forward off the shoulder onto the road. She held her breath as the engine hummed and the road slid away underneath her.

"Move the wheel side to side so you can feel your control. Give it some gas too. Feel that you're connected to the car. It moves how you want it to move."

She did as he asked, swaying the car left and right and tempting the car's full power by pumping the gas. Her held breath released itself in what sounded half sigh, half laugh. She turned to him, all the lights in her face beaming bright.

"All right, now hit the brake and get a feel for slowing down."

"Okay." She pressed down with her foot, giving a perfect amount of pressure to the brake to settle the engine into a full stop. Sidney looked at Charlie, thrill like a current in her expression.

"Now you got it. Go!" Charlie said.

Through her fear, Sidney pushed the gas and accelerated down the empty road, a crawl, to a jog, to a sprint. As the engine opened and the beaming on her face brightened, Charlie put the windows down, letting the wind blast through the car. Sidney giggled now, excited and nervous and terrified all at once.

"This is amazing!"

And then she screamed. A powerful roar. Of frustration, of thrill, of release. She laughed wildly, nearing on mania, pushing the car faster. Wind whipped their ears. The engine met her excitement. The road and the roadside grass and the trees blurred in her speed, their onlook seeming applause. When Charlie regarded his daughter he saw tears streaming down her face. Excitement and fury and sadness all spilling out. Pent-up months. Swollen years. Released in the speed. She went on like that, weeping and shouting and laughing, until they reached a bend in the road. She took the turn with both hands on the wheel. Charlie smelled the water in the air before he saw the land open up into a great river. Sidney slammed the brake and the car fishtailed, swerving and screeching as the Nissan whipped off the road and onto the shoulder. They crashed through bushes, small trees pelting the car on both sides.

"Brake, Sidney! Brake."

Sidney stomped the brake. The car ground to a dust-swirling stop in a clearing just behind the trees. Sidney kicked the driver's door open and ran away into the taller trees just beyond.

The water. Charlie sat in the car for a moment, contemplating the truth of the sea, the stories the water told, new and old; all the bodies the water held and all the baptisms the water gave, death and memory like an evaporation that somehow shimmers all beginnings, ends, and beauty of life. So much water that it could never ever be evaded. His daughter could fear that water for the rest of her life, or she could find in the sea's dark depths the power to absolve herself.

Charlie thrust the passenger door open to the sound of birds scattering away.

"Sidney!" he called out to her, and listened to the echo of his own voice until he heard Sidney whimpering in the silence that followed. Charlie found her slumped against a tree at the edge of the clearing.

"You're stronger than this," Charlie said. He could hear the river humming beyond. There were bodies in the river, Charlie was certain, and he would not allow those ghosts to possess his daughter as they had all those people walking, haunted by a need to be led, somewhere, anywhere, but here. "You hear me, child. You are stronger than this."

Her eyes rolled up to meet his. "When I look at the water, all I see is death. Loss. Loneliness. All I see is the end of everything I know."

"Do you want to know what I see? Resilience." He nearly told her every truth there was to tell about her mother, what her decisions had done to him, and after all the betrayal, he still stood on his two feet. He nearly told her everything, but he could only say, "Stand. Stand to your feet. We rise. That's what we do. No matter the pressure or circumstance, don't matter how high the tide of our troubles get, we rise above it. That's resilience. You may not believe that you are like me in any other way but that. Because you're still here. And I'm still here with you. So stand up."

Slowly, begrudgingly, Sidney rose. Just as she did, something shifted in the air. A warmth. A whisper. A tingle.

Sidney felt the sensation too and looked around like invisible bees swarmed her.

"You feel that?" Charlie closed his eyes and allowed the feeling to stand the hairs on his skin.

"Yes. What is it?"

"I don't know. Feels like . . . static, electricity. Come on, let's get back to the road."

Charlie took her by the hand and led her back to the roadside, where the feeling in the air grew stronger, weirder. The sensation offered such an unusual texture that even Sidney's sniffling firmed, alert.

The van remained, but Sailor and Zu were gone.

Charlie saw then, in the trees along the road, a yellow school bus tucked into the woods. He was wondering who put the bus there when he heard the footsteps. One pair charging through the woods, then another, then more on the opposite road coming right for Charlie and his daughter.

They were boys. At least a dozen teenagers surrounding them on all sides. Black hoodies with the sleeves cut; black sweats cut at the ankles. All of them carried weapons. Charlie reached back for Sidney, sliding her behind him. The boys carried knives, Charlie noted, axes, crowbars, and machetes, but no guns. The bus in the woods rolled to life, not with the distinctly diesel engine, but silently, as if the bus ran with no engine at all. The yellow beast pulled out on the road, the paint giving off an odd, if not glowing, coat, and stopped in front of them, and someone inside flung the back door open.

"Get in," one of the boys said.

"What the hell is going on here?"

"You're in Alabama," another boy said. "Get on the bus."

"Where are you taking us?"

The boys shuffled tighter around them, backing Charlie and Sidney against the bus so they had no choice but to get inside.

Once inside, Charlie saw the bus was not much of a bus at all, but completely refashioned, running on electric, cleared of most of its seats to offer extended storage space. In one of the few remaining back seats, Zu sat alone; their expression seemed to acknowledge that the fact that Sailor was the only one with a weapon was precisely why Sailor wasn't on the bus.

One of the boys, older but not more than eighteen, cleared space in the back seats, gesturing for Charlie and Sidney to sit down.

"We don't want to hurt you, but we will." The boy's voice rang sharp and sure beyond his age.

"I asked you a question," Charlie said. "Where are you taking us?"

When the boy smiled, a bit of magic happened. "I'm taking you to see the king."

19

WHEN THE WILD young boys arrived with their knives and machetes and axes, Sidney wasn't ready.

She wasn't ready when they surrounded her and sat her on a school bus, nor when the bus sped off, a secret hovering in the silent air between them as they headed for someplace unimaginable. Most of all, when her sensibilities returned and she looked up to make eye contact with one of those wild boys, she wasn't ready for the wash of warmth that waved through her body.

She looked away at first. But still, she could feel his gaze on her. And when, finally, she returned his stare, she saw how the light sparkled in his eyes with such glitter those deep browns looked silver. And she wasn't afraid. None of them would harm her, but him especially, the one who shined. For a moment she lost all sense of time and place. She could just as well have been on the bus back in Wisconsin, headed to school, crushing on the boy too cool to be popular.

She'd no description for the feeling. When her thoughts tried to simply analyze him, she warmed inside, like summer had breached within her stomach. She became more aware of herself in the small moment she held his watch. Not how she looked or sounded. But of a power she knew he could see. She turned to the window, to the lush green world wisping by outside. So far from Wisconsin. So far from the quiet house on a lake and the life her mother made for her, a life so unlike this one. But for a moment, however fleeting, this world didn't seem foreign. Some part of her understood the world into which she was headed, felt kinship to its vibrancy. And to look upon it was to open a door inside her, just as another one began to shut.

Let air flow now in a place that had always been still.

20

CHARLIE LOOKED FOR SIGNS.

With so many eyes on him, he saw little chance of escaping by force, not without losing flesh and blood to at least one of those blades. More than that, the memory of prison was still stiff in his bones, having taught him well the futility of fighting. So Charlie watched the road, looking for any highway signs, hoping for a sense of location. He did his best to conjure any rebellion left inside him to run for safety as soon as the chance arrived.

"Mobile," he heard Zu say, just as he saw the highway sign as well.

"*Mo-bill*," corrected a boy, the one with the smile. "It's pronounced *Mo-bill*."

"You said you're taking us to the king?" Charlie asked.

"That's right."

"Why? What are you going to do to us?"

"What happens to you is not my prerogative, sir."

When the boy looked away, Charlie observed how the boy glanced at Sidney. And Sidney matched him, her eyes glittering quickly and away. Charlie burned on the inside and turned his attention to the city as they neared. That distinct feeling, the one he felt crossing the border, yet pulsed in the air. Though he had no way of explaining the feeling, its quality nevertheless manifested into a different world outside. Some cities shut down after the event, becoming ghost towns; others lived forlorn, locked in their own grief. The best cities, like D.C. and Chicago, lumbered forward, though wayward, building a new world atop a damaged foundation. But Mobile was different.

Ease moved people in Mobile. They cruised sidewalks with a casualness Charlie couldn't remember seeing in any city before or after the event. People smiled when they passed each other, genuine, familiar smiles. Absent from their eyes was that roaming, searching look he'd come to see everywhere and in everyone. A striking contrast from Mississippi.

And Mobile's ease wasn't limited to people. Nature itself didn't clash with civilization. Wildflowers and plants grew up the sides of buildings and tilted over freeways. Plums and oranges, lemons and apples, hung from trees for people to pick at their leisure, a harmony of nature and society. Few cars toured on the road. Trolley cars zoomed past in silence without a cable line to power them. The storefronts bustled with life. Mothers and fathers strolled children along storefronts, couples hand in hand. And more than anything, Charlie could hear the smooth hum of the engines of living.

He realized then that he'd expected to find Alabama ruined under rule of a king. Sailor told him the south would be bad, so he imagined this kingdom to be a war zone, a dictatorship rapt in fear, ruled by force. But fear did not infest Mobile. In America everyone carried something, emotion strapped to their backs, trauma to their ankles. But not here. Not in Mobile. Charlie looked again at the boys around him, taking a second note of how they were armed. Tools, not weapons.

Charlie glanced over at Zu, whose expression suggested they'd arrived to similar revelations as the bus exited the main highway at the edge of downtown.

What Charlie saw next was even more bewildering. The view was as if they'd been transported from Alabama to New Orleans, right into the heart of the French Quarter. The road narrowed, made snug by two- and three-story Creole town houses on both sides. Galleries and balconies, wrapped in intricate ironwork, swept over the main street. People of all ages and sizes occupied those balconies, shouting down to passing friends, sipping wine and leaning over wrought iron, gossiping over tea, smoking from pipes in celebration, watering magnolias with care, and dancing, dancing in circles to the thump of drums. The energy of the people was intensified by the energy of the buildings, all bursting with different colors and textures, all luminously coated like the bus in red, violet, yellow—stucco, brick, plaster—all peaking rooftops and tall, rounded windows; the Mobile scene collected like a crayon box filled with poems.

Someone, somewhere, was shouting. Charlie heard trumpets playing out of view. Drums thumped, far off but near as a heartbeat. Charlie leaned close to the window to listen, sure, amid all the activity, someone sang tenderly. Music. All of it. The feeling he felt crossing the Alabama border was stronger now, revealing itself in all he saw and heard. A harmony of living so finely tuned as to make its own music.

"This is Dauphin Street," the young boy said, seeing the wonder in Charlie's expression. "Sister to New Orleans."

As the lively storefronts and city bustle on Dauphin slowed into a more residential pace, Charlie couldn't imagine what meeting the king might be like. Would he sit on a gold throne and wear a crown? The likelihood of coming upon a castle lessened the farther the bus rumbled, arriving to a neighborhood with houses and lawns just like any other.

When the bus came finally to a stop, they'd reached a corner lot holding a three-story Victorian house. Blue, coated with the same shimmer, the house's porch extended its full width, and its rooftops resembled church spires. Nevertheless, the house stood beautifully, though undistinguished. Certainly no place for a king.

"Out," the young one said, ushering them from their seats. Charlie paused for a moment, afraid of what he'd see when those doors opened. A fear he experienced oddly near to excitement.

As the door swung open, their young and dangerous captors transformed. Charlie watched them spill out of the bus, giggling like children just returning home from school. They were suddenly just boys. Charlie followed them out to a driveway extending to a two-car garage with the doors open and no cars inside, just three men fiddling about.

Charlie saw then how many people moved around the house, lounging on the porches, picnicking in the grass. He watched the three men in the garage come out to greet the boys, dapping fists and giving hugs. When the bright one reached them, all three men swallowed him in embrace. Two were his brothers, one thin and bearded, the other hugely muscular and bald, both twentysomethings. The third man was the boy's father. A fact less proved for Charlie than felt. The way the man palmed the boy's head and smiled, hugged him with purpose, Charlie couldn't help but feel a pang of fatherly envy. Responsively, he reached for Sidney's hand just as she withdrew from him, folding her arms in defiance.

One of the boys shouted a word in a language that Charlie didn't understand. Then, all at once, the boys turned as quick as soldiers to face him and the others. One of the smallest boys, no older than seven, scurried to the father's side and took his hand. He did this gently, formally, as a ritual act.

"I introduce you . . ." The small child had hardly any bass in his speaking voice, and yet his words resounded. ". . . to the land's chosen king, Hosea."

Charlie stepped back just as Hosea, the king, stepped forward. A stocky block of a man, Hosea stood exactly Charlie's height, with a graying beard and a short-brimmed fedora that matched his skin color. *This can't be the king,* Charlie thought. All the fear and worry about Alabama and its king, only to stand before a man. A man seeming no different from or better than Charlie.

Casually annoyed, the king eyed Charlie's lot. His hands behind his back and the rigidity in the king's posture gave Charlie the sense that he was a military man before, perhaps a general or maybe a high-ranking lieutenant. The king sucked at the back of his teeth just as one of the brothers, the thin one in well-fitting clothes, stepped forward.

"Excuse my father. He is more a man of action than words. Your name is Charlie? Is that right?"

"How did you know my name?"

"My father told me. He told me all of your names. Sidney and Zu, correct? But you're missing one—Sailor, I believe."

"Nobody catches my daddy unless he wants to be caught," Zu answered.

Charlie noticed the pride in Zu's voice. Pride that seemed to suggest Sailor would be back for his child.

Charlie glanced again at the king and then back to the son, who held back a most confident smile.

"My name is Herald. This is my brother Tau." He nodded toward the powerful-looking man and then at the teen who captured them. "And you've already met Fela, our youngest brother, who brought you here."

"Against our will," Charlie replied, a bit lost on what to say to them.

"Let me be clear, we don't aim to hold or harm you." Though slender, the man's voice offered a boom, deep and scratchy like his words sprung out of a speaker. "And I'm sure you being here is accidental?"

"Well, not exactly by accident," Charlie answered.

"Explain yourself." Herald looked into Charlie. "Truth is better. No matter how things turn out."

"We want to get to Orange Beach. We heard rumor that there is a colony there, and we hoped to see it."

"Are you one of those walkers?"

"Walkers? No, we're not here to do that."

"Good. We've been seeing more and more of them coming, headed to Orange Beach—"

"Them?" Sidney cut in, and Charlie gripped her hand tight as if to scold: *Be quiet.*

The king huffed then, more annoyed than before, followed by a sigh as if pressurized air had been let out of him. He touched his son Herald, and the young man made way for his father. When the king spoke, he looked right at Sidney, and his voice felt like a heavy boulder dropped between them. "You think you're white?"

"Doesn't matter." Charlie spoke too quickly, a realization he felt when Sidney shifted her feet. "But my daughter needs to see it. She needs to know."

"Know what?"

Sidney stepped forward. "If this is all there is. If my family is really gone. We need to know the truth."

"Truth?" he said. "Is that all? And you want to go searching for ghosts on Orange Beach to find it?"

Charlie reached a calming hand toward Sidney. "We're just desperate, is all."

"Desperation used to be the engine that turned the world. But it is not the engine of this new one."

A bit of sunlight struck something in the garage. The king and his sons had been fiddling about, working in that space when Charlie and the others arrived. Charlie assumed what shined was maybe a car they tinkered with or some sort of appliance like a dishwasher. But from the look of what he could see, the thing was too big, too blocky, and peppered with lights and buttons. Standing as tall as a grown man, the machine spanned the width of the entire two-car garage. That's when Charlie saw the obelisk out behind the house. The tall black foreign spike shot stone straight into the air, and Charlie realized he'd seen other obelisks all over Mobile as they drove in, standing as sculptures in the grassy pocket parks, in the center of turnabouts, and seeming not at all out of place at the king's home. When Charlie looked back at the machine in the garage, he identified the metal bulk.

"That's a radio transmitter in there," Charlie said. "It's the biggest one I've ever seen."

The king watched Charlie's eyes, giving away none of his thoughts. "Being nosy is how a nose gets cut off. That said, I know you came here to steal something. So you're nosy, thieving, and you think you're white."

Charlie shot a glare at Zu, unsure how this king seemed to have information they hadn't even thought to give him. He wondered what other knowledge the king held in his sturdy form.

"We just came for safe passage to Orange Beach, and yes, we need jet fuel, but I'm not here to steal it. Maybe there's something we can trade for it?"

"Trade, huh? We'll see." The king eyed Sidney. "As for you, I'm not the one who can give you passage to go to Orange Beach."

"But you're the king. If you can't, who can?"

"Understand, a king—any king—is little more than an adviser." Sidney could only regard him with confusion and curiosity. "You ever played chess, child? The most powerful piece on a chessboard most certainly ain't the king. So, you need to know what you're dealing with. If you want permission, the person you have to ask is the queen."

"The queen?"

"My wife. She's inside. Go on. Fela will take you. And you"—he flicked his glare back at Charlie—"come take a walk with me."

"I am not leaving my daughter."

"She is safer here than any place before or after our liberation. Now come with me, there is something I need you to see. My asking is a courtesy."

The timbre in the king's voice was subtle but certain, provoking the people around him to take action. Fela, the young one, gestured for

Sidney to follow him, and the two older sons maneuvered to separate Charlie from Zu, and Zu pushed back.

"Take your hands off me!"

Charlie had only a second to find Sidney's eyes, glad to see her more intent than afraid. The king's power spread out like the shadows of clouds. He wasn't simply the king of a neighborhood or even of the city of Mobile. The child had called him the king of *the land*. All of it. And, by all measures, he seemed just that, king, from one border of Alabama to the other. And as Charlie followed the king around the back of the house, he understood that the man's power, at least some of his majesty, had origins from whatever he was building in his garage.

21

INSIDE, THE KING'S house felt to unravel, room after room, hallway turn after hallway turn. Sidney gawked at all the ornately decorated spaces: framed art hung in clusters, sculptures, and patterns—so many patterns—invigorating the walls and ceilings in prints. The house seemed many times larger and more intricate inside than out, yet throughout the colorful amalgam retained a familiarity. For even the few seconds Sidney strode through the king's home, she witnessed dozens of people rushing up and down the sinuous staircases, carrying all sorts of shiny things: silver serving dishes, vases, and glass jars containing rich effects. She peeked into the kitchen and, for a moment, stood dazzled by the buzz of activity inside sizzling with light and movement. Even the perfume from flowers, bundled in halls and atop tables throughout the house in zealous bouquets, mixed sweetly with the spices of food cooking nearby, working together to warm the house in ways that made the busy space feel like home. But the king's home wasn't her home, and Sidney quietly punished herself for being even briefly disarmed.

"It isn't always like this," Fela said.

Thoughts she hoped to keep to herself leapt into words. "What is it normally like?"

"Slower. It's busy now because everyone is getting ready for the holidays, and then Mardi Gras."

"I thought Mardi Gras was only in New Orleans."

"The very first Mardi Gras in America was right here in Mobile. A Pan-African celebration—our carnival, brought here by way of Haiti. But like everything else it was 'commercialized and weaponized.' At least that's what my mom says."

"I don't plan on staying here long."

"Then you'll miss one hell of a party."

She followed him through a sizable living space, where chairs and couches were matched together in seating arrangements meant to inspire conversations.

"Is your mother really the queen?"

"Yes." Pride raised his chin. "You don't have to be afraid of her. But understand, we don't lie here. So speak true. She'll know if you're lying. She always does."

A wall of windows at the back of the house led to an indoor/outdoor courtyard that separated an entirely different section of the house.

"This place is massive," she said. They stepped outside into the courtyard, whose scale only emphasized her statement, opening onto a grassy area with a sprawling oak tree at its center. Sunlight from the open roof brightened the scene, and the house wrapped around all sides of the courtyard in causeways that people scurried up and down, carrying things and talking. Out in the yard, builders stacked materials for what Sidney assumed to be parade floats, and, along the edges of the grass, small groups of people sat at tables sewing costumes and patterned float skirts. Others practiced a choreographed dance, laughing, then focused, then laughing again. She found the activity wildly chaotic and, as a result, distracting. Until she discovered precisely what deserved her undivided attention.

Sitting under the shade of the oak, a group of colorfully dressed women lounged together in a circle. At Sidney's distance, the company of women looked like they'd just gathered together for a picnic, a rainbow of colors under a tree.

One by one, a line of people waited to step into that colorful circle. Fela led Sidney to the back of the line and stood with her.

"What are we waiting for?"

"This is a council. My mother and her advisers. So, we wait our turn to speak to them."

"Aren't you her son? You have to wait in line to talk to your own mother?"

He shot her a look, the marvelous shine in his eyes amplified in the sunlight. "That's right. I'm no better than any person in this line, nor are my needs any more urgent."

"They aren't *your* needs, they're mine, and I say they're urgent."

Intentionally, he gazed at her a moment longer than what was agreeable, before turning away. "Then I'll ask you to be patient."

Sidney folded her arms, huffing childishly, tapping her foot, but did as he asked. Together, silently, they waited as each person stepped into the women's circle, spoke a few minutes, listened, and walked away with resolution in their steps.

"These people really do whatever your mother says? Even if they don't want to?"

"The council advises. People heed that advice."

"What if they don't?"

Fela cut eyes at her, smiling, but did not respond.

"Look, I don't have time for this. I have to get to Orange Beach!"

Fela ignored her outburst but still gestured for Sidney to step forward.

Sidney studied the women of the council from close-up. They sat on low poufs, each one of them wearing a different-colored gossamer kaftan, yellow, orange, teal, and so on. Small tables rested between them serving tea, iced oysters, and fruit. There were eight of them, all middle-aged with natural, bursting hairdos that made them look as though they all wore crowns. Only one was younger, still caught in a youthful softness, with hair that did not go up but down in a waterfall of black curls.

When Sidney's turn came, she froze when all those pairs of eyes landed on her. She felt judged before a single word was spoken. And for a moment she rocked, dazed by the paralyzing beauty and poise looking back at her. All of them, Sidney perceived, immeasurably wise and dangerous, like stepping into a den of panthers. Though they all seemed to glow, the one in violet shined a little brighter, her confidence reaching out a little more sharply. Her instincts left little doubt: the one in violet was the queen.

Fela did his best to speak to all of them, but he couldn't help tilting every word in the specific direction of the queen. "This is Sidney. We found her, her father, and their two friends crossing the border, but one of them escaped. Her motives seem genuine, but she has business in Alabama that requires your consideration."

The women shifted from Fela to Sidney and paused as if they were waiting for Sidney to speak. Sidney swallowed hard, and just as she found words, the one in red, who was lean but muscular, cut her off.

"She wants to go to Orange Beach. Isn't that right?"

"How did you k—"

The woman curled a smile like a whip in the air. "I know it. But what I don't know is why. Tell us." The woman's accent, a bit French, a bit island, calmed Sidney enough that she felt she could speak true.

"Because something took my family. Took all of them. And it left me."

"Your father, did he not cross our borders with you?"

"Yes, but—"

"Is he not your family?"

"I barely know him."

"And who do you know in Orange Beach?"

"My aunt Agnes," she said, with more exuberance than she meant to. "My aunt is there. My aunt is waiting for me."

"Waiting for you? To do what?"

"To . . . I don't know . . . go back. Go back to the way things were."

"And how exactly *were* they?"

"I don't know." Sidney heaved, agitated, and winced at how small the impact of that heave made. So she went on. "Simpler, I guess. Better. Can't you just set me free so I can go back to my people?"

That had an impact. The women flashed looks at each other, incredulous, before giving all attention to the queen, who finally spoke. "'Simpler.' 'Free.' The funny thing about the way things were, child, is that they weren't."

She reached to whisper into the ear of the woman in pink next to her, who stood and darted away, then nodded to the youngest among them. Sidney saw the resemblance.

"This is my daughter, Nona," the queen said. "She will decide how best to resolve your request."

Near Sidney's age, if only a year older, Nona was the most beautiful person Sidney had ever seen. She had the same sparkling eyes as Fela, but the sparkle seemed to spread out and cover her whole being, making her dark skin like a silhouette backlit in glow. When she set her eyes upon Sidney, Sidney recognized the same regal quality of the queen, but different, harboring an eagerness that age had not yet contained.

Nona stood and walked up close to Sidney. She smelled of coconut warming in the sun. Sidney, once more, became aware of herself. Where her hair spiraled untamed and matted, Nona's hair cascaded with curled perfection. Where a year indoors paled her skin and darkened the space under her eyes, Nona seemed to exist as her own star.

The woman in pink returned holding a tray with three small dishes, each one containing a different dollop of food. She held the tray out to Sidney. Dog food—that's what the dishes seemed to hold. An ancient mush of leftovers that smelled as unappetizing as they looked.

"Do you know these?" Nona asked.

Sidney eyed the different speckles of meat presented to her. One dark meat in a red-black sauce, another with small chunks of white meat in white rice, and the last hand-rolled balls that looked part meat, part rice, like a bratwurst made with bits she couldn't begin to imagine. Not exactly what you'd get from TGI Fridays or her mother's casserole. Sidney kept her mouth closed out of fear the smell might make her vomit and just shook her head.

"Taste one."

"No way in hell I'm eating that. Any of it."

"You want to get to Orange Beach, don't you?"

Again Sidney huffed. The white meat at least resembled pork, and the familiarity of rice made the dollop mostly recognizable. So, as quickly as she could, Sidney took a spoonful and swallowed. A moment passed before the foul flavor washed through her mouth. Instantly she gagged, trying to spit out the taste. "What the hell is that?"

"That was chitlins. Made from the intestines of a pig. This one is oxtail, and that one is boudin."

"It tastes like garbage."

"These dishes kept our people alive when they were allowed nothing else to eat. Each one of these comes with a history you should know. And you will, because that is my decision. Sidney will stay with us until Mardi Gras and learn what we have to teach her."

Sidney gasped and nearly ran off, away from these people and their rules. "What? You can't keep me here!" She longed for the shape of the rifle in her hand. How easily the gun made the world change the way she wanted. She looked around at these women unmoved and understood she didn't have the power to change anything. "Please. Please, just let me go back to my family."

Then something happened Sidney didn't expect. Nona stepped closer and hugged her, embracing her fully in both arms. Nona whispered in her ear, "From here until you leave, I will be your sister."

Sidney sank into that hug, unable to even imagine fighting free. *Sister?* she questioned. And, in the instant she heard it, Nona's word, *sister*, blinded Sidney's thoughts in the shimmer of family. Then, with all her strength, Sidney pushed Nona back, but the princess hardly moved.

"Keep your hands off me! I'm not your sister."

Nona, more or less amused, smiled warmly at Sidney. "Follow me."

Two of the colorfully dressed women flanked Nona on either side as she marched back into the house. Sidney fell right in and was already in the hallway before she realized how easily she'd taken Nona's command. Sidney stopped where she stood, suddenly sick with rage.

"You don't tell me what to do. You hear me? I'm not your sl—"

Nona turned back sharply, a look of genuine surprise spread across her face. She made eyes toward the women at her side. The three women held back smiles that only sprinkled pepper on Sidney's temper.

"Well, go on," Nona said. "You're free to speak your mind."

"This is such bullshit. All of this. You can't just take whatever you want and start calling yourself royalty."

Again the young princess held back a smile. "You seem very familiar with taking what you want."

"It's not yours. None of this is."

"Then whose?"

"What?"

"You said it's not ours. Then whose is it?"

Sidney's anger curled inward, from boiling to simmering. "They're not all gone. They're coming back."

"I don't believe there has ever been a more terrible weapon in this world than the word *they*."

"You think you're so righteous. But all of this is fake."

Again Nona just smiled warmly, stifling all the things she knew and Sidney didn't. Sidney understood her fury wasn't aimed at Nona but at how little she understood her own anger. Anger made of grief, jealousy, fear, and loneliness. A concoction boiling together eventually reducing to an emptiness she knew of no way to fill.

"Little sister," Nona said, "hear me when I tell you my mother taught me to be kind and generous—treat others how I would want to be treated. What did your mother teach you?"

At that, Sidney's temper caught fire. She stepped forcefully into Nona's space, her hands reaching as though she'd kept her stepfather's gun. "Don't you speak about my mother, or I swear—"

"Swear what?" Nona pushed through the women protecting her and Sidney regarded her power like a storm about to crack. "Don't forget to whom you speak. My mother also taught me how not to be trifled with."

Sidney stepped back apace and sighed, Nona's influence blowing all the heat out of her rage. "Look, I just want to go."

Nona softened without reducing any of her power. "I keep my word. Now, you can wait in my room."

Once again, Nona's accent turned music in Sidney's ears, easing Sidney's tension. "Wait to do what?"

"To get all the dust off your sparkle, little sister."

Nona's bedroom took up nearly the full third floor of the king's house and spread out like a loft-style apartment. The smell of her room, fruit and spice and burned palo santo, enchanted Sidney within the first step. Nona's room offered no similarity to hers back in Wisconsin. No pink poufs, pastels, or fairy lights bedazzled her space with plastic magic. A maturity flooded Nona's room, with natural light that leaned against wood-earth tones and simple design. She had bookshelves stiffened with old books, original art on her walls, cabinets stacked with vinyl records, a sitting area softened with the memory of friends, even a claw-foot bathtub near the far window that cupped sunlight in its bowl. In the sanctuary of Nona's personality, Sidney's anger sagged into envy.

Nona's room felt settled. Intact. Who Nona was, her room made clear to Sidney, Nona had always been. Sidney clenched her jaw, tears hot under her eyes, at the thought of how so much self-certainty must feel.

The door shut behind her. For a long time she remained still, afraid to go any deeper into the bedroom. But envy evolved into inquiry, and she slipped into wandering, consuming all the things that made up a so-called princess.

Nona's bookshelves were stacked with familiar authors Sidney knew but never read, and, outside of the occasional photo of Nona's family and friends, the shelves avoided the busyness of trinkets or trophies. There were no kept birthday cards or encouraging notes to self. Not like Sidney's shelves, which displayed everything a shelf could to remind her she was worth something.

Sidney appreciated recognizing the artists of some of the vinyl records—Duke Ellington, Erykah Badu, Aretha Franklin, Prince—but sighed upon finding even more she had never heard—Joseph Bologne, Fela Kuti, Digable Planets—lining a long wood credenza topped with a record player. *The Miseducation of Lauryn Hill*, Sidney saw, was the last record to spin in Nona's player.

She made her way to Nona's sitting area, where plush couches surrounded a coffee table speckled with little bowls of stones and runes, a strange-looking deck of tarot cards, and a tea set made for six. The phantoms of shared laughter and deep conversations Sidney could almost hear still echoing in the space. She reached out, sighing as her fingers touched the bathtub near the window, which faced a balcony overlooking a pear tree.

Sidney realized she had expected the world of Alabama to be something very different than any of this. Why, so effortlessly, her mind had littered with images of riots and violence, crime and madness, confounded her. In Nona's simple, well-adjusted room, conscious or subconscious, the effect left her shamefully surprised to have found that the people of Mobile spoke intelligently, showed kindness, laughed, sang, created. What had she been imagining otherwise? Even if subconsciously? With sudden guilt, she understood she'd held on to and held up an image of what it meant to be human in which the Nonas of the world had not been included. Nor the Charlies. Who had she imagined filling all the homes across America to make the American people? How did her mind come to be just another set of eyes looking, ignoring, fearing, but never knowing?

Quietly, Sidney made her way to Nona's closet, a large walk-in space with a sink and a vanity. Inside, the colors and patterns of her clothes seemed to flutter, fabrics soft and made to be worn, like every item in her closet competed to be her favorite thing to wear. The vanity, light wood with a round gold antique mirror, held a wide array of bottles and trays. Sidney couldn't keep herself from touching them all. Rosewater spray, nearly a dozen different hair moisturizers, coconut oil, a range of wide combs and brushes, lotions, and essential oils smelling like magnolia and moss. Sidney imagined Nona sitting at the vanity every day, combing the cascade into her hair and polishing glow into her skin. There were no straighteners on Nona's vanity. No concepts of an elegant she could not herself achieve. Then Sidney gazed at her own face in Nona's mirror. Her hair matted down on one side. The tones of her skin uneven. What did Nona claim so much of and Sidney so little? What spells had been spoken into Nona's ears to help her find the source of herself, when the voice in Sidney's mind repeated the same verse: *You're not worthy*?

She couldn't bear to look at herself. She couldn't bear to be in a room constantly reflecting back to her how alone she was in the world. Within the cluster of Nona's life, Sidney acknowledged the hollowness of her own. *Who am I?* never shouted so loudly. And yet it still was muted by the boom of Nona's *I am*.

No, she didn't hate Nona. She wanted to be bold too. She wanted to wield a sturdiness of self just like Nona. She wanted the security of all her parts fitting comfortably together. She wanted her mother back. She wanted to stop collecting the stories of *everything else* in hopes that composite might make her a *something at all*. While Nona's room reflected shades of Sidney she didn't want to see, the room nevertheless reflected, making its composition irresistibly familiar. For when finally Sidney allowed her emotions to settle, she recognized herself in Nona.

She'd seen, before, something in the way Nona moved in the twinkle of stars at night. She heard, before, the sound of Nona's voice in river depths. She'd felt, before, Nona's skin flash in the soil breaking in her hands. She'd no name for that familiarity, but whatever the kinship could be called, she understood that the elusive attribute had lived in the glass house with her all along. Made small, insignificant, but nevertheless inextinguishable and ever present. She needn't have claimed that kinship for that kinship to have always claimed her.

The bedroom door creaked open.

"Sidney, we're ready for you."

22

THE CITY OPERATED with intention.

People didn't loiter in Mobile. No one tended block corners or painted themselves to the walls of closed gas stations. No unseen hands dragged people toward jobs they loathed. No one looked tardy for something, or impatient to get somewhere, or annoyed at having to be moving at all. A system, Charlie thought, operating without friction. Mobile's dynamism bordered on effortless, each person striding with purpose and grace. Smiling. Nodding. Confident.

Charlie walked ahead of the king into the downtown area, bookended on both sides by the king's eldest sons. Mobile showed itself to be a downtown unlike any he'd ever seen. No one walking with him spoke, the silence intentional, extending to Charlie the time and space to take in the city. The buildings had been modified into more natural forms. In many places, from roofs to windows, bamboo and thatch replaced glass and steel. Scaffolding scaled the sides of tall buildings, where craftspeople altered brick and metal edifices with ebony and stone. And the city tingled with color, once dull skyscrapers shimmering yellow and orange and violet.

Charlie saw no power lines, no solar panels in fields or windmills towering into white steel forests, yet everything pulsed with electric silence. And the obelisks stood elegant and powerfully throughout the city. Mobile's infrastructure was all a marvel to Charlie. Not solely that it all seemed to work so well, but that the effortlessness didn't feel new. Indeed, as Charlie gazed over the city, the technology, operations, all infrastructural underpinnings, felt familiar. Ancient even. As though this Mobile had long existed in a parallel reality, one in which the trajectory of these people's lives centuries of American cruelty had not warped. On this other plane of existence, the king and his people went on without trauma or fear, unbent to whips and guns, to be fulfilled in the wonder of themselves. Just over a year had passed since the event, and with the change, Charlie sensed, this version of Mobile was transported as though its genius had always been here. A city filled with resonant people and colorful energy.

"I don't understand how this exists," Charlie spoke out loud, more to himself than anyone.

"You're looking at this place like it came out of nowhere," the leaner son, Herald, responded. "But you can feel it, can't you? Been here. Always. Above and below."

Charlie stood in awe of all the faces as they passed—a bit of Barbados, Haiti, Egypt; a great spectrum of marvelous earth tones—and felt fortuitous to be there, among such wide-open boldness of black people. He'd never once considered that such a place could even exist, and he experienced the fact of his ignorance like a shameful treasure. And there was more. Beyond the buildings and underpinnings, something else subtly hummed with the breeze. Charlie had felt the same throb crossing the border. A charge in the air. But he could only glimpse the force in his mind, an idea fleeting, but evident. *Above and below*.

The presence of the king weighed on Charlie then. There was no fear in that weight, only respect, which surfaced whether he felt respect appropriate or not. Charlie turned suddenly to face the king. With the speed of a Bengal cat, the king's muscular son, Tau, stepped in front of his father in a protective stance. The young man's nose flared, and the tension in his shoulders tightened like the string on a bow. Charlie knew better than to challenge the king, but felt real fear at the thought of crossing the son. Every eye bore into Charlie. Even the king found Charlie's stare and received that with amusement a tick away from being bored. Then the king smiled, touched his son's shoulder to ease him, and stepped closer to Charlie.

"Speak."

Charlie realized he'd not been prepared to speak. His thoughts buzzed with questions, and not a single one could take shape. Finally, he said, "I want to understand."

"Understand what, exactly?"

"What you're doing here? How this place is what it is? What's going to happen to me and my daughter? Everything. I want to understand everything."

"Everything? No, I don't suspect you want to know everything. Knowing everything means you'll need to ask yourself questions a man like you isn't prepared to answer."

"A man like me? What does that mean?"

"You even stop to ask yourself why you're really going to Orange Beach?"

"I'm taking my daughter. You know that."

"What I *know* is that she's going because she doesn't know who she is. That fact is the fault of her father, who doesn't know who he is either."

"I know who I am."

"No, you don't. But you will." The king brushed past Charlie. "You will whether you're ready for it or not."

Charlie and the others followed the king off Dauphin Street through the next intersection, where he turned down a narrow road, made narrower by the Creole town houses, one next to the other, their height tilting shadows over everything. People bustled twice as busily on that street than any other, decorating the buildings, the bushes, and the trees in dazzling Mardi Gras decor. In front yards Charlie saw tremendous celebratory floats being built, one as a massive mermaid, another as a bushel of fruit, even one made in the image of a winged demon.

"Understand this," the king continued, "if it were solely my decision, a place like Orange Beach wouldn't even be there for you to pine after. And anyone fool enough to be chasing a world that never wanted you wouldn't be there either."

"We ain't walkers, if that's what you mean."

"You don't know what you are."

"And you do?"

"Don't I?" The king turned and punched a finger into Charlie's chest. "You ain't a man. You a knot. A conflict. Empty and full at the same time. I know what it's like to have to hold back everything you feel and feel that shit anyway. You're sad, you're lonely, confused, more pissed off than you know what to do with. But what you don't seem to understand is anger is a vital part of the human experience. Without understanding the shape of yours, you'll never be a full human being. I don't hesitate when I say I'm angry as hell. Will be probably until the day that I die. And more than that, I deserve to be. I'm still mad that every single person who walked into the water didn't get to *feel* what I feel—to know it. Because they deserved to. You and I both know what I say is true. Only one of us is able to accept that fact. But, as I said, you'll come to accept it. That I assure you."

Again the king turned away from Charlie, marching toward a house at the end of the street.

The house, unlike the others, wore no bright colors or decorations. No furnishings or ornamentation distinguished the house visibly, but something in the way of it could be felt. Dread in a wave coursed through Charlie just as a hand pushed against his back, guiding him forward. Wood, stained by age and nature, gave the house a fearsome quality. The small structure stood two stories tall, and the windows had no glass in them. Where all the other houses busied with people, not a soul occupied the wooden house inside or out. Quiet throbbed around Charlie like an omen, and his dread strengthened the nearer to the house he inched. When he reached the porch that feeling became physical. His muscles tensed, the hairs across his body stood upright, and his stomach soured. *Forbidden.* The word blazed in his thoughts. *You are forbidden here.*

Charlie stepped back, attempting to run, but the hand on his back became a grip, forcing Charlie forward.

"No, this place isn't right. Please. Let me go."

The king's voice was unnervingly calm. "Where you stand now was once called Africatown. Where the last shipment of enslaved people arrived to this country. Of course, by then slavery was supposed to be abolished, and yet the *Clotilda* came and docked just over there. For that, and for so many other reasons I can't begin to count, I'm angry. Understanding that anger, reacting to it, learning from it—well now, that's about the difference between walking around with your eyes closed and seeing what's real. Seeing what's true and what ain't. And, as you said, you're a man looking for understanding. This house is where you'll find it."

"Wait. Wait. You don't have to do this . . ." *Forbidden* again flashed in Charlie's thoughts. "King, I can help you. Just let us go and I will help you. In your garage, what you were working on, it's a radio, right? I can fix it. That can be my trade. I can do it, I swear, just let us go."

"You think I need you to help me?" The king laughed.

Again the grip on Charlie's back tightened, thrusting him forward, even as he fought to free himself. *Forbidden* again, again, and again. The hand on Charlie's back drove him into the dark house.

Inside, sunlight squeezed between the house boards. Woodsmoke blurred sight and smell, giving texture to the dim space. The hand shoved Charlie deeper into the house, pressuring him past ominous hallways into an empty space the size of a bedroom, so dark inside he could hardly see anything.

The door shut behind him.

All the alerts in his body flared red warnings. The space deepened with blackness, the lone window boarded shut, and smoke thickened the emptiness with a sweet smell. He imagined himself being chained and beaten in that room. Tortured maybe. Killed. That's when a voice spiraled out of the darkness. The voice spoke a word Charlie did not understand, then instantly, the warning in his bones evaporated. The room was no longer empty and he was not alone. Candles came to life in front of him, burning flames to make light in the space. A tin bathtub sat in the center of the room, steaming with fragrant hot water. So many smells and smokes filled Charlie's nose that his mind dizzied, but the voice speaking through the darkness steadied him.

"Take off your clothes," the voice said. "You don't want the water to get cold."

She didn't appear so much as came into Charlie's view as though she'd always been there and his eyes had lagged in adjusting to her.

"Who are you? What is this?"

"My name is Seraphin. And this is a bath."

Charlie took notice of her accent, specifically the yellow and green colors her voice left in his brain.

"Are you going to try and drown me?"

"Maybe one day, if you deserve it." She raised an eyebrow and continued. "But today we will only wash you. If you'll kindly take off your clothes."

Charlie saw the woman clearly in the low light. The sight of her triggered new alarms in his body. Not fear alarms or warnings, but something closer to thrill. She donned a shawl that gave her tall form a powerful effect. Her features Charlie couldn't quite settle on. She had eyes like the sun had light. A mouth like the sea had horizons. Features that existed in a space that could not be described, but more effectively used as a metaphor to describe other things—not beauty, but the variable elements that defined beauty. Only once in his life had he felt the same shudder under his skin he felt looking at Seraphin. And the affairs following that shudder changed the trajectory of who he became.

Stunned, Charlie did as the woman, Seraphin, asked, stripping down to his underwear, the humid air comfortable on his skin.

"I'm not sure what's happening here."

"I've told you. A bath. But that can't happen until you take off your clothes. All of them, down to what your mama brought you into this world wearing."

He took a deep breath, stepped out of his underwear and into the bath, adjusting to the heat and submerging himself up to his neck. She watched him carefully until he settled in completely.

"What do you hear?"

Charlie listened to the slosh of the water around him and the soft, weak air moving between the boards. "Water. I don't know. I don't really hear anything."

"Have you ever been baptized?"

"Can't say. If it happened, my mother would've done it when I was a baby. Just to be playing it safe."

"All right then. Take a deep breath and go all the way underwater. Like a baptism. Breathe in deep and go on."

Smoke in the room spiraled into Charlie's nose as he breathed in, filling his lungs, muscles, and out to his limbs. He glanced once more at Seraphin, closed his eyes, and sank down into the water.

And then the sun glowed warm over him, and dry grass in his mother's front yard pushed up against his thighs. His hands were small when he looked down at them. One hand held a screwdriver; the other hand held a CB radio. He hadn't yet figured out how radios worked. Not really. He'd taken the machine apart under that sun, but he couldn't reconcile how the mechanics functioned. He was familiar with the soldered connections, had an understanding of the printed circuit board and, to some degree, the variable resistor and tuner. But he could make little sense of how the machine pulled voices out of empty space to possess the speakers, a possession anyone could hear. To young Charlie, the act still teetered nearer magic. Such simple parts. And yet, they were capable of delivering messages from anyone, anywhere. Young Charlie sat there pondering magic until the sun burned into afternoon, extending the shadows of his mother's live oak tree like clawed hands reaching toward him. He looked up at that sun, absorbing heat and energy into his skin, and all of a sudden the machine made sense to him. He'd not learned anything new, nor did the circuit board or the tuner decide, abruptly, to reveal some secret answer. He just knew. Same way the big, bright sun sent invisible waves of heat into his skin, words hung invisibly in the air. Old words, new words, lessons, stories, information—all hovering above him filling up the sky. The machine itself possessed no magic. The mechanics were designed to simply tune in to that which broadcasted already. Imperceptible to the eye. Unknown to the ear. Sky full of messages. The radio could grip on to the signal. Such thoughts fascinated Charlie, and he imagined lifetimes of messages above him, transmitted and receivable. Charlie went on fixing the machine until the stars broke out and his mother turned the porch light on.

The stars, Charlie saw, were not exclusively stars but messages too, reaching through the blackness of space. Looking up at the dazzle of lights, briefly Charlie understood those messages and himself within them. *He* could be a radio, tuned in to the knowledge above him—all that *was*, *is*, and *will be* was his to hear. Fleetingly, he knew any problem he could solve, any question he could answer, because he had access to all the lessons in the history of the world. And one day he'd transmit his own. He'd be a frequency moving freely through space and time into which someone else could tune. The stars pulsed a rhythm. A beat. Music. Charlie reached up toward the night. The stars were so very close. And as he reached up, the sky reached back. The blackness of space clothed tight around his hand and pulled him. Up. up. There, he gripped on to something he thought he'd lost forever, and the blackness enveloped him completely.

Charlie sucked in air as he burst from the surface of the bath. He'd no idea how long he'd been underwater, but remembered everything the waters showed him. Seraphin was still there with him as she'd always been, holding back a smile.

"Where was I?"

"You'd know better than me," she said, handing him a thin sliver of soap. "Now, go on, wash."

She moved around behind him and draped a wet towel over his shoulders. Under the warm water, Charlie washed his chest and arms, though he felt more than just his skin being cleansed. Layers of fear, pain, and sadness seemed to wash away in that bath. His darkness, the truth of it, sturdy and marvelous, polished like obsidian. With her bare hands, Seraphin washed the beady naps across the crown of his head. Charlie closed his eyes. The memory of his childhood remained fresh in his mind, the proximity offering him a sense of wholeness. More than a decade had passed since he last saw his mother's face; even then he had to piece together her features from behind prison bars and a sullied glass window. The king had said anger, or at least an inability to process the emotion, had kept him from a wholeness. When Charlie reflected on the memory of his mother's yard and all that he'd lost since then, he *was* angry. He was angry when his mother said goodbye for the last time, and they were unable to comfort each other. Anger long suppressed. Angry for more reasons than he could fully comprehend. Anger he'd smothered all his life only to be made even that much angrier for having done so. For once, in that bathtub, Charlie allowed the anger to wash over him too. To his surprise, anger surfaced in tears, not rage. In stillness, not violence. Anger like a gateway to feel so many other things all at once.

Charlie thought of his daughter. Not thought, but *felt*. Wherever she was, whatever she was doing, he *felt* that she was safe. A message in a signal, pulsing like stars in the dark.

"Now," Seraphin asked. "What do you hear?"

Charlie let his vision swim in the darkness behind his eyes. Again, the stars. Pulsing. A beat. Music. For what is music but rhythm? And what is rhythm but a system? Again, as he had in his mother's front yard, brief but sweetly, Charlie understood everything.

"Music," he said. "I hear music."

"Good. We'll see if you remember how to dance to it."

She took him by the hand and raised him, renewed, from his bath. He felt looser and tighter at the same time, freed, somehow, in that smoky room—unraveled, shaken, and put back together. Seraphin slid a simple dashiki over his naked body, and he followed her back into the city now dipping into twilight. Into the talking stars. Into the music of Mobile. He could hear that hum much clearer. And he knew the energy he felt, the gyration of the people, and the knowing in his bones had everything to do with the machine, still broken, in the back of the king's garage.

23

SIDNEY COULDN'T STOP looking at herself in the mirror.

A herd of women had taken her into a bedroom deep in the house. Soft music played. The women lit candles and incense and hummed a tune in unison. The effect calmed Sidney enough that when they drew a hot bath, she couldn't resist undressing in front of them and soaking her body. She hadn't showered in more days than she could remember, and the curls of her hair had nearly matted into dreadlocks. But the women worked her, two of them gently washing her clean and three more cleansing, combing, and oiling her hair. She fell asleep in their hands. When she woke, she'd been moved to Nona's bedroom, draped in a purple shawl. She went straight for the mirror in Nona's closet.

And couldn't stop staring at herself.

A mountain of red curls, her hair, shiny and thick, towered up and out and down over her shoulders. Beautiful, she thought, and at the same time she saw herself as someone else. The same, maybe, but another version from another dimension. Her skin shined with fragrant oil. The muscles in her shoulders glistened; her cheekbones revealed precision through the softness of her age. She'd never thought of herself as beautiful. But the person in the mirror was like seeing a bud in bloom. She smelled different, felt different, and looked activated.

She couldn't stop staring.

"So, how do you feel?" Nona appeared in the mirror behind Sidney, wearing the same color shawl. Sidney started to speak, but could only burst into a smile.

"I don't believe it. I don't feel like me. I don't look like me."

"You look more like you than you probably ever have." Nona sat down beside Sidney and they gazed together in the mirror, ends of a spectrum, different, but the same. Whatever tension between them that had existed before eased into vapor.

"I used to hate the way I looked. My nose. My lips. My hair. It was just so . . . different."

"Different from whom?"

They stared together into the mirror awhile longer until glares broke into giggles. Sidney realized she wasn't fighting anything inside herself. She wasn't carrying any weight or steeling herself against the world. She felt looser and tighter at the same time. That bath, she thought, was more than a bath.

"Different from everyone, when different was the last thing I wanted to be. I miss my biggest worries being, y'know, who liked who, what to wear to the prom, getting into college—simple stuff that made me feel a part of something."

"I used to like all those things too. Used to dream about my prom dress and pulling up to my high school in an all-white G-Wagon. But all that changed. I sort of realized that it was all just stuff people told me I should like. Couldn't be a part of something without learning myself."

"So, what kind of things do you like?" Sidney asked.

"Well, I love to dance and sing like my momma. I like trying new things. I like helping people. I like it when boys think I'm intimidating, *which they should*. But I also know I'm still young, so I'm giving myself space to learn all the things I like. And not being hard on myself for not being what somebody else wants. That's all. Trusting my instincts. Never making myself small for other people. And no judgment."

"That sounds perfect."

"Not perfect. In progress."

A knock at the door took them away from the mirror.

"Yes?" Nona answered.

"Sorry to bother, just bringing snacks."

"It's all right, brother. Come in."

Fela entered Nona's room carrying a basket of colorful fruits and a decanter of what looked like juice but smelled like wine, and nearly fumbled the offering when his eyes found Sidney. He froze, gawking.

"Something wrong with your eyes, Fela? You know better than to stare."

"Sorry," he said, but kept gawking, making no adjustment.

Sidney, drunk on borrowed confidence, raised her chin and held his eyes, and those eyes sparkled so she could see in them the qualities of stars. "What's in the basket?" Her voice rocked sense back into Fela.

"Um, sorry, it's orange slices . . . and some pecans. Grapes too. And, um, I brought you rum punch. I mean, maybe you don't drink . . . I don't know. Just a snack before dinner, is all."

"Thank you." Sidney mustered a swell of strength to keep herself from smiling.

"All right, brother, you can go now."

Fela nodded dumbly, smiled, and stumbled toward the door. As he stepped out, he stopped as if he'd forgotten something important and turned back. "Um, Sidney, I just want to say you look beautiful."

The door shut behind him. Sidney and Nona doubled over with laughter, heat reddening Sidney's cheeks.

"What was that all about?" Sidney asked.

"Look at you, putting spells on my brother. That boy is smitten."

"No," Sidney replied, still warm in her cheeks. "He just likes seeing someone new in town."

"No, he's seeing someone he likes. And if I didn't know any better, I'd think you were too."

"No. I don't know. He's cute, but I'm not gonna be here long." Orange Beach rose back to the surface of her thoughts, as did a desire to cover her shoulders and straighten her hair.

Nona's smile turned serious. "All right then," Nona said. "Go on and tell me the story of Sidney."

"Not much to tell."

"Tell it anyway."

"Grew up in Oshkosh, Wisconsin, with my mom, stepfather, and two little half brothers. The event came and took all of them and left me. It's hard for me being here with you and with my birth father, because, I guess, until it all happened, I always believed I was just as white as my family." She paused and looked away, views from inside her glass house. "No, that's not true. I didn't really know what I was. But white was normal, so I just thought that maybe after a while I would be too."

"Be white?"

"Seems silly now, I guess. After everything."

"But isn't that why you want to go to Orange Beach?"

Sidney struggled to look back at Nona, suddenly aware of how the idea sounded to be pursuing something in this world she couldn't have in the last. "I want to go to Orange Beach because a part of my family is there. Maybe that'll help me make sense of why I'm still here."

"And what does your father think?"

"I barely know him. I called him to help me because I don't have anybody else. I guess I just . . ." She nearly stopped herself from speaking her truth, but there was something about that bath, the room, and Nona's presence that opened a door in her chest. "Listen, I've never known how I fit in. I'm two things at once, which means I'm never fully one. Half of two different worlds. I'll never be whole."

"I can't imagine what it must've been like for you growing up. And I'm sorry you had to go through so much. I like to think we are all just a recipe of different parts. My mother says that no one can give you your wholeness. You just have to claim it."

"What about you then? How did you become a real-life princess?"

"My mother would tell you I've been a princess since the day I was born. I guess, in a way, she's right. She's the queen of Mardi Gras. My father is the king. They have been every year since I can remember."

"I wish I knew things about myself."

"Turn around, look in the mirror, and tell me something you know about the person you see."

Sidney took a deep breath and did what Nona asked. "I barely recognize myself right now. I look so . . . natural." Sidney examined her features anew. A nose she'd wished off her face gave her definition. The lips she'd feared too big to kiss puckered pink and lush. Even the muscularity of her neck and shoulders looked radiant under the sheen of oils. "I know I am not special and I know I'm not elegant," she said. "I know I've spent my whole life just trying to convince myself I'm worth the trouble of my own existence."

"Can I tell you what I know? I know you're strong enough to endure what you endured and still make it to Mobile. I know you're beautiful enough to turn my brother to mush. Your energy is my energy. I made the decision to make you my sister because I felt it. Energy that's way past anybody's value or definition. Strong, beautiful, and precious. That's you."

"You could say that a million times and I'd still not believe a word of it."

"Well, lucky for you, I can show you better than I can tell you. C'mon." She extended her hand to Sidney. "Dinner's ready downstairs. I promise it won't be chitlins this time."

24

CHARLIE SAT AT the center of a storm of a dinner table.

The table, lengthy with seating for more than twenty people, couldn't itself contain the amount of food, people, and energy rousing the dining room of the king's home. The king sat at one end of the table, and the great queen, almost blurred in the distance, at the other; their three strong sons marched back and forth from the kitchen delivering dish after dish of food. And there was so, so very much food, warming the air with spice. Grilled corn and tomatoes, seasoned mushroom tops, fire-baked potatoes, patties made of black beans, baked macaroni and cheese, shrimp and grits, corn bread dressing, sweet potatoes warm in coconut and bourbon, salt fish, rice and peas, a whole burst of different slaws and salads, and a second table just for the sweet stuff, crowded with beignets, peach cobbler, lemon tart, and white cake.

All of that good-smelling food passed, hand to hand, from one side of the table to the other, laughter and conversation bouncing back and forth like a celebration for the joy of every second that ticked past. Happiness. Movement. Color. Leaping and yawping. Even the queen's laughter spilled out of any expected formality to bless the table as plates piled high with food.

Charlie hadn't even scooped a single dish, but he looked down to his plate already made, flowing over. Charlie just smiled. *Nothing in the world like breaking bread with black folks,* Charlie thought. He hadn't enjoyed a proper family-style dinner since before prison. Delight tingled through him to be able to fall right back into the speed of it. No, not speed. But pulsing: the evocation of the very rhythms of being alive. He looked around at all those faces, even seeing Zu, and blushed a little after a wink from Seraphin.

Conversations flowed, many of them, Charlie overhead, talking about New Years and Mardi Gras: where the best parties were happening, who would make the best float, and music—who played and sang where. Charlie overheard deeply focused conversations as well about work: trolley repairs, building maintenance, and the dates of different shipments arriving, as well as new art gallery exhibitions and theater shows. Charlie listened, fascinated, aware that every second of those imprisoned years kept him from experiencing the simple joy of a round table dinner.

He'd come to learn so much more about Mobile in a short span of time, even as the notion of time itself seemed to expand and accelerate and slow down all at once. The sun rose and set without clock or calendar to frame the days. The city proved to be vastly different from other thriving cities like D.C. and Chicago. Where they clung to previous ways, Mobile created a new lane for itself. No system of money ruled over them, no classes or levels of life separated one group of people from another, nor did any definitive religion guide the masses with a firm hand. Indeed, a system of sorts had revealed itself to Charlie in the way people moved, interacted, and thrived. He thought of George Washington Carver's scientific papers and overall fascination with mushrooms. As Carver saw them, fungi were the oldest and largest organisms on the planet, perfecting a harmony with the world no other organism had achieved. An advanced intelligence, Carver might say, in the art of living. From the dirt a little mushroom carried the power to feed you, to heal you, even to take you to a higher consciousness. The people of Mobile, as best Charlie could gather, maintained a similar, supernatural cycle. They gave, they grew, and they communed, a three-part existence that played out in their days.

For a third of their day they seemed to freely give what was in them to be given, whatever passion woke them each morning and just spilled over. From what Charlie saw, those passions included building things, growing things, teaching, dancing, learning. People seemed to almost become themselves simply by offering what they loved doing most. Another third of their day dedicated time for growing, strengthening the body, the mind, the heart. All over the city, people gathered together in groups talking, eating, training, learning history, planning futures, accepting all the things others had to give. The method of erudition struck him as similar, in many ways, to Howard, where classrooms and schedules could not contain learning. And there was so much to learn, new things and old, equaled only by a willingness to teach. Spirituality, in the last third of their days, played a formless role in the lives of the Mobile people. Some prayed on their knees to gods in the earth. Some shook runes in their palms and dipped bones in blood to access the lessons of the dead. Some stood face up at the bases of obelisks, their serene expressions brightly painted in the light of the sun. Charlie acknowledged the spirituality in everything, an awareness of magic and gods and spirits. But no defined religion. The people of Mobile dreamt. They meditated. They communed with something higher, seemingly capable of sensing the subtlest energies. When Charlie questioned what power the king and queen wielded to force these people to abide by their principles, he settled on the hypothesis that the flow of the city required no force at all. No more than how he knew to come home when the streetlights came on, or if he were to lie down with dogs he'd wake up with fleas. In simplified form, Charlie gathered, axioms turned principles had always passed through generations of black folks, leaving him with but one answer: *It's our nature.* Still, there was something more to the city. Something profound and longing. Something he couldn't analyze, only feel.

A hush brought down the noise at the dinner table. Charlie looked up to see his daughter arrive side by side with whom Charlie assumed to be the princess. He hardly recognized Sidney. And though her hair was conditioned and done up, and her skin shining, her essence itself beamed, like she'd been plugged in and powered up. All he could do, like everyone else at the table, was look on in awe. Sidney smiled with bashful brightness. Charlie's heart swelled in his chest. Whole. That's what Charlie thought, taking Sidney in. She looked whole.

Then the queen stood. Silence became attentiveness. Looking at the queen was like gazing at mountain ranges in the night. He stared, speechless, certain he'd never felt anything so powerful as her presence.

The queen scanned over the full table, taking care to make eye contact with every person. She said nothing and didn't need to speak for her weight to be felt. She quietly stepped aside and made space for her daughter.

"As always, family, we give gratitude for all that has been given to us," the young princess said, and all the heads at the table nodded, even Charlie's. "Everyone here knows that my mother's table is open to anyone in need of a meal or good company. But today, we have new arrivals to break bread with." The princess glanced at Sidney, and Charlie could almost feel Fela, standing near the kitchen, shift in place. "My sister Sidney and her family have arrived to experience the world that we've made. I am grateful they're here, for however long they stay. So, I invite Sidney's father to speak if he chooses."

Every eye turned to Charlie. Terror nearly put him under the table for how woefully unprepared he was to say anything. And he wouldn't've spoken at all, if not for Sidney's eyes, among those all around him, glassed of hope.

Charlie stood and just started speaking, unsure where the speech would lead. "First, well, thank you all for having us. I'll be honest, I didn't know what to expect coming down here. Well, no, that's not entirely true. I expected the worst. The last thing I thought we'd walk into was what I see all around me. Everyone here seems so . . . alive. I don't know what it is, must be something in the water." At that, the faces at the table held back smiles and chuckles. "We was all doing whatever we was doing before the event. None of that matters anymore. We are here now. And, for me and mine, in this moment, Mobile is starting to feel like it's the center of the universe. So, thank you for allowing us to be here with you."

"Not just *with* us, Uncle Charlie," Herald shouted. "You *are* us."

Charlie canceled his move to sit down, seeing Nona still standing. "Uncle Charlie, one of my dad's traditions is for someone to have a question for the table. Do you have a question you want to ask?"

"Um, well, I have so many. I guess my main question is how is all of this . . . all of this?"

A flutter of laughter lightened the room.

The smile on Nona's face seemed to glitter. "It is what it always has been, Uncle Charlie."

"Well, daughter," the king interrupted, "I think what Charlie means is how did we all get to this moment, doing what we're doing? And that's a story best told by your mama. Vivian, baby, would you?"

Hands beat against the table and feet stomped the floor, making a drumroll that shook the house, everyone anxious to hear the queen speak. The queen nodded gracefully, an act that made Charlie's skin warm. She milked the rumble until the thunder grew so loud Charlie couldn't help but join in. When finally she stood, a hush smothered the table. The queen looked to Charlie, her voice like a song in the room.

"Charlie, Sidney, I want you to close your eyes and imagine a paradise.

Rich land that can grow anything you put in the soil. Shade trees, mangoes, bananas, corn. Anything. Imagine a beach so blue and sand so crisp, a beach where you can cast a line from anywhere and bring up fish. Wide-open sunshine. Imagine absolute freedom for as far back as you can remember and having your entire history intact going all the way back to the first woman to give your line a name. A place where your ancestors can still speak to you. No worrying about status or schedules. No shame, no conflict, nothing but blue sky and clear purpose. Everything that you have ever done, created, mastered, sang, screamed, and sacrificed to nourish the old world is to be savored only to nourish you every day of your life. Everything you've got to give, given to just you and your family. Can you see it?"

Charlie didn't want to open his eyes from the picture the queen painted in his mind. "Yeah? Can you tell me how to get there?"

"It's not hard. For me, that place was Haiti."

"Haiti? The little island?"

"Oh yes. That island. Charlie, did you know that Haiti's slave revolution is the only one that has ever won back its freedom? They beat the French back so many times and so badly those Frenchmen ended up just selling Louisiana to America along with all the gateways to the west. All so the French didn't have to go back and fight that little island again. Without Haiti, America wouldn't be America, y'know, *Manifest Destiny* and all that. Haiti changed the trajectory of the world."

"I didn't know that."

"Neither did I. That's why a few years ago Hosea and I left and took our family to Haiti. To learn all the things we didn't know. We discovered there were other ways to live. When our time came to come back to America, we brought those ways with us. And, no, Mobile is not the paradise you imagine, at least not yet. But we came to learn paradise is the mind. What you believe about yourself. What you *know* about yourself. We have a lot of work to do, and we know it will never be perfect. But better is a direction. As long as we progress, together, we will be all right. Mobile is movement. We are all movement."

Again, the room rumbled with sound until the king stood and raised a glass. "To movement. Progress toward better."

Charlie raised his glass along with everyone at the table.

"Now, please, can I eat? I'm starving." Tau's voice blasted through the end of the toast. "Y'all torturing me with this food."

The table exploded in cheers and raised glasses. Charlie received a stiff nod from the king, a big smile from Zu, and the subtlest raise of her chin from Sidney, then sat down and put a fork in his plate.

Hardly any time passed for the conversations to find their way to Charlie in the form of the king's youngest son, Fela, scooting close to talk. Charlie saw through his attempt to win favor, abstractly making pathways to his daughter. Still, Charlie entertained the boy in good nature. Fela asked Charlie about being a professor at Howard and who inspired him to know the things he knew. Charlie, naturally, fell back into being a teacher, talking with Fela about power sources and how he'd spent years reading from the works of Granville T. Woods, Frederick McKinley Jones, and Shirley Jackson.

When he wasn't talking like his throat was greased or chewing down forkfuls of food, Charlie looked around the raucous dinner and, equitably, just felt good. The scene, chaotic and wonderful, reminded Charlie of a live oak tree in the height of summer, where the leaves applauded every breeze, and the sun and the birds and even the clouds sang. Trees that sprawl out untamed and free, executing the whimsical program for which they were made: nature's most beautiful chaos. Family, Charlie saw, in skin, in bone, in spirit, impossible to bury, chain down, or educate out of the mind. Only in pieces could he remember the last meal he had with his mother. He couldn't remember what they ate or what they talked about, only the feeling: family. Twenty years in prison did everything it could to erase family from Charlie's heart. And yet, as good roots often do, family remained.

Charlie's eyes found Sidney barely eating. He understood her pain and how her hope for a colony in Orange Beach was less inspired by race than by a sense of belonging. The world took him away from her before she even knew he existed, so she'd spent her life trying to belong to something that never fully embraced her. He glanced around the dining table, stirred in his heart with hope to finally show his daughter all the things that belonged to her.

25

SIDNEY HAD LEARNED to make her mother's green bean casserole as a way to contribute every Thanksgiving. The recipe wasn't particularly complicated, just a can of cream of mushroom soup, green beans, and onions. Once she'd all but perfected the technique, she added a pinch of paprika and cayenne to give the dish a spark of flavor. Every year at her home, the ceremony of Thanksgiving played out the same: Rick would fry a turkey, nearly burning down the back deck; her mother would make fresh mashed potatoes, Stove Top stuffing, and a pumpkin pie. The family would say grace, taking the time to announce all the things for which they were grateful, then eat and watch football with full bellies, while the twins raked the fall leaves outside just to wrestle in them. Indeed, on the very last Thanksgiving as a family, the only break in decorum came with Rick commenting, absently, on how the green bean casserole that year was too spicy. Nevertheless, Thanksgiving could be counted on as the one meal where the whole family sat at the big table and ate. Together.

What Sidney experienced in Mobile, however, had no space in her mind to even be conceived as a way to eat together. So much noise. So much food. So much *everything*. The smells, the flavors, the laughter, the conversations, like being caught in the most appetizing tornado. And while the food looked and smelled delicious, she hadn't developed the tongue to appreciate all those flavors, nor the mind to decipher all those conversations. Overwhelmed, Sidney just studied her plate, trying her best to imagine how dinners might come together in Orange Beach. They'd be much quieter, she imagined, and less seasoned. When, finally, Nona asked if she wanted to take a night walk through the city, the opportunity for fresh air came as a relief.

Mobile at night sparkled. Not a large city, what Mobile lacked in size the streets made up for with an unseen energy. Night magic. Every alley, every pocket of dark between trees, even the space between the clusters of stars, seemed to be breathing. Watching. Waiting. So, as they walked, Sidney stayed close to Nona, even as their night outing picked up a crowd. First, some of the younger women joined in, friends of Nona's; then Zu and even Charlie, walking stride for stride with a tall, beautiful woman who made eye contact with Sidney, smiled, and kept walking.

As they strolled toward the downtown, Sidney stood amazed at how developed the city felt. Modern and timeless at the same time, different from Chicago in almost every way. The shapes and forms of the building architecture, the slow-moving trolleys that seemed to almost hover, and nature, nature most of all, seemed to harmonize, as though the roads, the technology, and even the people had grown right out of the soil no different from the peach trees.

Music thumped in the distance, swelling louder the nearer to downtown they walked. Didn't take long for Charlie to appear beside her wearing what looked like a dashiki and an easy, easy look on his face.

"Hey. I just wanted to tell you that you look lovely, Sidney. Got your hair done and all fixed up. So beautiful."

"Thank you." He seemed somehow different, Sidney considered. Relieved, maybe, of a long-carried heaviness. "I saw you walking with that woman."

"Seraphin." A light flashed in his face when he said her name.

"Oh, so you weren't just walking, you like her."

"I do. I think—hope—she likes me too."

"Didn't see that coming."

"Didn't see Mobile coming. I thought this place would be a war zone."

The music nearby ballooned loud enough for Sidney to avoid responding. She still very much planned to make her way to Orange Beach. There wasn't much of anything Mobile could show her that would change that.

Around the corner, the source of all the music was revealed at the end of the road, a street party throbbing with lights and sound.

"Listen, Sidney," Charlie continued, forced to speak louder over the music. "Sitting at that dinner table, I realized the world really is a new place. Everything before doesn't matter. What we need is family, and, I guess, I'm saying—asking—if maybe I can be your family. For real. If you'll have me."

Before he even said the word *family*, Sidney's anger swelled up to her eyes. All of a sudden she was back in Wisconsin, sitting at the shore of the lake, trying to will her body to drown like her family.

"My family drowned and that matters! So, no, you don't get to ask family of me. You can't even tell me where you were all this time. Why you left us. We can't be family, because we've never been family."

And then hands grabbed them both, Nona pulling Sidney in one direction, Seraphin pulling Charlie in another. She glimpsed the pain on her father's face, and just knowing she could hurt him turned her anger raw. Raw anger that sparked of regret.

By the hand, Nona pulled Sidney down Dauphin Street, where music in the air carried the last elements of twilight into night, and a party exploded in front of them. Music thumped deeply, and hundreds of people danced in the street. Lyrics were chanted in unison. Balconies shook with bodies leaning over the crowds. Sidney heard drums and brass horns—a full marching band kicking thrill like a voltage through the boulevard. A voice boomed over the whole scene, singing in a call-and-response:

"Aye yo, aye yo!"

And the crowd responded in howled unison bordering on holy: "Aye yo, aye yo!"

"Shout it up to the clouds, say 'aye yo, aye yo'!"

"Aye yo, aye yo!" Call-response. Wild, feverish, but spiritual all the same.

Aye yo, aye yo!

Aye yo, aye yo!

The dynamism stopped Sidney where she stood, her anger lost in the fray. "What is all of this?"

"Have you never seen carnival?"

She had never even heard of carnival or anything like what convulsed before her. "This is crazy."

"It's not, Sidney, it's a party. C'mon!"

Nona dragged Sidney out into the throng. The heat of that party warmed Sidney before she entered the crowd. Heat revealing itself in colors: red, yellow, violet, orange. Revealing itself in smells: flesh, flowers, wood, asphalt. In lights that weren't lights but darkness made to shimmer. And there was so much sound, activating the air and rattling in the narrow stretches under her skin—everything a percussion. The scene was a spell, enchanting the frenzy to lose itself in dance. Hands pumped and swung like the tips of flames. Hips ticked side to side. Heads dropped back and throats opened wide with delight. Even Nona, under the spell of the street party, broke out immediately into dance.

But Sidney didn't dance.

Her body squeezed down on the modicum of abandon alive in her chest. She didn't move and wouldn't dare gyrate as fast and free as the people around her. So she squeezed tight, her hands at her waist, her knees nearly touching, and her tongue swollen in her mouth, accounting for every tooth, the roof and base, and the depth of her throat to assure all allegiance to silence.

The night began to boil around her. Stars spun into orbs hovering at her brow.

Sidney feared closing her eyes.

A skirt swished against her knees. She heard the sound of a man's thighs clapping together. Though she didn't move and didn't speak, she felt herself heating up. The heat started in her soles. The heat moved up though her shins and her stomach, and by the time its burn reached her head, it was a current pulling her up. Her shoulders, her ears, her hair. Up and up.

She shouted out, "No," and ran off the street, leaving everyone behind. The first empty alley drew her into its darkest corner. There, she burrowed herself in the refuge of her glass house.

Sidney covered her ears, shut her eyes tight, and tried to imagine herself back in her bedroom, her brothers bumping against the walls in the next room, the smell of lavender breezing through an open window. She tried to imagine her mother, and, through her, access enough sadness to swallow her whole, and, with it, take up every emotion she had. Until there was nothing left. No sadness, no happiness, no color, and no longing, just her face reflected on glass walls. But she was no longer alone in her glass house.

"It's okay." Nona's voice lit up the darkness behind her eyes. "I won't leave you. It's okay."

"I'm not one of you." More anger than she intended fired her words. "You hear me? I'm not your sister. I'm not one of you."

"You're angry?"

"I'm a hell of a lot more than angry."

"Sad? Confused? Ashamed? Afraid? Let yourself feel it. Feel all of it. Then dance with me until it burns up, until you can finally stop apologizing for being who you are. You can't go backward and there's nothing you need to settle to go forward. Let go of it, Sidney. Just let go." Nona took Sidney's face in both hands. "If you're here with me now, you are us. You don't have to know how to dance. Listen to that beat. That's our calling. Our rhythm. You have to move and move with all your body, because it's how you give those feelings inside you a way out. Don't worry about where you've been or where you're going. You are here right now. But you have to let go. Come on. You have to let go."

By the hand, Nona led Sidney back out into the middle of the crowd. Having Nona's eyes on her offered Sidney the only point of relief in the swirling mania. Nona dropped her arms around Sidney. Smoothly, Nona started to sway, catching on to the rhythm grooving around them.

"You have to let go. Move with me, Sidney. Close your eyes and feel all that anger, sadness, loneliness—all of it—and let it shake out of you. Dance until what haunts you can't haunt you anymore."

Then the beat cut to a rumble, heat again rising up under their feet. Just as the beat dropped deep, Nona grabbed both of Sidney's hands.

"Now, dance with me, sister."

The beat flurried upward. Sidney closed her eyes and let herself ascend.

Arms first, then shoulders, hips, then knees. Moving proved easier than she expected, familiar even. Before long the spell of rhythm worked through her, spinning her in circles, expelling laughter and tears. And there was so very much to expel. So many questions. So many fears. So much longing. Cracking. From the inside. Breaking, burning. Sidney danced harder, aware of how the movement blended her into everyone dancing in the street. And the riling felt so very good. To cry, scream, sweat, and laugh through the physicality. Remaking her in the therapy of something primal. The more she danced, the more a tremendous lump inside her gave way. The beat bopped in her bones. Her muscles swelled of joy. Freedom. Laughter as a form of movement that popped, rocked, allowed her to slip free of herself and be gone into the rhythm. Burning up. Boiling. Steaming. So hot she spiraled upward. They all did. Far away from everything. Hot and bright as stars. Together in cosmic unity. A constellation right there in the streets of Mobile.

Sidney welcomed the sensation. That she could be both alone and together. Down to the core. Down where everything and everyone blended into the dimension behind her eyelids, connected, finally, in a living darkness.

While the rhythm lasted there were no sides.

No lines in the sand. No walls. No them. No they. Only us. Alone and together.

Like the fine molecules of a mountain.

26

SIDNEY SHOT AWAKE, again panicked by the smell of something burning.

She was alone in Nona's bed when she opened her eyes. The music and dancing from last night left a headache that went on pounding its rhythm in her pulse. She'd done as Nona asked and let go. She'd danced with Fela. She'd caught a glimpse of Charlie dancing with Seraphin. She'd chanted along in the call-and-response until her voice worked itself ragged. And those memories would've been a delight to wake up with, except the smell of something burning spoiled the air.

She crawled out of bed and into the hallway of a morning-quiet house. Where, in the daytime, the house rumbled with people, morning settled upon it the same sensation of being in a church outside of service, solemn and silent with spirits.

Sidney tiptoed down the stairs and through the kitchen, following the smell, and found its cause out in the courtyard. Behind the staircase, she hid where she could see outside. The queen and her council lounged under the live oak tree, smoking together from a long pipe. They passed the pipe among them, coughing and laughing, even the queen, suddenly seeming less regal. Hidden away, Sidney watched them puff and giggle, certain what they were doing was illegal and aware there were no police anywhere to do anything about it. The way they passed the pipe, clicking on mouthpieces to breathe in and blow out smoke, had a ceremonial quality. Nevertheless, she'd discovered a flaw in Mobile's perfect society. And seeing that flaw came as a comfort to Sidney. Orange Beach, she imagined, wouldn't ever break the law.

"It's called Inqawe." A voice spooked Sidney from behind, and she whipped around to find Nona standing next to her looking out at the older women.

"I wasn't spying."

"There is nothing wrong with being a little curious. What they are doing is a traditional Xhosa smoking ceremony. Some of the women in my mother's council came from South Africa and shared the old ways, which we try to reintegrate into the new way."

"Old ways? Aren't drugs bad?"

"Drugs are made in labs. What they're doing is maintaining relationships with the ancestors. You want to try some?"

"God, no. Have you ever tried it?"

"No. The ceremony is supposed to only be for older women or women who've borne children. My friends sometimes do it anyway. I haven't yet, but, if you want, I'll try it with you."

"Are you insane? No way. I mean, we'd lose our minds, right?"

"Probably. Or at least find some trouble to get into. And my trouble is that I've never been afraid of anything. Didn't always think that was a good thing. Now, my trouble is my superpower."

"You don't think smoking is wrong?"

"What if you just let go of everything you've been taught about right and wrong—forget what your schoolteacher said, your church pastor; forget about your Girl Scout leader—and you just tried to *feel* right and wrong in your bones, in your heart—would you still think what they are doing is wrong?"

Quietly, Sidney remembered herself nearly shooting a child on the lawn of her home. She remembered Little and all the houses along the way with their doors wide open. She remembered the tenor with which Rick said *elegant*.

"Nona, I don't think my bones know how to feel."

"We can fix that, little sister. Come with me, I want to show you something."

27

PANIC WOKE CHARLIE.

Instinctively, his mind reached to find Sidney and apologize for miscalculating her state of mind, a state made more complex by the truths he kept from her. But even as his mind reached, his body remembered all the sensations of last night and where those sensations delivered him—a dream he feared waking up would repossess. He could still smell the incense as he turned over in a warm, cozy bed. A few feet away, Seraphin stood naked at the window, pulling back the curtains, sunlight bejeweling the curves and muscles of her form. At the sight of her, the night before returned. The dancing, the celebration, the way the moon transformed longing into lust.

"Good morning," Charlie said, aware of all the years since he'd lain with a woman, or woke up with one.

"Good morning, Charles Brunton."

"Last night was . . ."

"As all good nights should be." And it was. Good that filled Charlie to the brim and spilled over. He'd danced like he hadn't in decades. Danced like his body wanted to shake something out of itself. The magnitude of what he felt last night wasn't his alone. It was everyone's. Big love. Broad, sweeping, and all-consuming. Love that made you dance when you didn't want to. Made you laugh so hard you stopped breathing. Made you *want* to feel everything, pushing him to hug, and dap, and hold on to the person next to him like magnets wedged between his joints. Charlie, over the course of one night, felt that he'd recovered something profound and unnamable. And as he looked over at Seraphin's luminous black-gold body, he knew what he'd found last night he yet retained.

"I must be the luckiest man this side of the Mississippi."

"It's sweet that you think luck had anything to do with last night. And don't think I don't know we aren't that far from the Mississippi River."

Morning light showed Charlie qualities of her bedroom the night veiled. A yawning space, more lounge than a quarter for sleeping, Seraphin's room sat at once full and vacant. Smells of long-burned sage and perfumes mixed together to make Charlie imagine deer rolling in jasmine. A big velvet couch and chairs sat in the center, and there were so many fat-leafed plants that the space could resemble a jungle if the room weren't so dim and the carpet so lush and the windows stalled by curtains as thick as duvets. Her bedroom came together like some part of her mind made real. And in it, Charlie felt as comfortable as he did uneasy, surrounded by all the shelves sagged with hoodoo things. Bones, sticks shaped into creatures, stones that glistened with quartz, jars stuffed with dead things floating in murky liquids with their eyes open looking right at him. Bottles of wine with no labels, looked as old and dangerous as wine could look. A small apothecary of spices, dried leaves, and roots. A few feet from where Seraphin stood, between the long velvet couch and chairs, a coffee table sat loaded with an assortment of spiritual baubles: piles of runes and stones, small silver bowls to burn things, and several worn decks of cards.

"Are you some sort of shaman?"

"Manbo. A conjure woman."

"So, magic?"

"Science. Magic is just all science at once. Chemistry, physics, medicine. All the ones you know, and others you don't."

"Have you always been a . . . manbo?"

"Yes. My mother was manbo, and my father, houngan. Been in our family. In my blood. I couldn't avoid it if I wanted to. I can just feel the world. And hoodoo is a method of processing those feelings."

"Did you put a spell on me last night?"

Seraphin strode over to Charlie and kissed him. "Depends on what you call a spell."

"Must be my luck then."

"You're special, Charlie. I can feel that without even trying. It's like a heat warming the air around you."

"I ain't ever felt special my whole life."

"What did you feel?"

"Hard to explain. Felt like the opposite of special. Like a big black void moving through the world. Empty, if not for all the people trying to fill it with their own judgments on me."

"The thing about voids, Charlie Brunton, is ain't nothing inside of them but light they can't figure out how to free."

"Last night felt pretty freeing. Maybe we can keep doing that?"

"Maybe we can. And I'd like to read your cards for you, Charlie. Maybe an ancestors spread. Let the spirits remind you how special you are."

"I wouldn't mind seeing you use your magic."

"And you will. But right now, you have to go." She gestured toward the window. "They're waiting for you."

Charlie slid out of bed, looked out the window, and saw what she'd seen. He rushed back on last night's dashiki, and as he found his shoes, he heard water running into a bath and saw Seraphin was gone. His body ached to stay, to climb into the bath with her and spend the day naked in bed. But, as she'd said, there was more for him to discover, and more waited just outside.

Out in the front yard, standing with his hands behind his back, was the king's son Herald.

"Well, come on," Herald said. "You want to see it up close, don't you?"

"See what?"

"What my father's working on in the garage." He smiled then, almost by accident. "I'm sure in your life you've seen all sorts of things, Uncle Charlie. But I'm willing to bet a dollar to a doughnut that you've never seen anything like what I'm about to show you."

He walked ahead of Charlie, who could hardly see straight.

"Just hold up a minute," he said. "None of this makes sense. You don't use any money. The power running everything from the streetlights to the trolleys seems to be coming out of thin air. And the people . . ." Charlie paused, seeking the words to describe suffering a lifelong conflict no one in Mobile seemed to endure. "It's like y'all enlightened or something."

"Enlightened?"

"You heard me. Y'all black just like I am but don't carry black like I carry it."

"That's because you got it wrong, Uncle. Black carries us."

"You talk like it's magic."

"Always feels like magic when the light comes through. We just benefiting from our hard work, that's all. No magic. We work off value, not money. We rebuilt the power grid to make it free like it's supposed to be. We're still trying to figure out food, making sure we have enough and getting it from place to place—the big dinners help keep things from spoiling. Pops is working hard on infrastructure, clean water and so on. Mom says 'better is a direction,' so we just headed that way, is all."

Herald's eyes, Charlie noted, had a shine to them that seemed less a reflection than a source. "I want to understand it. All of it."

"I heard you the first time. Some things you won't know until you know. So come on, my pops is waiting."

28

ANOTHER SCHOOL BUS idled out in front of the house. More than a dozen people, all of them around Sidney's age, dallied just outside the bus. Near the door, she could hear them cracking jokes, laughing, and talking louder than necessary to be heard. Nona strode out ahead of her, easily absorbed into the fray, laughing and talking just like the rest of them. *Them,* Sidney still gnawed. Them *not* me.

Then a familiar voice rang out louder than those of any of the people out in the yard. "Sidney!" the voice shouted. "We left hell and landed smack in the middle of heaven."

Zu, sunlight dazzling their skin, charged through the small crowd, drawing every eye to them and eventually to Sidney. All those eyes on her at once sank her heart, but Zu's familiarity gave her buoyancy. Felt good to know someone in the crowd. Even better to be known by them.

Zu almost looked like a shaman, wearing a toga patterned similar to a dashiki. Seeing them felt like seeing an old friend, and Sidney suddenly felt the separation of time. She realized she had no idea what day it was or just how long they'd been lingering in Mobile.

"Don't you love it here? I know you do. I do." Zu hugged her like they'd known her all their life. Zu's eyes swelled big and inquisitive. "Tell me you danced last night?"

"I danced," Sidney responded, barely able to hold back a blush. How happy Zu seemed, considering Sailor left and hadn't come back, surprised her. "I danced with Nona."

Zu spun her around and did a little samba, their moves so nimble Sidney danced along with them before she realized what she was doing.

"Oh, I wish I could've found you. We would've danced until the sun came up. Or until the rum put us on our asses. Which is exactly what it did to me."

Sidney laughed. "Do you know where we're going?"

"Out to the countryside. That's what they told me. Could use a little fresh air."

"You think where we're going is close to Orange Beach?"

Sidney witnessed the disappointment shudder through Zu's expression.

"You still thinking about Orange Beach?" Zu curled an arm around Sidney's arm to walk together toward the bus. "Child, I can't imagine a world better than the one we're in right here. Because it's ours. And it's beautiful."

Sidney knew better than to respond. Instead, she swam in memories of boating on the lake, wrestling with her brothers, and picking lavender in the spring. *There are better worlds,* she thought, just as Nona appeared to her left and hooked her other arm.

"There's my sister."

Zu stared all around Nona like they could see her aura. Sidney was sure Zu saw things she couldn't. Performatively, Zu unfurled a hand like a servant and said, "Princess Nona, may I speak in your presence?"

"You know better than to ask me that. Zu, right?"

"Lord a mercy, a princess knows my name. A whole princess knows *my* name."

"Don't be silly, Zu," Sidney added, feeling suddenly embarrassed.

"Ain't nothing silly about it. She gonna be the queen and rule over the whole world one day. And, allow me to add, you'd be the most beautiful queen anybody's ever seen."

"Thank you, Zu, that's very kind. The only thing I want to rule over is myself. Same as you. Same as Sidney. That's more than enough for all of us."

The school bus horn blasted, and inside Sidney saw Fela at the wheel of bus number 303. Seeing him sent a flutter so strong inside her, she was certain that Zu and Nona felt its vibration. As much as she wished to deny the fact, she liked Fela being near her.

"Load up!" his voice bellowed out over everyone.

As the small crowd loaded onto the bus, Sidney observed her peers, all young, all strong, all moving with a stride so sure of itself their gaits did not betray any sense that they had ever been anything other than certain. Certain of who they were. Certain of what they could accomplish. Certain that any world they stepped into, be it an inch wide, a mile, or the full size of a planet, that space would sprawl out before them like a canvas to paint an image no amount of cruelty could keep from stupefying all to behold. Sidney wondered if they saw her differently. She was sure she didn't walk with the same swagger. She could not speak as brashly or embrace someone with her whole body. As she boarded the bus, she tried to conjure in herself what freedoms she experienced last night, tried to hear the same rhythm, thumping, thumping like the music of the universe.

"Welcome aboard, Sidney." Fela's voice breezed through her thoughts. "I'm glad you're coming with us."

She felt the rhythm then, still inside her, when she said, "And why are you so glad?"

"W-well," he stumbled. "Um, because, uh . . ."

"Gracious, y'all better stop before y'all set the whole bus on fire." Zu laughed, and the three of them found seats in the back of the bus.

Warmth filled Sidney to the brim as she sat down. Orange Beach quietly, bleakly, slipped to the back of her thoughts. Several others came to sit nearby, each one introducing themselves and shaking Sidney's and Zu's hands.

The bus rattled into motion, and within the group, conversations began to flow. A little gossip about who liked whom. A bit of excitement about what Mardi Gras would be like this year. A bit of wonder about taking a road trip west to the Grand Canyon. Sidney had never seen the Grand Canyon, and a tingle coursed through her at the thought of driving herself to see it.

She listened in on the dizzying conversations or casually looked out the window to open countryside and farmhouses surrounded by roaming animals: cows, horses, and goats. Twice, she saw groups of people raising obelisks out far from the city. She'd been lost in the blur of it all when Zu nudged her halfway through a question posed for her.

". . . Wisconsin?" she heard the girl in front of her say. The girl was younger than Sidney by a year or two, with eyes so big and sharp they wrapped like wings around the sides of her head.

"Sorry? Yes, I'm from Wisconsin."

"You're the one who wants to go to Orange Beach?"

"Yes." Sidney felt exposed.

"You'd be the youngest person there."

"You've been? Seen it yourself?"

"Of course. We all have. We serve the people there just like we serve everybody else. Bring them food, rehabilitate the ones who want it."

"What is it like?"

Nona cut in. "Sidney, what do you think it's like?"

Again Sidney felt exposed. She knew better than to say she expected it to be more like the world used to be. Even as she thought about those words, she recognized she had fewer and fewer memories of what those days were like. Indeed, she feared she could recall only the shiniest parts.

"I don't know. But my family is there, so that's where I should go."

"It's strange, every time I go there," the girl continued. "Like being in one of those old folks' homes, you know, where people aren't really in their right mind. Looking for something, somewhere, that ain't here anymore."

"I'm here," Sidney said, with a little more attitude than she intended. "So that means what was before still very much is."

She braced herself for a judgment that didn't come. They all just nodded their heads somberly around her.

"Identity is a struggle no matter what world we're in," Nona chimed in. "We are all sorry for all that you've lost, Sidney. Can't really imagine what you're going through. Grief is grief. We can all understand that, right?"

Again, they all nodded, a series of empathetic eyes flashing at Sidney. All except Zu, who chewed on a question they couldn't swallow. "Can I ask you, Sid . . . what do you think happened to them?"

The question felt like a black hole punctured in Sidney's chest, sucking in all the air in the room. She didn't know how to answer. Indeed, she hadn't once, at least not deeply, tried to answer the question for herself. Did the Rapture and God just take them? Did some signal tuned to their ears call them out of this world? Without an answer for any of her questions, Sidney spoke freely.

"When I was a little girl, my mother would take me to church service. One of those days we were supposed to go to the bad side of town. The preacher said, 'We have to help the people less fortunate than us.' I remember how the word *less* just turned a light on in my mind. For someone to be less, there had to be someone that was more. We went to this rec center and brought food we didn't care to eat and clothes we didn't wear and made packages to give to the 'less fortunate.'

"At one point I got separated from my mom and ended up in one of the back areas. One of the women from my church, someone I knew—someone who had seen my face before—gave me one of the packages we were giving all of the less fortunate because she thought I was one of them. I was one of the *less*. And the people from my church, my friends, even my mother, was more. More wealthy. More respected.

More intelligent. More deserving. More in their skin. More in their eyes. More in the way they talked and moved. More wasn't even something they ever needed to say. They just knew it.

"I could never be the same kind of *more* no matter what I did. Maybe it was the more that took them. Maybe it was being less that left us. I don't know. I don't even know if going to Orange Beach will answer any of it for me. I just don't want to be less. Only I'm not sure I know how to be anything else."

Nona took Sidney by the hand and examined something at the base of her eyes. "Your value is decided on all the things you are willing to accept about yourself. And what you won't."

Sidney nodded, aware somehow that Nona's words did not punch, but soaked, like a wave absconding on the shore of her thoughts. Still, neither Zu's curiosity nor impudence had been satisfied.

"You were there, weren't you? When your family died." That Zu spoke less in question than in realization softened the blow of what they aimed to know. "What was it like? Being there, I mean."

Sidney surprised herself with how easily she spoke. How distant, how like what happened to her happened to someone else. "It was like they heard something I couldn't hear. Like they saw something so far away I couldn't see it. And then they started walking. My mother, my brothers. Walked right into the lake behind our house. I tried to stop them and I couldn't. Even when they got into the water. It was like they turned to stone. They didn't float. They just walked on the lake bottom, deeper and deeper. I tried to go with them. I tried to drown myself in that water too."

"But you couldn't."

"I couldn't." Sidney looked from Nona to Zu, then scanned the eyes of everyone now staring at her on the bus. "No, I couldn't. But I wanted to. With all my heart, I wanted to go where they went. I wasn't good enough to die."

Her words spread out over the rumble of the school bus engine. No one spoke again. They looked at each other, exchanging silent conversations, before turning toward the windows, where nature could console their mortality.

They rode on awhile longer before Fela turned off the main road and arrived at an open farm, active with people moving in and out of a one-floor building with a sprawling pavilion.

"Everybody out," Fela said, shifting the bus into park.

One by one, they filed out of the bus with the zeal of schoolkids. Sidney remained near Nona, magnetized by equal parts fear and familiarity.

They stepped out into the pavilion, greeted by some of the same boys who had captured Sidney on the bridge as well as one man who stood tall and wide over the others. Shirtless, his muscles made rugged terrain of his torso, all abs and shoulders and arms put together like they were meant to move the world. Sidney recognized him as one of the king's sons. Fela's brother Tau, she recalled. His face knotted with tension that never seemed to unravel. Even when he hugged Fela and dapped the others, no joy entered his face. His stoicism, or rather something within that it hid, reminded her of her father.

Tau's expression didn't change until he saw Sidney. Tension tightened into anger. The brawny man marched toward her until he loomed as big as a skyscraper in her airspace, wide and menacing.

"What the fuck're you doing here?"

"Leave her alone." Nona stepped in front of Sidney but did nothing to diminish Tau's looming, sky-darkening presence.

"She shouldn't be here, Nona." He turned his eyes on Sidney, and she nearly crumpled under the force. Like looking at the sun, or, better, the moon mid-eclipse. "You don't belong here," he snapped. "You're not one of us."

"She's my sister."

"Calling somebody 'sister' don't make them kin. You should know better. Can't just be letting anybody have what we have."

"I won't say it again, Tau. She is my sister. And you will treat her like it, you understand?"

Again his eyes found Sidney, and again she shrank under his intensity.

"We'll see how much of a sister she is when she gets to Orange Beach. She starts thinking she's white again, and you won't even exist to her no more, guarantee you that."

Fela appeared to her left and had to spread his arms nearly as far as they could go to grip the broadness of Tau's shoulders at once. "Relax, big bro. Sidney is good people."

"Good people? You don't even know what that means."

"I know you're the grumpiest person on Earth and you're still good people."

Tau's expression, only subtly, loosened, and he grabbed Fela, lifted him easily into the air, and carried him off into the pavilion. Sidney remained still, paralyzed by her nearness to a power supreme.

"Don't worry about Tau," Nona said. "He can just be a grumpy old bear. All he wants to do is protect me, which means, in his own way, he will protect you too. He won't do you any harm."

Sidney struggled to reconcile how such power could also be protective. "But he's right, Nona. I don't belong here."

"You belong where you decide you belong."

Nona coolly walked ahead of Sidney. Nona possessed a profound gravity, a gravity that seemed to pulse around her with every step, and everywhere she went, Sidney couldn't stop herself from following. A gravity so sure in its influence, Sidney didn't *want* to stop herself, but keep as near to Nona as she could. That pull was enough to skip her out of her paralysis to catch up.

"This is Redemption Farm," Nona said. "We come here every week to help till and harvest the land and get things packaged up to distribute all over Alabama. It's also where many people come to be rehabilitated."

Sidney saw, throughout the pavilion, the difference between the people bopping about, energetic, and those who tried to keep up, fighting themselves from casting their eyes downward.

"Being in nature helps them get through their traumas."

"What kind of trauma?"

"The trauma of being black their whole lives."

"I don't understand."

"Sure you do," she said, and Sidney experienced the words *in your own way* added in her thoughts.

And she did understand it, in the same way she understood a church hymn or the formation of rivers; it was life's needlepoint where beauty and suffering were as indistinguishable as they were endured absolutely. Sidney didn't fully understand her version of this, but she could always recognize its quality. The impalpable line in the world demarcating more from less.

"How do you help them?"

"Talk to them, empower them, remind them that they're not alone. All of that, and more. But nothing helps like nature. Fresh air, sunlight, trees, watching things grow. Even the storms when they're so big you can smell them coming—it gives them something back. Gives us something back too."

Sidney followed Nona out into the field. Southern sun warmed her differently from sunlight in Wisconsin. Heat she could breathe, even in winter, making the inside of her body more alive. Gentle air breezed over hillocks of collard greens, obscuring the somehow perceptible rumble of root vegetables reaching down into the earth. Faraway trees whispered, and there was water in the air—bayous somewhere, creeks, bays. Sidney angled her face up to the sun and closed her eyes to an orange-black darkness. She breathed in deep without any desire to exhale, just keep drawing in those warm breaths on top of each other. Life atop life.

"We farm the way the ancestors did. It's important to feel connected to the world and to have it connected to you." Nona handed Sidney a stone rake to walk a furrow. Her job was to turn dirt for future plants. Nona followed the line of a different furrow, and they rarely spoke at all over the next few hours.

Sidney found a rhythm in how she tilled the land, each stroke, swift and deep, crunching black dirt and pebbles forward and back, amused by her inability to fully perfect the act. But the act itself offered something else entirely. Time slipped away, or rather felt to consolidate all past and all futures into the stiff present of her rake's sharp dig. The simple deed of something to do, and the manner with which that deed consumed her thoughts, made a tonic for all the unanswerable questions. Sun and trees and dirt made her no more and no less than the ants that scurried about. No more and no less than the birds sliding against the base of clouds. No more and no less than anything else stirring on the earth. A truth she needn't think, but felt. And the feeling comforted her.

After an unmeasured knot of time, Nona appeared to her right carrying a basket of pears. Sidney took one and bit into it, juice bursting in her mouth, the ecstasy of its sweetness forcing her to close her eyes just to savor delightfulness in every possible dimension.

"Come with me," Nona said. "I think it's a good idea that while we're here you sit with one of the newcomers."

"One of the ones to be rehabilitated?"

"I like to think we are all in some form of rehabilitation."

Sidney followed Nona back to the pavilion, where people sat together in groups of two. Even Tau, sitting upright and still as stone, coupled with someone, a woman with dreadlocks down to the floor. Anger still tightened his face, but he listened to the woman, Sidney saw, listened and nodded and even touched her knee to emphasize the impact of her words. She saw Fela too, sitting with a man three, maybe four times his age. She noted how Fela spoke with his hands, the length of his fingers like batons, conducting words as they came out.

"Will you sit with Malcolm?" Nona pointed to the far side of the pavilion, where a man sat alone, angular and tall, his eyes closed in a meditative state. Even sitting, Sidney could see his might, like a ballet dancer, lengthy veins visible and stretching the distance of his shins and forearms. The sight of him, and the potential intimacy of sitting so near to a stranger, intimidated her.

"I don't want to do this. I don't even know where to start."

"Start by talking. Just ask him how he feels."

"That's it?"

"You're making space for him to express himself. All a person needs sometimes is to be asked how they feel. Go on. It's as much for you as it is for him."

Sidney stepped forward, careful not to say just how much she didn't need to be rehabilitated. She hardly looked up as she walked across the pavilion and sat down in front of Malcolm. He kept his eyes closed at first, and she thought for a moment that he might be asleep. *He's handsome,* she mused, his copper skin unblemished and his hair cut straight up like a tower. She was imagining him in pirouette when she saw his eyes were opened, two hazel gems glittering right at her. Like a child, she cut her eyes away.

"I'm Sidney," she mumbled.

He nodded gracefully and smiled in a way she was sure had melted many hearts. From a deep part of him, his voice rumbled out: "I'm Malcolm."

"Malcolm, I'm here to ask you, how do you feel?"

"Fine," he said. "How do you feel?"

"Fine." Silence squeezed then swelled between them. "Yours wasn't an honest answer."

"No. But isn't that just it? Who's ever really honest about how they feel?" He smiled again, that smile proof that the last smile was a mask, the vulnerability of it releasing tension in her shoulders.

"All right then, let's change it. I'll ask the question differently, and you answer honestly. You can ask me anything, and I'll be honest too."

Her small hand completely disappeared into his palm when he extended his hand to confirm the agreement with a handshake.

"Good. Then tell me how you felt . . . after the event happened."

"Sad," he answered, and she felt him sit down inside himself. "At least at first. I lost a lot of close friends, a few lovers, teachers, mentors—a lot of what helped make me *me*. Then I was happy. I mean, I walked into any bank, any store, any experience, and did whatever I wanted, only to realize none of it mattered. Nothing was like it used to be. So, I guess I'd say everything just feels like one of those days when the sun comes out. No clouds or rain, just bright sun. You can still be sad on a sunny day—happy, angry, scared—whatever you want, but it's still sunny. Clear, you know. No more days under pressure. Not anymore. Still trying to figure out what that means. I'm guessing since you're multiracial, you feel differently?"

"I don't really know. I feel . . . lost. The truth is everything about my life has changed, and in a way nothing has. I never knew who I was—what I was. Where I fit in. Where I didn't." Her heart became a finch in her chest, her tears collecting and drying at the base of her eyes. "So while my heart is broken for my mother and my family, I felt disconnected before and I feel disconnected now. That's the truth."

"Before the event, I was an actor. A good one too—Shakespeare, that was my shit! Played all over the world. *Hamlet* at the Globe in London, *The Tempest* in Beijing, the Scottish play in New Zealand. I liked being onstage because no matter who I played, the people loved me. They always raised their glasses to me. Because, on a stage, I decided who I would be. I determined the shape of me. And I was always the most beautiful thing anyone had ever seen because I decided to be."

"I just wish we could go back to when everybody was happy."

"When was everybody happy? What time was that? Did I miss getting on that train?" He leaned a bit into her space. "No one was happy, Sidney. We were just a bunch of people getting on with it, living our lives with monsters on our backs. No, nobody was happy, and nobody told the truth."

"What was the truth?"

"That the world wasn't ever equal. And the white folks who made it that way—the ones who fought, silent and spitting, to keep it that way—refused all responsibility for what it meant. You can't imagine the inhumanity, horrors on top of horrors. People shot in the streets, in their homes, at grocery stores, so much that after a while some white folks just kind of shrugged. No one was fighting for our bodies. And it went on like that for so long I think we all started to believe that was just the way life was supposed to be. Trust me when I tell you, I've been black all over the world and I always knew what that meant. Not welcomed anywhere, and yet there ain't nowhere else to go. Damn, what a storm in the mind."

"On my way down here, a black man dressed in a Klan uniform attacked us. He was crazy; he said I was like him. He was out of his mind."

"That man was probably out of his mind long before the event, chasing something he can't see because it ain't real. I'm no different. Maybe not on the same scale, but life's made me just as crazy."

"No, you seem so normal. Not crazy, not like that man I saw."

"*Normal* is an illusion. It can turn people crazy just trying to get it."

Sidney nodded without thinking. "After it happened, I used to sit out at the lake behind my house. I'd put my stepfather's rifle under my chin and try as hard as I could to pull the trigger. I would pray to God, any god, for the strength to go where my family went. I wanted to die so bad, Malcolm. That's crazy. And it's crazy that I am here with no family left."

"That's not crazy, Sidney. That's suffering. And suffering makes kin of all of us." He took her hand, smiled that truthful smile, and gave her the space to return a smile of her own. "Now, let's speak of happier things, little sister. Today is a new day, and the sun is out."

They talked together for a while about food they missed, movies they wished could somehow get a sequel, places they wanted to see, homecoming dances, and how much they both loved Madonna and Taylor Swift. They laughed some and cried some. When their time had ended, the act left Sidney relieved and exhausted, like she'd exercised a fever out of her body.

As the sun began to dip, nature called her and others back out to the field. Not to work, but to lie back in the whispering grass and observe in silence the sky transition from lilac to periwinkle to mulberry. No one spoke. Wind moved across the tips of yellow grass, and when Sidney closed her eyes, her nose filled with the smell of lavender.

It was then that Nona popped up unexpectedly, raising her voice to recite what sounded like poetry.

"'And you will understand all too soon / That you, my children of battle, are your heroes.'"

"That's Nikki Giovanni," one of the girls from the bus shouted.

"Correct. Who knows this one? 'The impatient idealist says: "Give me a place to stand and I shall move the earth." But such a place does not exist. We all have to stand on the earth itself and go with her at her pace.'"

In the silence that followed, the only name that rose in Sidney's thoughts was Shakespeare. But she dared not speak.

Zu raised a hand. "Can I guess that one?"

"Don't guess, know," Nona replied.

"Hemingway?"

Nona just smiled that warm smile. "The correct answer is Chinua Achebe. And now that you know the name, I expect you to know his words the next time you hear them. So, who wants to go next?"

And they did; one after another people stood up and quoted poetry and literature from more names Sidney didn't know or had ever heard before. Beautiful words that seemed to stick to her ribs. Poems went on until day pulled a curtain back on the stars, who offered themselves in clusters and dust that stirred in Sidney the sensation of enormity and insignificance at once. She couldn't stop herself from feeling a part of something. Stars in a constellation.

Then the smell of smoke filled the air, and Fela, mimicking what Sidney witnessed his mother do, lit the same pipe she used for the Inqawe ceremony. The wooden pipe was long and adorned with jeweled beads. Without asking, Fela passed the pipe to Sidney.

"Breathe," he said.

In that instant, Sidney understood right and wrong in her bones.

And, before, felt it in the tilling of the earth and in listening to Malcolm's stories. She'd felt right and wrong in the faces of all those people in Mississippi and in the strength of Little's grip. How deeply buried that feeling throbbed inside her. Not just buried, but fractured, broken into so many parts over so many years that right and wrong might never again be redeemed, and yet she could still feel its certainty. Like how all stars could seem a universe broken into shards or, on a clear night, the singular luster of that which refuses to be forgotten. Sidney experienced right, however fleeting, and right spurred her to take the pipe and breathe the smoke.

She lay back in the deep grass. Smoke moved into her blood, and the stars began to bob and speak. Her eyes swayed in and out of her mind.

All those stars above, the great broken unknowable now luminous.

Shining and shining and shining.

All at once.

29

THE GARAGE DOOR was closed when Charlie and Herald arrived at the king's home.

He'd arrived midmorning, just in time to see a school bus drive away with Sidney aboard, dousing him with equal parts delight and jealousy to see her making friends.

Through the narrow window of the garage, Charlie saw the king and the queen inside. They danced together to music he could not hear, love as tangible as a steam between them, desirous eyes and smiles enduringly curled.

Watching, Charlie feared he'd glimpsed an intimate moment not meant for his eyes.

"Come sit with me in the shade awhile," Herald asked, sensing perhaps the same intimate violation. Charlie followed Herald under a sprawling persimmon tree jeweled in sunset-colored fruit. Herald picked two ripe ones and handed one to Charlie. Down into an Adirondack Herald slid, where flecks of cool sunlight glittered through the tree leaves like a sprinkling of pennies. Herald said nothing, tilted his face up to the light, took a deep breath, sighed, and closed his eyes.

Charlie regarded Herald with the same wonder he had his students back at Howard. No war of darkness inside him. Charlie found himself struck by just how bright Herald seemed to be. And comfortable, most of all, in his skin, in his time, in the radius of his being. His darkness did not gnarl up inside of him. Indeed, his darkness was his aura. And his darkness wasn't dark at all, not in the manner Charlie had resolved himself to believe, but thick and lustrous, a refined transmission of space itself. At once Charlie envied him, glorified him, feared him, and loved him like his own son. But Herald paid Charlie no mind. He just munched away on his persimmon, his face tilted up at the sun. *Young black boys,* Charlie thought, *the most marvelous beings in the universe.* As nonchalantly as Herald bit into that fruit did black boys ever ponder their influence on the whole world. How effortlessly they rounded the shape of the earth with their swagger and illuminated its days with their creativity. Their hope, Charlie mused, offered even the bleakest parts of our planet a second sun.

"I've always thought of it like a sky full of elephants," Herald said absently, as though he weren't speaking to Charlie but to different versions of himself. "It's up there, been up there, heavy too. All wisdom and memory . . . sorrow. A weight so heavy it would damn us all if it came down. But you can't see it 'til you see it. No matter how many times I tell you they're up there, you can't see 'em until you see 'em."

Behind them, the garage door clattered open, and Charlie could hear the thud of the king's footsteps. He glanced one last time at Herald, still cool and bright, then spun around out of his chair to meet the king at the edge of the driveway. The man didn't extend the look of one who'd just enjoyed a romantic moment, but the scowl of being yanked too soon out of one.

"You said you're a fixer. That right?"

"I can be."

"Well, are you or aren't you? No sense in talking small."

"Then, well, yes, I guess I am," Charlie answered, noting how both vigor and wisdom made shadows over the king's expression.

The king sucked at the back of his teeth, and Charlie heard Herald walk off quietly behind him. Charlie kept eyes on the king.

"You ever been to Africa, Charles?"

"No," Charlie answered, following the king to the garage entrance, where he could see the machine and the shelves of tools and miscellaneous parts. "Never been to Africa. Never even been out of the country."

"I played trumpet in Vivian's band, see, and went once on tour. Years ago. Flew into Cape Town. Got to see Zimbabwe, Zaire before it was the Congo, Pointe-Noire, Lagos, Sierra Leone, and even got up to Cairo while I was there. Unbelievably big, unbelievably beautiful, that continent is. Old too. Older than you can imagine."

"I bet," Charlie responded, unsure where the conversation was headed.

"One of the things I saw there was something called the Ishango Bone. Ever heard of it?"

Charlie shook his head.

"It's not much bigger than a pencil. Got markings on it that they told us were mathematical. Said it was like holding an ancient calculator. Now, when scientists first dated the bone, they put it at four thousand years old. Ancient Greeks were about three thousand years old, which means Africans in the Congo understood arithmetic for a long, long time. But turns out the date on the bone was wrong. Years later, they dated the bone again and learned it wasn't four thousand years old, but somewhere closer to twenty-five thousand years old. *Twenty-five thousand*. You believe that? That's a hell of a long time to be doing anything, let alone measuring the sun and moon, learning, growing—evolving. Wouldn't you say?"

"I guess so. But I'm not exactly sure why you're telling me this."

"Because history didn't start with slavery, and stealing us here cut us off from twenty-five thousand years of memory. Charlie, if you're going to help me, you have to understand what we're doing here, how long we've been doing it, and why I did what I did."

Charlie was no longer a teacher in a classroom, but the one doing the learning. "All right."

"Now, I'm gonna say a lot of things in the next ten minutes. If you can keep up, then maybe you can help me. If you can't, well, then, you can't. You got it?"

"Got it."

"Good. Now, sit down. I understand what you believe is in my garage is a radio. And, in some ways, it is, but radio waves are not the only kind of waves. There are electromagnetic, ultraviolet, gamma, infrared, and on and on. These are just the ones known science can quantify. There are a lot more. In fact, every person alive radiates their own waves. Our thoughts, our intuitions, and our feelings are signals we give off. We pass those signals to our children and family in the form of lessons, knowledge—an intuitive awareness that informs our consciousness. It's what we believe and how we experience the world, understand? Collectively, we all carry so many of the same memories. How we ran around in the yard or the streets as kids, how our mamas whipped us with a switch, a belt, or the flat of her hand, how our fathers and our brothers looked at us when we made mistakes . . . like they were afraid for our lives. The kind of food we ate, how we played, how we couldn't stop ourselves from dancing if the right song hit—hell, even how we talk shit to each other. We're connected. We all know it. In every city where black people live, so does that subtle consciousness. Togetherness. *Us*-ness. How we dance, how we love, how we hope. Everywhere it's basically intuitive, as these are the manifestations of a signal buzzing all around us, all the time, all over the world. You follow?"

"Yes, so far."

"Good. Back in 1902, Nikola Tesla built the Wardenclyffe Tower. It was made to create access to wireless power transmissions. He built it on the basis that the earth itself could be tapped to conduct energy, signals, visuals—anything. Without getting too scientific, he theorized that he could utilize the earth as a power source and charge the sky, making it possible to tune in to any wave, anywhere. Now, while this may seem impossible now, the man built the thing one year and had it torn down the next. I suspect that's because he found more than he bargained for. He didn't *invent* something as much as *discover* something. Something that's been there a long time."

"You mean Africa? The bone."

"The bone is a single coin in a treasure of knowledge. Old, old knowledge. Even the Greeks would go to Africa to learn. Pythagoras himself spent twenty years training in Egypt, and we called him the 'father of mathematics.' He went to learn African science, which as best I've been able to understand it was based in resonance. Frequency. Sound."

"Music."

"That's right. What Tesla discovered Africans already knew a long, long time ago. They understood how to tune in to everything, everywhere. A fully connected world. A collective consciousness. They weren't out conquering the world because they didn't have to. They had power before electrical grids, connection before the internet, unification before continents had names. They had it. And it was taken, broken apart, sold, buried, burned. Destroyed."

"I mean, what you're saying is really incredible, but I don't understand what it has to do with what's in your garage."

"Maybe I gave you too much credit then. What I built is a way to tap back into that power and history I'm telling you about. A radio that tunes in to black consciousness."

Charlie stared at him while his words took root. *Tunes in to black consciousness*. He went back to being out in his mother's front yard, imagining himself as a frequency moving through space and time. "A sky full of elephants," is what Herald had said.

"Show me."

30

THE STARS WERE still out when Sidney woke.

Morning had but just completed its first strokes, painting the sky in a violet indistinguishable from twilight. She'd slept in the grass with the rest of her peers, rising just as the grass's yellow tips perfumed in sweet-smelling dew.

She could hear no cars in the distance, no creaking of buildings, and no rumblings of industry. Just nature in its most tender form.

A hush purred through the morning, and a sudden terror lit up in Sidney. She sensed ghosts in the land. Their whispers. Was she awake or dreaming? Fear and questions messed her mind.

Sidney sat up straight. She saw her mother standing in the field, close enough to smell. Her back was turned to Sidney as she reached down and picked lavender from the ground, grouping it into bundles. Sidney thought to call out to her, but when her mother turned, she was no longer Sidney's mother but a dark-skinned woman, dressed all in rags, and it wasn't lavender she picked but cotton. Then the woman was no longer alone in the field but surrounded by others, more women, children even. And then there was a sound in the air, a cattle bell clanging in the distance. All the expressions of all the people in the field transformed, just like her mother's had at the stove that morning, hearing the sound of fate that could not be stopped. Nothing any of them could do but walk toward that sound. Death one way, death the other. Walk. Nothing they could do but walk. Only one of them stopped and turned back. The dark-skinned woman looked right at Sidney, the terrible sadness on her face too much for Sidney to witness—so much so she nearly got to her feet if only to stand shoulder to shoulder with the woman, company to soften a terrible fate. The woman nodded and Sidney understood. Right and wrong. The *us* in her blood. The roots in the dark.

Ancestor.

Sidney closed her watery eyes to an unsolvable conflict as black as the morning.

31

THE KING'S GARAGE smelled sweetly of oil. Tools of all sorts lined the walls, everything from power tools to garden tools, and three different drafting tables covered in various blueprints took up most of the space. Hosea led Charlie near the machine on the back wall, where a polished trumpet sat atop a stool. On that trumpet, Hosea blew a single, lovely note.

"When I met Vivian she was stump speaking about racial discrimination in our school. She always talked about changing the world, and man, I believed every word she said. I fell in love with her instantly. Fell more in love when I heard her sing. It was at this nightclub downtown, jazzy place. She sang like nothing I'd ever heard, and I'd swear to you she pulled God down into the club that night. Before I tried to even put a move on her, I asked her if I could play trumpet in her little band. She kissed me right on the spot. She told me that she was meant to find me, like a vision. Right then and there, she said that one day I would ask her the biggest question of my life and her answer was, would be, and is yes. From then on we were inseparable. When we weren't speaking at rallies or marching for justice, we played together in every jazz club we could. New Orleans, Chicago, Montgomery, even New York. Always together, just like she said. We didn't have much, you know, and activism is grueling work, especially when ain't nothing changing. So when our band got that chance to play in Africa, she jumped at it. And, you know, where she goes, I follow. Our Mecca, she called it."

He walked over to the machine, which spanned the length of the back wall in four large sections, each with a small glass face for tuning knobs and buttons. It was old, rusted in some places. Half transmitter, half receiver, Charlie noted, but the machine was a great deal more. He could see the simpler parts—amplifiers and limiters, oscillators and filters—but he couldn't fully understand how the radio turned on, let alone how the mechanics functioned in the way the king explained.

"We learned many, many things in Africa, the bone being one of them. But nothing stuck more than learning about our lineage—what happened to us after our people were stolen. Vivian learned her family ended up in Haiti, fought side by side with Toussaint in the revolution. She was to inherit land, farmland, that even had access to the beach. When we got back to America, black folks were still fighting in the streets for crumbs; our kids, like everybody else's, were tired of fighting and just wanted to give in. But we always swore to make a better world for them, so Vivian decided we should leave and try to start a new life in Haiti. Now, don't mistake it, Haiti wasn't some paradise, that place has been through hell like no other maybe ever—dictatorships, economic ruin, even hurricanes done tried to wipe it off the earth. It's beautiful land, but it's in a far worse state than America. In a terrible way. But its history was still intact. Grounded, still, by ancestors connected to the homeland—the closest a black American can get to Africa without going. We had our own plot we could farm, we had community, and freedom most of all. We wasn't 'black' there, we just were. You could feel the difference in the air. And I mean really feel it. It was the signal. Just standing still you could hear it like whispers or a breeze. Like something just vibrating all around you. So while Viv, Nona, and Tau went off to the houngan and knowledge keepers to learn as much history as they could, me, Herald, and Fela went to work trying to make scientific sense of that feeling. We discovered all sorts of things in the process. We worked until we built a prototype."

Sitting on top of a stool next to the machine was a heavily modified boom box with a six-foot antenna and a knot of wires protruding from the back. Upon the boom box, the king laid a heavy hand. "The prototype captured just enough of the signal for me to understand what we were dealing with. First couple of times I turned it on, at its lowest possible power of course, I already felt it, was healed by it. And it was more than enough to make us certain we needed to make the full thing."

"I think I'm still with you . . ." Charlie said, though he wasn't certain.

"What Vivian might've called a vision, I would call a frequency or a wave. She'd say things like magic and the voices of the ancestors, and I would say chemistry and broadcasts. But it was all the same stuff. You see, the full machine here is grounded deep, deep beneath us, and the obelisk out back activates the charge in the sky, like Tesla's tower. Piece by piece, my sons and I put this beast together, and Vivian guided me every step. We all knew we needed to hear it."

"Hear what? What is it?"

"The signal of our fractured consciousness. All those emotions, memory, and vengeance heavy as a storm in the sky. It's a message. A feeling. A signal. It's everything we felt and couldn't say repressed in a frequency. Just here in America, we're talking over four hundred years, man, generations upon generations, tortured, raped, possessed—all the violence and evil possible in this world inflicted upon our people. Horrors that all a man could do was bite down on, teach his son to bite down on too. And his son and his. It's forgotten flesh and bone, lost memories, so much anger wound tight like a bomb stuffed in a bottle. And we ain't ever been given even a moment to process any of that pain, that grief. So, over time, it broke the connection and in a lot of ways broke us. With just that prototype, I could tune in to that signal and see the connections we used to share were like shattered glass. And I knew if I didn't help put them back together, we might never be whole. Of course, Vivian knew that all along. She saw it long before I did. If I turned the full machine on, it could fix us. Give us back to ourselves. She knew I would have to choose. Turn it on, let loose all that grief, and repair our broken selves. Or leave it be and continue on as lesser people in a fucked-up world. She knew it would be the most important question I would ever ask her."

Heavily, the frightening realization settled on Charlie and nearly took his breath away. "You're talking about the event, aren't you? The machine, when you turned it on . . ."

"She said when I asked, her answer was, would be, and is yes."

"My God, you killed them. You turned on that machine and it started the event."

"That's what happened."

"You killed all those people."

"I didn't kill them. We did. All of us. All through time. Everything they'd ever done to us was pent up, and it just poured out. It had to. I didn't choose to have what happened to them come to pass. I just chose us. To heal us. And healing us meant reconciling all of that shit, you hear me? That's the only decision I made. When no one else would, I chose us!"

"Jesus Christ, man—I can't believe what you're saying to me."

"I kept thinking, *What a strange fruit we are to have never ripened.* Hung, dangled, sweetened, eaten, but never just filled up with the miracle of ourselves. We had to heal, Charlie. We had to. What other decision was there to be made?"

"You chose to kill half the country!"

"And how many of us have been killed, Charles? How many of our bodies are in the sea, in the soil—and not a cross stood up or a name remembered? I chose to give us back something that was taken, and that ain't got nothing to do with them. All that emotion, all that rage in the sky, poured out the way it did because for so long no one tended to it. No one cared about our sadness, or grief, or pain—none of it. And you know exactly what I mean. To be left in the darkness so long you become darkness. All I did was open the door and set it free the way it deserved to be."

"This is unbelievable."

"But it's true. You feel it same as me. Felt it the moment you crossed the Alabama border. The signal heals you, Charles. It connects you back to everything we lost, and it heals you."

Charlie wedged his face in his hands and shivered at the thought. All those people. It was madness. Madness that spun around in Charlie's head, bouncing off a knowing he refused inside himself. There was anger. There was sadness. There were so many feelings no one ever processed. The machine spilled it all out like a flood across the nation.

Behind him, the king closed the door to the garage. "When I turned the radio on to full power, it surged, popped every breaker in Alabama, and burned the grid out entirely. I haven't been able to generate enough energy to get it back on. So while the people in Alabama started to be connected and thrived off just a flash of the radio's signal, I aim to fix black collective consciousness everywhere. All over America. All over the world. And I will do it. One way or another, I will. It is the decision I made and will spend my life trying to fulfill just like Vivian saw. Somewhere in there she also saw you too, Charles. That's why you're here now. So, I'll ask you again, are you the person to help me?"

"This machine destroyed the world. I can't be a part of that."

"You already are a part of it. And this signal didn't destroy a world or a people. It destroyed an idea. The very idea and the lies it spun that had warped our sense of self into something you couldn't even recognize. The machine destroyed an idea, Charlie. And in so doing, it took all the people who clung to that idea as fact. All I did was tune in to what was already there—the signal of us hovering in the air."

Charlie shook his head, not disagreeing as much as trying to shake that truth out of his mind.

"There's a lot more than just anger in that signal," the king continued. "It's complex. Remarkable. Far too beautiful for words. You've heard it before, though. Felt the sensation of being tuned in. You hear it when Miles plays, when Etta sings, when Nas raps. Power you can't explain saying things you feel deep even when you don't have the words to speak them. I could keep telling you about it, but the only way for you to truly understand is to tune in for yourself."

"I can't. I won't."

"Charles, the only thing that makes me a king is what I decide to claim. I claim my body. I claim my family. I claim my past. And I claim my future. Every man is a king of his own choices. So what are you going to claim?"

Charlie watched the king hit a few switches on the prototype boom box, which illuminated its LED lights, then twist all the knobs down to their lowest setting. He picked up a set of headphones next to it.

"It's just the prototype. Took me a week to store enough power just so you can listen for a few seconds. I'd ask you if you're ready, but you are, and you always have been. That's what my wife told me and that's what I'm telling you."

Charlie looked up at the king, his vision blurred with tears. He felt he'd arrived at the center of his darkness, the conflict resolved in a single moment, a choice he understood to be both noble and malevolent, necessary yet against the good in his nature. He thought of Elizabeth, how he loved her in all the ways he knew how, and how little that love mattered. Sidney, his mother, Little, Ethel—so many people wound up tight in the fists of this way of life. Relief. That's all Charlie ever wanted. Relief from innominate feelings haunting his life.

He nodded his head like a bow, and the king draped the headphones over his ears. Charlie closed his eyes.

In the dark, he heard trumpets.

What came next, Charlie knew no words capable of describing.

Enormity is what it felt like. Something so colossal it galloped like chariots, surged like a wave, spread out and towered at the same time. So much, so wide, so deep. Ferocious ecstasy. Emotion. Wisdom. Mania. Heavy and primal. An ocean of teeth. Time sharpened into needles. Blood. Soil. Water. All the dark magnitudes of space crystallized into a single sensation. All of that resonance descending on Charlie at once. And yet, what he felt in that incomprehensible enormity was his. Personal. Filling him and swallowing him up simultaneously. More than anything, the sensation released him. God, did it release him into a place beautiful only in that it was exquisitely complete.

The enormity took Charlie's breath away, and he felt for once the holy fullness of his own denied reactions. His darkness, now whole, bursting forth.

Charlie fell to his knees. Tears streamed down his face. He sucked in breath like he meant to hold himself together, but couldn't stop breaking apart. Impossible clarity. Too much. Far too much. Charlie cried out everything inside of him. Spilling. All of that enormity spilling out. All of that enormity spilling out.

It was the king who took him. Raised him to his feet and held him. Charlie's spillage and fractures the king held in embrace. Hugged him tightly so Charlie might finally let go. Weakened. Overwhelmed. The king held Charlie as a friend. Held him as a guide. Held him as his brother. The enormity broke Charlie apart, but his brother held him up.

"I know," the king whispered. "Brother, I know."

The enormity broke Charlie apart, but his brother held him up.

32

NEARLY A YEAR AFTER *it happened, Vivian found her voice.*

"You have to understand, Vivian," Hosea explained, "even if we could turn the machine back to full power, there's no way to calibrate it. We turn it up and . . . all those people in Orange Beach, the walkers—hell, maybe anybody who ever even dreamt of being anything other than black—might end up at the bottom of the ocean. You want to risk that?"

"Risk it?" Her voice, for the first time in years, even as a question, exerted the power she'd used to move the masses. "The signal, it heals us."

"Yes, but—"

"Heals us, Hosea. All the pain. All the suffering. All those bloodiest of years. You think anybody with their hand on the whip ever cared about the risk *to us? I am tired, Hosea. Have we not sacrificed enough? Why do we have to consistently hold ourselves back? Why are we forever the bottom priority? Healed. That's what I want.* Healed! *All our people, everywhere. Healed in their minds, their hearts. I want to give them the power to claim their history back and their future."*

Hosea shrank, the passion in his wife's voice both paralyzing and provocative. "If we turn it on again, Viv, we could be hurting our people as much as helping them. We have to figure out how to calibrate—"

"When do we stop trying to calibrate being black!" she shouted, her eyes boiling with an intensity Hosea had never seen before. "Manifest our *destiny. Sure, we can believe in us, Hosea, we can believe that we are worth the risk—but belief without action is a shallow mistress. Healed. You understand?* Healed. *By any means necessary. Because we must believe that we are deserving of a mercy to ever actually have one. Don't just believe. Act!"*

Hosea had grown accustomed to filing away his anger. Hosea had grown accustomed to filing away his hope. He had grown accustomed to filing away his power. Her voice spilled those files out before him to see. And all those filed away truths, seen and not hidden, came together as though he'd rediscovered himself.

"I will."

"Then go on. Keep working. So you can have mercy, for once and for all, on us."

33

"WHAT THE HELL are you doing in the middle of the street, man?"

Sailor found Charlie flat on his back looking up at the stars. The signal had rewired Charlie. What he experienced, out of the smallest measurement of what the king's machine offered, felt like salvation, like being in that bathtub with Seraphin, the darkness within him polished and shining. The signal infiltrated Charlie like aloe on a wound, pulling emotion from his body, and in a flash showing him everything he'd lost, everything he'd gained, and all the potential of his life. And, for once, he saw himself enormous. Not a temporary sensation either. Not fleeting. Rewired. And the feeling left him flat on his back staring up at the stars. A moment passed before Charlie realized Sailor stood before him, holding the same big gun he had before.

"Sailor?"

"Get up, fool, I thought you was dead."

"No, I was . . . What happened to you? I thought you left."

"You thought I was gonna leave my child here? You crazy. I told you to get a gun when you had the chance. Now, get on up. I got a tip on the fuel. We gotta go."

"Go?"

"You heard me. This is our chance to get out."

"Sailor, we can't leave."

"What you mean? That's the deal we made." Sailor adjusted the gun on his shoulder.

Charlie sat up, his senses settling back into place. "You don't understand. The king. He did it. It was all the king."

"Did what?"

"The event, Sailor. That machine in his garage. It was the bomb, the bomb that went off in people's hearts."

Sailor held his breath, staring blankly at Charlie, unable to find words to respond. When finally he spoke, he could only muster a faint "What?"

"He was trying to help us. All of us. But now the machine's broken. I'm going to help him fix it."

"Fix it and then what? Huh? I should've known better than to trust you. You really are a fool. You can stay here if you want. I am getting what I came for and leaving."

"You don't understand. What's happening here in Mobile is incredible. And I know you're a better man than what this world made you out to be, same as me. Look, I promised you I would help you and I will, but I have to help the king first. I have to. If you don't want to wait, I understand." Charlie stood to his feet. "I won't try to stop you from going your own way. But last I saw your child was with mine, so maybe you can tell me where to find them?"

"Why would I do that?"

"Because Sidney has to know the truth too. About all of this here in Mobile. About what she's probably going to find in Orange Beach. She needs to know the truth about me."

34

"CHANGE IS COMING," the queen had warned her, "and memory always prevails."

The bus ride back from the farm, for Sidney, had been deeply contemplative. The land healed, just as Nona said, and renewed Sidney. The woman she saw, whether real or dreamt, nevertheless lingered in her thoughts as memory and a reminder of an ancient disconnection.

The bus arrived to a quiet Mobile afternoon and a flock of black mothers waiting in the queen's driveway, giddy to ensnare their children in *welcome back* hugs. Even Nona and Fela transformed into kids as they stepped into the queen's embrace. And just as loneliness knotted up inside Sidney as tight as ever, it was the queen who gripped Sidney by the hand and asked her to take a walk. Nona's command to treat Sidney as a sister extended all the way to the queen, who was kind and exuded a motherly energy that Sidney both relished and evaded. The queen asked Sidney about her stay so far and told her about the Mardi Gras celebrations to come. Sidney enjoyed the walk and the company of the queen, a woman who seemed to almost float with every step and yet carry a presence as heavy as an elephant. Even her voice purred with a certain heavy huskiness, and yet fell on Sidney's ears with the gentlest tone. In any time and on any continent—anywhere she stepped—Sidney understood the queen would always be a queen.

As they walked together, she told Sidney that her ancestors fought for their freedom on Haiti only to immigrate to America, free people, and be treated as second class or worse. Sidney sank into the music of the queen's voice and listened to her chronicle just how bad the country was for her grandmother and her mother, and that even as a child she could feel what all those years did to people's minds. Their spirits. Their sense of self. Generation after generation of people running away from themselves just to try to belong to something that had affirmatively defined them as *other*.

"That had to change, and it did," the queen had said. "One day soon you will know all the stories about your family that go all the way back to the beginning of them. Healing stories. And you'll be made whole."

When they'd toured a loop around the block, the queen took Sidney by both hands.

"You are welcome here, child."

Sidney's response required no thought. The answer was preprogrammed and would've played itself out no matter whose ear listened. "I have to go. I have to see it for myself."

The queen offered the same warm and knowing smile as Nona's. "We are, all of us, in search of ourselves. My only ever desire was to make sure we all are afforded the space to find it." She found the deep black in Sidney's eyes. "Child, hear me when I tell you memory matters. It is the anchor that keeps us tethered to substance, else we are powerless and set adrift."

What the queen said next she said without cruelty, but matter-of-factly, which for Sidney made it that much more frightening.

"There is no amount of deceit that can erase memory in the bones. We have never forgotten. Change is coming, and memory always prevails. My dear, be free to choose your own way, but try your best to really understand where it is you're going."

Sidney spent the rest of the afternoon struggling to find footing in the queen's warning. *Change is coming. Memory prevails.* She refused to see anyone at all. Nona, graciously, gave Sidney the space she wanted, and when others came knocking at her door, Sidney left altogether, walking the house grounds, seeking enough solitude to wrap her in a thin comfort. And though she held fast to her mission, get to Orange Beach, she couldn't deny the storm of her own conflict brewed by all she'd seen and felt.

The courtyard was quiet and emptied of all the Mardi Gras wares. Sidney resolved herself to the dark cloaking under the live oak, night rising at the edges of the world. From there, she listened to the buzz of Mobile, the constant movement and laughter, music that chirped and popped and sailed. How their lives felt to overflow, spill out loud and colorful like their existence couldn't be contained, and yet was. How little she understood their plight. She'd no real sense of how much they'd been through and for how long, nor the powerful efforts to keep their lives tied up in a struggle.

She listened to them gathering not far, hearing the drums and rallying sounds. She questioned whether suffering, as Malcolm said, connected them. She suspected that connection far more profound.

Then, appearing out of the shadows, came Charlie.

"Been looking all over for you. You didn't come down for dinner, so I brought dinner to you," he said, holding out a plate of food. He seemed even more different from how he was the last time she saw him. Something about him illuminated the air around his shape with glow.

"What happened to you?"

"A little bit of a lot of things. Mostly just finding my way back, I suppose."

"Back to what?"

"Back to a better version of myself." He smiled in a way she'd not seen him do before. Carefree. She knew her father just well enough to assign him many attributes: hard, focused, strong. But not carefree. The smile registered in her with the subtle distinction of having witnessed a modest miracle.

"I was hoping we could break bread and maybe talk for a while. Would that be all right?"

"Fine," she said. "You mind if we eat out here? Just don't want to be inside right now."

Charlie nodded, smiled again that startling, carefree smile, and sat down next to her against the tree. The lilac in the sky had thickened to wine, stars already peeking through.

"I love when the stars come out," Charlie said. "I used to imagine they were messages, like radio signals moving through time."

"They're just planets and stars."

"Maybe. But I never had enough time in my life to really look at them, y'know. To just stare and wonder." He sighed, turning to Sidney and looking at her with the same wonder he regarded the stars. "I see you've been spending time with the princess."

"Yep." Sidney cut her words short by biting down on a soft, sweet butter biscuit.

"She really seems to like you. She told me how you were helping rehabilitate a man down at the farm."

"Nona is sweet. She keeps calling me her sister, which is a little strange, but it's growing on me, I guess."

"She means it. She's like her mother. She don't strike me as a child who says many things she don't mean."

"Yeah," Sidney responded, pushing down the unintentional sting of his words and how they made her ache for him to say the same about her.

"And that boy, Fela, I see how he looks at you. Seems like he is just following you around, standing in all the places you leave like it's a field of flowers."

She blushed lightly and looked away.

"I used to be that smitten with your mother."

Her blush turned cold and she found Charlie's eyes in that twilight. "What did you say?"

"I loved your mother. Gracious, did I love her like I loved nobody else. And I was sure she loved me too. No matter what happened after, it's important you know you were born out of that love."

"Then why did you leave? If you loved her so much?"

He shifted off the tree to face her, and what he'd say next, she felt, was the real reason he'd come to find her.

"I didn't leave you, Sidney. The truth is I was in prison your whole life."

She expected him to look away from her in shame when he said those words, but he didn't.

"I was lost in the system, nowhere near getting parole. The only reason I got out when I did is because the event happened. We all broke out and got free."

She saw prison then, having shown itself in the way he moved and talked, the strength in his hands, the way his eyes flicked nervously at the world around him. "Why were you in prison? And why didn't you come looking for me when you got out? If you loved my mother and you knew about me, why didn't you come?"

He reached into his pocket, took a deep breath, and revealed a letter that he sat in the grass and slid across to Sidney. "Your mother wrote this letter to me after I was locked away. I only read it once in all those years. Just couldn't listen to what it had to say anymore."

Sidney held the letter in her hands, able to see her mother's handwriting bleed through the folded envelope. "What did it say?"

"Your mother and I fell in love at first sight, but it was our secret. Back then, a rich white girl and a poor black boy didn't have much of a chance. Wasn't but three days. But it was the best three days of my life. We never left each other. We hid where we could, at the movies, walking together at night. Wherever, whenever. One night, we ended up in what I thought was her dorm, but it was her brother's, your uncle Thomas, and he walked in on us. He screamed out how I was trying to force myself on—rape—Elizabeth. And then there were so many people, I was surrounded by all these white faces, punching me, kicking me. I tried to fight back—tried to stop them. I heard the gunshot before I felt the pain. Thomas shot me in my side. They pinned me down and held me until the police came. Here I was, bloodied, beaten, and captured like a rat, and when they asked Elizabeth what happened, she chose to save her brother. I didn't do anything but love your mother, and I got put in prison for twenty years. Marked a rapist for the rest of my life."

"That can't be true."

"It's truer than I'd ever want it to be. I thought she loved me. And maybe she did in her own way."

"No. No. That's not true. My mother would never do that. She never said a bad word about you."

"Why would she? I told you, I never did a thing to her but love her. And that one love, however small it might've been, was big enough to bring you into this world. You're proof of what was possible. I guess when she looked at you, she remembered me. Telling you more about me meant she would have to give up a truth she had to hide. The only communication I had with her after it went down was that letter telling me about you and how much she regretted what happened that night."

"And you didn't think to show it to the guards or a lawyer? Use it to get out?"

"I tried. Nobody listened to me. Nobody cared. Judges, lawyers, all of them, just telling me over and over how the system worked but how it didn't work for me. After a while, I just stopped thinking I deserved to be out. I didn't deserve freedom."

Shame surged inside of her. Shame that she'd hated him for all these years. Shame that even if she'd known, she was powerless to do anything to change his fate. Tears filled her eyes, tears she knew could not turn back time, nor her empathy return to him all that he'd lost. She felt shame so strong it turned itself inside out, leaving the sole emotion in her body a sudden, red-hot frustration.

"Why are you telling me all of this? What's making you tell me now?"

"Because my past does not make the sum of me. I'm free to move on and let my life lessons put the wind behind the rest of my life."

Slowly, steadily, her annoyance barreled into resentment. He'd lain his trauma at her feet. A knot of traumas was all he had to offer his only daughter.

"I lived so many of my days mad," he said. "Mad at the sun, the stars, the sky, and everything they allowed to go on under their watch. I ain't mad no more. I forgive your mother, and Thomas, and all of them involved. And I forgive me. Because I can be filled with rage and grace at the same time. And even after forgiveness, that rage will go on smoldering. That's my burden, but it doesn't have to be yours."

"But it is mine, isn't it? That's why I was treated like I was my whole life. All I am is her shame and your anger."

"No, Sidney. You're the very best of me and your mother. Darling, you're all of us. You never have to choose between us or them. Choose you. *You*."

"Wait, this is about Orange Beach, isn't it? You don't want me to go. But I don't want your trauma and I don't want your stories. You promised me you would take me to Orange Beach. If you won't take me, I'll do it myself."

And then she was running, out of the courtyard, through the house, stopping only to snatch a set of bus keys while the dinner table still stirred with people. She rushed out of the house and into the streets of Mobile.

Anticipation of Mardi Gras charged the Mobile night. Sidney ran down Dauphin Street where a brass ensemble blasted a jazzy tune and groups of people lounged about drinking rum, talking, singing, and enjoying the charm of the evening as Sidney sped past.

She'd no sense of how far Orange Beach was, but she aimed to go the distance. Not far from Dauphin Street, a gated lot housed more than a dozen buses. She slid open the gate and walked in the silence between the buses until she found bus 303.

Inside, the bus smelled woody and warm, reminding her of Fela. She plopped into the driver's seat, recounting the driving lesson her father gave her. She glanced at herself in the rearview mirror. The girl ironing the curls from her hair, fearing the troubles her nose and her lips would have fitting into a Wisconsin college on the day of the event, wasn't who looked back at her anymore. Her curls were no longer untamed but perfected. Her lips were no longer for pouting and whispering, but to shout and sing and kiss, and yet she could not overcome the gravity that pulled her toward Orange Beach.

She took a deep breath, slid the keys into the ignition. Her father's voice played in her thoughts: *Best way to make it do something is to make it do something.*

Just as she turned the ignition key, the back door of the bus swung open. With a wide grin on his face, into the bus cab climbed Fela.

"So I guess you're intent to leave."

"I am," she said, swiping the wet of tears from under her eyes.

As he neared, the heat of his refulgence resembled her father's, and she wanted away from that heat too. Nevertheless, an element in Fela's presence made her not want to be alone.

"I am not here to keep you where you don't want to be. I know my parents and sister want you to stay, but if you want to go, you don't have to steal a bus to do it. My truck is over there. Can I give you a ride?"

"To Orange Beach?"

"To wherever you want to go."

Mobile sparkled in his eyes. To choose Orange Beach meant the inexorable forfeiture of a world bursting with colors.

Fela's truck packed so densely with silence, Sidney let the window down to keep the quiet from smothering her.

They drove over a wide bridge and turned south along the edges of a shoreline plunged in night. The quiet of the dunes outside her window reminded her of being back home on the lake and how nature made all such places seem like both the beginning and end of the world.

"Pull over," she asked, a ringing in her mind tolling, *A shore knows, a shore always knows.*

Where Fela pulled over, moonlight bounced off the white sand, making the night feel haunted. In the window, just cracked, she could see herself reflected, familiar and foreign at the same time. Outside, the growl and crush of the ocean went on. On and on, like a speaker for the dead. She wasn't afraid of the water. Not anymore. Whatever the sea had to say, she wanted to hear the message.

Fela cut the engine. Sidney sat in that heavy silence, allowing the quiet to settle around her.

Eventually, Sidney said, "I thought my whole life my father wasn't worth anything to me. I thought he left me and my mother, which meant I must've been worth less than nothing. Not worth the trouble of being brought into this world." She turned away from her reflection. "But my father just told me he went to prison for my whole life because of a lie my mother told. So, now I have to deal with the fact that I was raised by a mother who lied and left me with no father at all. How fucked up does that make me?"

"Doesn't make you fucked up at all. No more than anyone else put in fucked-up situations."

"But everything I've ever been taught was a lie."

He reached into his pocket and revealed three items he displayed one next to the other on the center console: a lighter, a rectangle of rolling paper, and a metal trinket box packed tight with marijuana. The weed's tart, grassy smell wafted into her nose as Fela opened the box. Expertly, with a pinch of green, he rolled the weed into a joint. She watched him with the same curiosity she'd watched the queen and her council handle the Inqawe pipe.

"Every medicine *on* this earth came *from* this earth," he said, his focus on the sealing of the roll never wavering. "And this here was planted, watered, sunned, and picked. Can't get much more earth than that. For what you're feeling right now, Sidney, you'll want all the medicine this plant has to offer you."

He rolled the window down, lit the joint, and drew heat, closing his eyes as he held in the smoke. He looked like a statue to Sidney, still, beautiful, and obsidian. When at last he moved, the smoke came out of his nose and mouth, wisping up in prophetic loops, a snake in a gray curl, the wing of a crow come and gone, a cut of one of Saturn's rings.

As he turned the joint over in his hand to pass it to Sidney, he said only, "Breathe," the ceremony of his movements very much like Inqawe's distant, modernized cousin.

Sidney did as he did, small puffs first, then a long drag that made fire in her chest. She couldn't hold the heat as effortlessly as Fela, coughing out billows of smoke, but immediately craved again the warmth the smoke offered. Twice more they performed the same ceremony, and by the third time she could close her eyes and see the universe in smoke behind her eyelids. She kept her eyes closed until she was outside of time, flowing in that living darkness. Again the face of the woman from the field swam in and out of her vision. Her face captured irrational pain and purpose in equal measure. Sadness. Exhaustion. Sidney could see those feelings become her father's and eventually become hers, caused by a singular force. Same force that drove Little to madness and took years of her father's life in prison. A force that would never relent and never atone in its grand design, spanning more years than she could fathom, reaching out wider and more powerful than the ocean itself. She'd given everything to that force. Memory. Identity. Possibility. Fought for it to endure. Was willing to die for the force to exert its pressure. At once, Sidney endured the most astonishing shame, a shame eased solely by a connection she could only describe as *us*.

When she opened her eyes, *us* visible like patterns of light, her entire body seemed to apologize at once. "I'm sorry. So sorry for so many things."

Then Fela, as beckoning to her as the incarnation of music, coolly responded. "Don't worry 'bout it." And the cool masked all the power it took to be so forgiving. Maybe it was the heat of the smoke under her skin or the way his cool triggered her, but right then she reached across the car and kissed him so quick it popped the air.

Sidney pulled back, surprised at herself. She expected him to be surprised as well. But again he just smiled coolly, the act like a gravitational pull of which she found herself at the verge. She kissed him again, slowly, thoughtfully, aware of how well their lips fit together, of the tension in the muscles of his jaw—how his hands sailed toward her. And it felt good. In the tips of her elbows. In her kneecaps. In the balls of her heels. Good in impossible places. And when finally his hands touched her she knew she was of the earth. That she could be watered and lean in the direction of a sun.

A gun fired somewhere near, snapped her out of the moment. She turned to see fireworks, not gunshots, tinseling the night air.

"It's just Mardi Gras celebrations," Fela said. "There's a party happening damn near anywhere you go."

"I want to go down," Sidney answered, feeling parts of herself awakening. "I want to dance."

A smile was the only hesitation he gave before flinging the truck door open, speeding around to the passenger side, and letting Sidney out to a night that surged from silent haunt to sizzling.

Music blessed the air. Fela took Sidney by the hand, and, together, they skipped down the dunes toward the water, kicking off their shoes along the way, moonlight reflecting off the crush of white caps splaying out onto the shore.

A great bonfire gave the night a golden sheen. Dozens gathered around, music soaring and fireworks bursting, making a scene that looked as wild as it did irresistible. The dark heat burned deep in Sidney, already flowing out of her before she reached the crowd. She welcomed the dark heat to consume her, releasing all command of her hands and feet, stepping into the crowd, closing her eyes where she could ascend with the joy of the music. Again, time peeled away from her, the thumping rhythm proving the only cadence left to tether her to space and time. There, she danced. She wasn't running toward something or away, wasn't knotted in questions or unraveling with answers. The heat and the dark and the music took her with neither shame nor sadness. Fela's hands gripped her waist. She felt the tremendous pull of *us*, of a *we* undivided. Dancing. No longer alone. Dancing on the pulse of roots. Dancing in the dark, dark heat.

And then she was moving, running, her feet wet in the splash of tide, Fela leading her up the beach, away from the music and the heat of the bonfire.

Sidney fell asleep that night on the beach dunes thinking about her father. Was he a good man or a criminal? Did love guide his heart, or did revenge sharpen his mind? Was the sum of him all of those things she believed and more, her father's blackness as multitudinous as the stars in the soil of the sky? As darkness deepened into dreams, she spoke back to the stars: *I don't know him, but I'd like to.*

Knowing him is knowing me.

Knowing him is knowing me.

When the morning came, Sidney woke on the beach before Fela.

Others from the party also made beds of the sugar-white sand, their bodies stretched out comfortably across the dunes like beached mermaids. The sky was just finding a morning shade, a coming sun making cotton of sodden clouds. Toward her, the ocean pushed its glory, offering to her its barely visible horizon and the early gulls brave enough to make a claim. Beautiful, though never lost on her how many people walked themselves straight into that blue and never came back.

Hiss whispering between the sea oats through the night was now a roar, morning wind strong and warm. Sidney got up and, with her mother's letter, walked down to the water's edge. Where the lapping water could wet her bare feet, Sidney opened the letter.

The familiarity of her mother's handwriting, specifically the way she crossed her *T*s with the most confident stroke, nearly gave Sidney tears enough to match the ocean. She unfolded the letter and read its contents. The first read ended in more of a skim, a sharp unwillingness to truly absorb the letter's message. The next few reads were studious, examining, retaining, but intent not to feel. Not until the fourth read, or fifth, did the contents take the shape of one human speaking to another. Love charged her mother's words, profound love, and regret in equal measure. Elizabeth, as far as Sidney could sense, truly hated what she'd done to Charlie. The lie she told. The betrayal. The impact upon his life. But there was no real understanding of that impact beyond a personal reaction to something far, far away. Because while every word Elizabeth had written proclaimed her remorse, the words quivered with astounding ignorance. She didn't really understand the decision she'd made because she had no awareness of *why* she made the decision at all. She didn't know what she'd sacrificed a man's freedom to protect. Even the astounding ability to do so was assumed effortlessly in her mother's pages. She said that the *universe did not have enough ways* for her to regret what happened to him, and yet she did nothing in this world to change the outcome. She did not leverage that same assumed power for his betterment. The letter offered no path forward for Charlie. No way out. No sense of how little she planned to tell his daughter about who he was and how much the vacancy of his identity would fill in with stereotypes. What befell Charlie was an outcome her life had prepared her to accept and his to endure. Indeed, the letter did not even ask for forgiveness.

She imagined her father, still spending years in the punishing deformation of prison, years without hearing his daughter's voice, and all he had was this letter as a receipt for his sacrifice. And for what? Her uncle was no good man. Why was his life more valuable than Charlie's? Sidney knew the answer but found no acknowledgment in her mother's letter that she knew. Her mother's brother represented an idea whose belief and maintenance meant more to her mother than regret, more than honor, more even than love. An idea she'd blinded herself from seeing. That blindness, Sidney understood, was why her father never read the letter a second time. A blindness that confirmed for him his nightmare had an architect. Layers and layers built on top of him, professing how a prison for him made for others the sturdiest foundation. He was always the villain in someone else's story. And his innocence didn't matter. Her mother's letter, for all its regret, read more like an oath she'd promised in the air of every breath she'd ever taken.

Sidney stuffed the letter in her pocket, charged back up the beach, and woke Fela. "Wake up." She nudged him with her foot. "I want to get over to Orange Beach."

"I thought after last night you would've changed your mind, maybe not want to go anymore."

"Oh, I very much want to go. But I am not running *to* Orange Beach, I'm running *at* it."

"At it, huh?" He rolled up to his feet. "Then I guess we'd best giddyup."

35

ORANGE BEACH, ALABAMA.

Daydreams and nightly conjures had filled her mind since the day she found Agnes's note. Orange Beach took shape in her heart as a hope. She realized she'd been imagining summer in Oshkosh, when warm wind billowed out American flags wide enough to see all their stars. The air hummed of boat motors trolling over still waters, and the sun glistened grassy fields into eventual memories. The color of chlorine pools, the smell of fire contained in charcoal, peacefulness to the edge of sedation. Hope idyllic. Edgeless. A rainbow of neutrals. She imagined her arrival like a climax, to cross a threshold or step right into some sort of ticker-tape parade. Alas, Orange Beach arrived unexceptional, listless if not for the shine of memory. Her welcome was not a parade but a snaking line of cars, which circled a working McDonald's drive-through.

Along the beachside, dozens of people shopped gift stores with lighted signs and, next to them, booths selling snow cones and cotton candy. American flags caught air over the arched sign at the boardwalk. And there was grass cut along the edges of sidewalks, and chlorine in the air, and charcoal burning somewhere. Still, Orange Beach was not like Oshkosh, but ill made in its model: an old world apotheosized.

Fela slowed the truck down for Sidney before asking a question she was already thinking. "You expected everyone to actually be white, didn't you?"

We are not all gone, Agnes's note had said. The *we* she meant and the *we* Sidney saw arrived upon her with as much surprise as relief.

People, she saw. Every shade of yellow, beige, red, brown, in a spectrum of colors in between extremes. White was an identity independent of color, and it lived out on Orange Beach.

"I don't know what I expected." She looked around at all those faces.

"White isn't a race, it's an idea. People who still cling to it, they're here."

Sidney scanned the busy but hushed city, aware of the pronounced difference between it and Mobile's electric streets. She could feel the tension. A collection of laws, beliefs, and stereotypes wound tight with the maintenance of its own form. Wound tight with all the ways a thing should be, tighter still in the faith that this was the way things had always been: a world safe in a firm grip. She didn't see *white*, but she felt the force of it. Like seeing a childhood toy as an adult, knowing all the places you've changed by seeing how an old thing hadn't changed at all.

"When people came to Mobile and saw what the city was . . . what the city was becoming, they didn't want things to be *that* different. My father wanted to send them to Nashville, but my mother knew they wouldn't have access to the care, food, and supplies they'd need. My sister, Nona, was actually the one who created this town for them. A place where they could just be, kind of like what we used to want. But to me, I don't know, they're out here like little white candles in the sun."

"But your mother said 'change is coming.'"

"It is. They can't live in a dream forever."

Sidney looked out to see a police officer in full uniform. She saw pretty girls jogging in yoga pants. She saw mothers pushing babies in strollers with little dogs leashed to them. And then she heard a different kind of music in the air. "Do you hear that?"

"Sounds like gospel music."

They followed the sound and noted small crowds marching in the same direction. Along the shoreline, where the gulf began to curve, the music grew louder—singing, she heard, and guitars played like harps. Tall white tents spread out along the beach under which the crowds gathered.

"It's a church revival," Fela said.

Sidney never thought of Agnes as the heavy churchgoing type, more for the social experience than the Holy Spirit. But Sidney knew Agnes well enough to know she would go where the crowd went. And Sidney wanted to see her, needed to, if only to see what her own longing looked like.

"I want to go," she said.

"We can, but you should know they don't like it when people from Mobile come around. Don't bother me too much, but you'll feel it going down there." Fela pulled the truck over a distance from the other cars.

"Feel what?"

"Like you just turned the lights on at their movie."

"Maybe the lights need to be turned on."

Out of the truck, Sidney stepped into the beach air. Together, she and Fela flowed into the crowd. Sidney watched the eyes around her flick to Fela. Color alone didn't draw their eyes to Fela, but the silent, invisible invasion his energy seemed to have on them. The nearer they came to the music and tents, she felt the eyes slide from him to her, acknowledging that she too brought something different to their world.

Ahead, the music from inside the tent softened to an end and a voice reached out over the speakers. Sidney didn't recognize the voice but knew the cadence well. Preaching.

"Stay close to me." Fela took Sidney by the hand.

They strode together into the largest tent, where rows and rows of pews filled with people gathered around a stage wreathed in flowers. Behind the stage, a grand painting of the Last Supper hung, and a lone Latino man idled with an elbow on a podium. He held his hand out as if stroking the animal of the crowd. Every head was bowed in prayer. Instinctively, Sidney stopped to pray along with them. Her reaction to that sudden respect, though delayed, was like touching something hot from which she needed to quickly step away. *Whose god am I praying to?* She kept her eyes open while the prayer went on, the preacher professing sadness for the event, celebrating Jesus's will in bringing his children home to his father, and expressing gratitude in knowing one day the congregation would be cleansed of sin enough to go with them in time. Sidney scanned the audience in search of Agnes. She saw the crowns of heads, long hair pulled back in buns, short hair shaved down tight. She felt the girth of her curls in that moment, sprawling out, and how the fragrance of the oil on her skin arrived steps ahead of her. Where such realizations in such places might've shrunk her before, she felt emboldened. Indeed, she swelled with pride as the prayer ended and the many, many pairs of eyes danced until they found her, stoking that new satisfaction in her with every glance.

Ahead of her, ambiently, the slick preacher welcomed his congregation and invited his wife to his stage.

Still holding her hand, Fela stepped back toward the exit. "We should maybe wait outside until this is all over."

Then a microphoned gasp sucked the wind out from under the tent, and the voice that followed splashed the still air.

"Thank you, Jesus! The Lord has brought my niece home."

Agnes stood on the stage with her hands spread out, tears already warping her mascara. Her hair, pulled back tightly, allowed darker roots to show through the blond. But Sidney saw her. Unmistakably. The one relative left in the world with her last name.

"Our God brought her safely to us. Come up here, Sidney! Oh, you're so welcome here to this new home with us. Come up here."

The crowd around her burst into applause so loud the sound frightened Sidney's hand free from Fela's. Embarrassment warmed her face pink, and suddenly she wished all those eyes were miles away from her. The odd, inescapable magnetism of the moment pulled her onto the stage. There, she embraced Agnes, her nose tickled by Agnes's lavender perfume emphasizing itself in the attempt to mask the tang of cigarettes. The crowd went on cheering, and the preacher hugged Sidney hard enough to leave the impression of his weight across her body. Words were said all around her that blurred into gibberish. And before she could process any of it, she sat hand in hand with Agnes while her apparent new husband, the preacher, gave an hour-long monotone sermon, not a memorable phrase of which stuck to Sidney.

Dumbfounded, Sidney sat still, suddenly thrust back into a place that felt and sounded like something it wasn't.

She couldn't see Fela from the front row, but instead rows of people dressed in white, with tense, frightened looks on their faces.

Sidney turned and looked at Agnes, remembering the last time she saw her. A month or so before the event, Rick had taken the family out to Red Lobster. Adam and John had just finished playing baseball, and the restaurant was packed with families in colorful T-shirts and all the other boys still in their uniforms. Sidney and her family entered just as Agnes left in a fit with several restaurant employees orbiting her with apologies. Agnes shouted about the food and screamed over the service until her meal was reimbursed. Unsatisfied, she was also given vouchers for a return meal. Sidney remembered how Agnes winked at Elizabeth as she passed, gave her the then crumpled vouchers and a smile baring her teeth. "Let their favorite aunt Agnes take care of dinner tonight," she had said, and strode out, half drunk, into the sun. Now, for reasons Sidney still didn't understand, after everyone else was underwater, out in the sun Agnes still stood.

Sidney observed the stretch of her aunt's smile and listened as she fastened an "amen" or a "praise him" to the end of every other thing her husband said. The woman held Sidney's hand but did not look once at her. An invested performance.

As the sermon ended, the preacher made his call to salvation, asking those in the audience who had not been saved to come and surrender their lives to Christ so they might finally have access to the Kingdom of Heaven. Sidney remembered those dressed in white back in Mississippi whom Sailor called "walkers." Just then, the people in the congregation dressed in white jumped to their feet.

"Will you take the walk?" the preacher asked, as the white-clad party gathered together at the base of the stage. "Will you take the walk and find your salvation?"

Agnes turned to Sidney, the performative excitement in her face betraying her green eyes with a sheen of brown. Into Sidney's lap she slid a white linen frock. "Put this on. Step down that aisle and get saved, honey. Walk. Just like the others. Walk until you reach the waters and wash all this sin off of you. When Jesus comes back for the rest of us, you will have made a way for all of us to walk through those pearly gates together."

"Saved? Agnes, what are you talking about?"

"Well, isn't that why you're here? To walk?"

"No, I—"

"That's what this revival is all about. You walk. Sacrifice for all of us. This is a good thing, Sidney."

"You think I came here to walk myself into the wa—"

"Forever. You'd be walking into a forever with no more pain or sadness. Just forever."

"Are you crazy?"

Agnes froze momentarily, stunned equally by realization and annoyance. "Well, now, I've clearly forgotten my manners," Agnes said, her smile widening from stretch to strain. "You just made it home, and I'm pulling you right into the deep end before you've had a chance to get settled. You were probably terrorized all the way here carrying all sorts of questions you want answered. Come on, then. I'll get you a Coke and we can talk."

Sidney steeled herself, looking back at Agnes. She nodded, for she did have questions, but more than that she had things she wanted to say and the space to voice them. Agnes yanked her along, outside and into a smaller, personalized tent fashioned like a lounge complete with puffy chairs, cold drinks, and a basket of expired potato chip bags. Inside, Sidney felt Fela's energy just before he appeared at the tent's entry. Agnes clocked him too.

"Thank you for dropping off my niece, young man. You can wait outside, and I will pay you for your troubles."

"His name is Fela. And he is with me."

Agnes released Sidney's hand then, suddenly loosening the strain in her face and shoulders. She plopped her weight on the puffy chair and sighed a sharp reset of a sigh. "I promised you a Coke. Go ahead and—"

"No thank you," Sidney responded.

"That stuff is as good as gold around here. Especially the bottled ones. You should—"

"I said no thank you."

"All right then. Go ahead and ask your questions."

Sidney shuffled her feet until she felt sturdy and unmovable. "Agnes, how are you still living?"

"Ha!" The woman laughed something nearer to a bark. "You call this living?"

"You're not at the bottom of that beach out there. Like my brothers. My mother. Your husband."

"Believe it or not, I'm more like you than I am your uncle and your mother. Just luckier, maybe, and obviously a lot smarter."

"You're black?"

"No, I'm white because I say I am white. But I have a grandmother, down the line, from one of the islands. She boated here, put my mother up for adoption, who, of course, put me up for adoption too. My adopted family lived in Wisconsin, and, well, that's who I am. But my mother's little sin, just like you, is the only reason I am still here. Still suffering for it."

"You passed all this time being white?"

"I wasn't passing, niece, I was *being*. I didn't know my mother or my grandmother."

"But how did you know to come here? About your family?"

"Word travels when it's important. But I felt it too, like trumpets in the sky. Telling me things. It took me a while to decide. But when I saw how the world was going, well, I came to where I could be of some kind of service. The more people I bring to take the walk, the better chance I have that God will have mercy on me. Invite me into his heavenly kingdom with the rest of our people."

"You called me here to be one of those walkers?"

"I thought that's what you wanted, darling. You were just squatting in that big house by yourself suffering. The more walkers we have, the better chance the rest of us have to be saved. Sacrifice, that's what salvation is all about."

"You thought I wanted to die?"

"Didn't you?"

"But you left a note for me."

"I did. And now you're here, alive and well, when the rest of your family is dead. This is the only way to get back to them."

"I can't believe you, Agnes. You knew I was alone in that house when you left that damned note. You want me to die, but you couldn't even bring yourself to see my face after."

"Oh, don't be dramatic. I've been to that house of yours more times than I can count. Was like my family home too. And now it's just another cemetery. You think I wanted to see that? The fact that I left you a note at all was a courtesy. Consider yourself lucky it was on my way out." Agnes cracked a Coke bottle open, sipped, and cut eyes at Fela. "So this boy here brought you all the way from Oshkosh, or did you pick him up along the way?"

Again Sidney shuffled, rocked by a barrage of feelings landing on her at once. About the confirmation of her own darkness. "He didn't bring me to Alabama, my father did."

The way she said *father* and the sudden standing up of a pillar of pride inside her reattached a connection Agnes's words had sought to sever. That same word, *father*, sat Agnes up in her seat.

"Your father? The rapist?"

"My father is not a rapist."

"If he went to prison because the law said he's a rapist, then he's a rapist. Your mother would turn in her grave if she knew you were with him."

"My mother isn't in a grave. And my father was no rapist."

"I suppose all sins are forgiven when the world is full of devils."

"And who exactly are you calling devils?" Fela roared, stepping farther into the tent, his energy a spike in temperature.

Agnes did not react to him, but recited, flatly, "'There will be a time of distress such as has not happened from the beginning of nations—'"

The preacher's smooth voice cut Agnes off as he breezed into the tent behind Fela: "'But at that time your people . . . will be delivered. Multitudes who sleep in the dust of the earth will awake: some to everlasting life.' Daniel twelve, verses one and two. That's our word here. And, Sidney, that is the word that welcomes you."

Again he embraced Sidney in too firm a hug, and she felt Fela's heat rise again.

"Can I get you a drink?" the preacher asked. "We have Coke here, y'know. Even the ones in the bottle."

"No, I don't want a Coke."

The preacher shrugged, sat down next to Agnes, and placed a hand on her leg. "I imagine your trip getting here was horrendous. I've heard all kinds of horror stories."

"My father took care of me, thank you."

"And where is your father now?"

"He's back in Mobile—"

"He left her, I'm sure." Agnes kissed the top of her Coke bottle for a sip. "Her real father—the only man to take care of her—was Rick. And Rick is with God."

"Wherever Rick is," Sidney responded, "God isn't."

"How dare you say such a disrespectful thing? That man kept food on the table, raised you in the church—hell, he even taught you to shoot a gun and hunt for yourself. And you weren't even his blood."

"No, I wasn't his blood. And he made sure I always knew it. Just like Uncle Thomas."

At Thomas's name, Agnes gasped, dramatic. "You will not shame my Thomas in this place."

"You think he feels shame from whatever level of hell he's in?"

"Don't you dare—"

"What? Tell the truth about him? How he shot my father and my own mother kept his lie? They put my father in prison for my whole life! Isn't that something worth being shamed over, Aunt Agnes?"

"You're wrong, child."

"I stopped being a child when my family died in front of me. And I promise you"—she held out her mother's letter—"I am not wrong. Even my mother admits it. My father suffered—I suffered—for Thomas's lie."

"Dear, the court found your father guilty. That's a lot more facts than some old jail letter. If the court of law said he did it, then he did it."

"And when has a court of law done anything for us?"

"Us?"

Us had bloomed from Sidney's mouth as leaves on branches. *Us* was in her and outside of her now. Standing there, she imagined Zu and Sailor, Vivian and Nona, her sister. She imagined Malcolm's beauty and Tau's rage. And last she saw her father proudly shouting, "Go!" with her at the wheel. Passionate people, creative and feeling people. People forced to be alone and in the dark, but who taught themselves to shine so bright they could always find each other. Sidney illuminated along with them. *Us.*

"You heard me right."

"So why come here then, if you've got so much against our way of life?"

"I came because you think this is the only way. I came to tell you there are so many other ways, Agnes. There always have been. I came to save *you*."

The preacher shot to his feet. The slickness of his mannerisms warped into something more devious. "Enough with this," he shouted, stepping toward Sidney. Fela rose to her side to meet him. "You will not come into my house with this nonsense!"

Fela's voice came steady, but sharp with defensiveness. "Not a word of nonsense came from her mouth. And I'd advise you not to let any come out of yours."

"I only speak the truth, boy." And then the slickness returned to his face, as he cut eyes to Sidney. "I don't suspect your friend here told you that this rapture didn't just happen, it was man-made. And he can tell you just the man to blame. He can tell you who is responsible for killing your family and mine and so many others."

Fela's steadiness wavered, his voice nearly cracking with anger. "You're the one responsible—you and your people."

"My people . . ." The preacher slid around them until his back shielded the exit, blocking either of them from leaving. "We weren't the ones with all that anger."

"Who do you think instigated that anger? All the things you did to my people and let fester because you wouldn't do a damn thing about it. So caught up in your fake fucking utopia you couldn't even acknowledge that any of it ever even happened."

"You people were already killing each other like animals."

"You love to think that everything you put in a cage is an animal. But I know there's no cage that will hold me if you call my people animals again."

"See? Anger, like I told you. Ask him, Sidney. Ask him who is responsible for killing your family."

Sidney turned to Fela, who refused to look at her. "Fela, what is this man talking about?"

Fela kept the anger in his eyes beamed at the preacher, who went on smiling like a fox.

"Go ahead, boy, tell her about what's in your daddy's garage."

Fela bowed his head, and when finally she saw his eyes, her heart sank into her stomach. "Fela, I need you to speak to me."

But Fela couldn't speak. Sidney watched him until her hope shifted into despair. She charged for the door, but the preacher blocked her path.

"We can't change the past any more than you can. So what do you want us to do?"

Sidney met his eyes and felt her father in her shoulders, disappointment becoming strength. "I want the same thing people like me have always wanted: for you to get the hell out of the way."

She blew past him out of the tent and up the beachside where the gospel music sang out. The sun loomed at its great height, spotlighting her in a futile attempt for distance. Where could she run? Where was there to go where that sun wouldn't also loom? And that's when she stopped. No more glass houses. No more running. She whipped her head around, and Fela was there, a step behind her.

"Tell me. Tell me the truth."

"It's hard to explain."

"Try."

She watched nerves turn him into a pacing, stuttering mess of words. "It's us, Sidney. It's all of us, y'know? Up there. And it's all time, all history—a deep, deep wound. All the trauma of all our lives. All of us, you understand? Since the day we were stolen and kidnapped here on this land. Herald says it's like a sky full of elephants."

"A what? Slow down and try to make sense."

"It's black consciousness."

"What is?"

"Everywhere is. All around us. Fractured, but connecting us, inspiring us, giving us hope. It's every repressed emotion we've pent up over centuries. My father's machine—he was just trying to heal us by reconnecting us all back to it. But he . . . It was like cracking a dam wide open on everything."

"That's what killed my family?"

"Many, many people were killed, people who were innocent. But so were we." He shook his head and shivered. "For centuries. So were we, and horrors went on happening anyway."

She took a step back. She needed space to truly understand what Fela had lain between them. Space for lies and lessons, truth and torment, to untangle from each other, and their grand scrolls outspread and made legible.

"Fela, I need you to give me the keys to your truck."

"Where do you—"

"I don't know and I don't want to talk. Just give me the keys."

Slowly, he reached into his pocket and did as she asked. "Stay. Don't go."

Sidney studied Fela with eyes she hoped showed more than anger. Eyes that said, *I am going, but I'm not gone.*

Without speaking another word, Sidney marched away from him, back to his truck. There, she sat inside with the windows up, remembering what her father taught her. Ignition, mirrors, gas and brake, gear shift, speedometer, the lights, and the wheel. Shift into drive. Feel the connection to the machine and its connection to the earth. She had no room for any other thoughts but driving. *Drive until everything makes sense.*

Let the wheels set you free.

As the truck idled forward, she gazed out at the beach and the surge of waves in ceaseless crush. Clouds blocked the sun in parts. A storm brewed out there in the deep. Swollen and cankering, darkening away all the glisten of the sea, eventually that storm would come down. *Elephants,* she thought, *that rain would come down as heavy as elephants.*

She stepped on the gas and heard her father's voice:

Best way to make it do something is to make it do something.

36

SPACE AND TIME.

The light inside the garage snapped on, and a few seconds later the garage door rumbled to life. Tau and Herald stood at the opening, and Hosea stepped out to the front.

"Don't make the mistake in thinking just the three of us worked on this," Hosea said. "This town ain't nothing but strong minds and strong bodies. They come here throughout the day to put in a few hours of work here and there. Not many come at night and never this late. But here you are, so I reckon you're ready to work?"

"Ready," Charlie clamored, honored to be among them.

"Good. Come on in."

Inside the place, the tartness of metal, dirt, and oil reminded Charlie of home.

"This was my great-grandfather's land," Hosea told him. "He built the first house on it with his own hands, not much bigger than this garage. He might've gone on living in a shack of a place if it weren't for my great-grandmother. She taught him how to see—further, wider, clearer.

A good woman always does." And then his face softened, a smile filling his eyes as he drifted off looking at something behind Charlie. The young men turned and Charlie followed to see, standing out in the driveway, moonlight collecting at the edge of her form, Vivian.

Night seemed to have evolved her. Hers was a strength no man could deny. And yet it was vulnerable, accessible, capable of being damaged and never show it. Because real power doesn't protect itself. Real power allows itself to be used for something greater. Wife. Mother. Guide. Grace. *Protect the black woman,* Charlie thought, and every bone inside him wanted to fall down in shame that he hadn't protected them before. That prison took away his ability to be there for his mother, as well as his daughter.

Vivian smiled. "What is the purpose of the work you are doing here tonight?" Charlie heard Nina Simone in her voice and music that seemed to play even in the way she spoke. She turned to her son Herald.

"To commune with my ancestors," he answered.

"To empower black people with a vision of their own self-determination," Tau followed.

"To heal black consciousness," her husband replied.

And then they all turned to Charlie. He stood in that garage for a different reason for every day of his life. But all those reasons condensed to a singular, personal cause.

"To connect to my daughter," he said, "in ways the story of my life can't seem to."

Vivian peered into the dark emptiness just outside the garage. "And what say you?"

Out of the darkness, sheepishly, as though he'd been caught stealing candy, Sailor crept into the light looking to Charlie like a young army man. Sailor hadn't left Mobile. Such was the power of the connections the radio could repair. "Been fixing planes for over ten years and hated every second of it. But ever since I got here, my hands've been itching to get to work on something. I figure if I come here asking for something,

I should be giving something in exchange. It's only right. So I just want to help. If nothing else, maybe I can help make it to where planes can fly over Alabama again . . . and we can have more folks come see what you've made here."

"Then you have my blessing to continue forward until the work is done."

She blew a kiss to them all, winked at the king, then stepped out into the dark of the night.

Charlie extended a hand to Sailor. "You're still here."

"You said it's worth staying, didn't you?"

"I did. And I am sure we could use all the help."

"Good. What are we looking at here?" Sailor asked.

Hosea began gathering books and tools for Charlie and Sailor, Herald getting down under the machine and Tau moving a fifty-pound transistor.

"Better to get your hands dirty first. Herald and his team built the first power system. Maybe that's the best place for you to get into understanding it. Follow their path so you can see where things started to break down." Hosea slammed a stack of books, blueprints, essays, and patents on the table in front of Charlie. Charlie recognized some of the names, but others were lost on him entirely: Granville T. Woods, who outwitted Edison in the development of the telephone; Lewis Latimer, without whom air-conditioning wouldn't exist; James E. West, who invented modern microphones; Mark Dean, who helped create the first personal computer. Some names weren't names at all but symbols of more ancient languages. "Before you start asking questions, know you already have what you require to find the answers yourself."

For the next few hours, Charlie disappeared in the work, discovering where the machine existed, partially, before the king. He could see where Hosea layered his build and where Herald came in, adding more sophisticated parts. With his hands on the machine, Charlie felt himself fit within their family as though he'd always been there, a brother to the king, an uncle to the sons.

The power source Herald built could, by all accounts, run a city without issue, but the energy the machine needed to run at full power would require thousands of times more wattage. As far as Charlie could tell, to achieve what the machine required, they'd have to slice out a piece of the sun itself as a power source. Finally, Charlie tilted his head down to Herald, still tinkering at the base of the machine.

"Herald, what other power sources have you tried? Water, solar, nuclear?"

"Yep, all that and more. Followed Tesla's work as closely as I could. Most of his stuff is lost. What you see here, we learned about back in Haiti. But a lot of that got lost too crossing the Atlantic."

"Not lost, erased. That's why I say fuck 'em," Tau, ever angry, chimed in as good as a growl. He slapped his heavy hand on Charlie's back. "Your daughter, Sidney, her mother's a white woman?"

"That's right."

"She betrayed you, didn't she? They always do—even in death they still fucking us over."

"She did, but I don't believe they always do—or did. Some rose to their better natures, some didn't. But you, do you ever laugh or smile? You seem angry all the time."

"The fuck I got to be smiling about?"

"All kinds of things. Surely you have good days. Or do you just forever hate everyone? Especially white people?"

"I don't hate white people. I hate the whole world for letting what happened to us go on the way it did. You telling me hundreds of years of torture and couldn't nobody stop it? And ain't *nobody* want to rectify it? Hell yeah, damn right I'm mad and I'll be mad forever, until the day I die, and even then I want them to set my coffin on fire so I can be mad in the afterlife. Because what happened to our people deserves that kind of mad. And if won't nobody else feel it, I'll goddamn feel it enough for everybody. That's my liberation."

"Liberation is a lot more than anger, son, I done told you that," Hosea said.

"Who here is thinking about what comes next?" Sailor asked. "I mean, say this radio comes online, what then? And what about everywhere else in the world?"

"Well, we've already started new trade routes with Cuba, the Dominican Republic, and Haiti. We're negotiating with Mexico now too, around the Yucatán," Herald answered. "But our liberation only happened here in America. Hasn't happened in the rest of the world."

"I'm surprised everybody else hasn't tried to invade already, try to take it all back."

"Only a matter of time. I'm sure they're coming."

"Probably scared of the water."

"Real question is what will the rest of the world do when they find out that black folks and other people of color have a way to heal themselves—to be fully redeemed for everything they've been plundered of? Oppressors really hear us, they very literally couldn't live with themselves? Knowing that, you think they would want our wounds to be healed? I don't think so. They will do everything to shut down even the possibility of us being whole."

"See?" Tau interjected. "More reasons to be pissed off."

"Be angry, son, but be more too," Hosea counseled.

"More is what this machine gonna have to be if we're gonna fix it." Herald slid under the machine, his legs jutting out like half a body.

"More?" Charlie asked. "Seems to me like the kind of power this thing needs don't exist on this earth."

"It's like a circle," Herald said.

"Oh no, here we go with this shit again—"

Herald rolled out from under the machine. "Tau, there's more things between heaven and earth—"

"I'm not sure I'm following," Charlie interrupted. "What does the circle part mean?"

"It's like this," Herald continued. "Right now I could get a compass out of my father's toolbox and draw you a perfect circle. Perfect circles are all around us. But mathematically, a perfect circle doesn't exist."

"You mean pi?"

"That's right. The equation for the circumference of a circle makes a number that goes on forever, which means, mathematically, the circle never closes, which means a perfect circle is nonsensical—doesn't exist. So, some things in this world are and aren't at the same time. I'm a scientist, so that's where everything I know falls apart. My father's the one with all the philosophies."

"Don't you go throwing me under nobody's bus." Hosea laughed like a car starting. "I'll tell you what you need, you need to go sit under a woman—feminine energy in whatever form you can find it. The feminine is sacred because the feminine is still connected to the universe."

"Oh, Pop, why're you always talking that shit?" Tau huffed.

"Nah, son, if you learn anything from me before I leave this earth, that's it. Sit at the feet of feminine energy and just listen. Woman'll tell you everything we need to do, everything we want, is here already. Been here. It's just we've been using the wrong tools to access it."

Herald slid back under the machine. "Pop, I ain't sure what you're talking about, but it sounds gross."

And they laughed together. Healing laughter that felt good and warm. Hosea cracked open beers and they drank together, talked, worked, and kept on laughing. Charlie hadn't felt such brotherly love in all his life, though he knew such tenderness existed. Like the circle. A thing seen and felt, but unquantifiable in its impact. If he could get the machine to work, this feeling, the special sense of connectedness, healing, would be felt all over the world. Healing, and so much more, was what he felt when the signal, from just the prototype, surrounded him. It would transform rage into creativity, despair into ingenuity. Everyone elevated by being connected. Charlie imagined all the people who still worked the earth with their hands, who talked to its roots and leaves, who knew the current of its waters, the smell of storms, and how to slow time down in the heat of summer. He imagined people who understood the science of the soul, people who spoke the language of magic—leaders, makers, adventurers, warriors, and healers. Charlie wanted to be connected to them all and have them be connected to him. To have been plundered such that we hid away our greatest treasures, even from ourselves. The signal would reveal that power to everyone. And Charlie would work until that job was done.

Nevertheless, even with all the hope and ambition he could conjure, he tried that night and failed.

In the end, he fell asleep with a book in one hand and a screwdriver in the other.

That night Charlie's dreams were less reverie than what felt like a download of information. Indeed, ever since the king exposed Charlie to the signal, whenever he closed his eyes, dipping into the deep black of his mind, information made a meteor shower across his thoughts, illuminating his mind with ideas, insights, and memory. That night, Charlie's dream detailed the functionality of the machine. As Hosea had explained to Charlie, the machine tapped into black consciousness, its signal liberating memory, oppression, anger, discontent, fear, and all other repressed trauma. Technically, the machine drew its power from the obelisks, coated in specialized solar cells, installed throughout the city. The spiked monoliths drew power in, pulsed energy into the ground until the frequency matched the resonance of the earth itself. The tip of the obelisks shot the resonance just above the clouds, charging the ionosphere, making energy and information accessible nearly anywhere the sky could reach. Nikola Tesla's tower accomplished the same achievement, if only temporarily. But even his work was based on ancient African resonance technologies, which powered ancient societies. Charlie *felt* those truths in his dreams encoding his waking life. What he could not reconcile was just how exactly the city of Mobile came to know, build, and activate such a remarkable invention.

When finally Charlie woke, Seraphin stood next to him with a cup of coffee, biscuits, and fresh fruit. The sun blazed its midmorning form, and he wasn't exactly sure how much of last night he'd dreamt and how much was real.

"Did you fix it yet?" Seraphin asked.

"I'm not even sure if I can."

She cupped his face in her hands and kissed him. Charlie knew no moment in his life happier than what he felt there in Mobile. But his dream lingered, curiosity hot in his veins.

"Have you seen Herald?"

"Out back," she said. "Go do your work. Find me after?"

"It'll be the most important thing I do today."

Charlie found Herald lying on his back in the grass at the base of the obelisk. Blue sky above him contrasted the towering black spike unnaturally under its clarity. All around Herald glittering bugs leapt out the grass, clicking and whirring, seeming to Charlie like the mechanization of epiphany.

"Good morning, Uncle Charlie. How'd you sleep?"

"Not even sure you can call it sleep."

Herald spun his head around to see Charlie's expression, smiling, aware. "So I guess you want to know where the idea for the radio came from, huh? Well, same place most ideas come from: the past." As Charlie sat down in the grass beside Herald, feeling, as he had with the king, like a student, Herald continued. "Crazy the kinds of things you discover when you reconnect to your history."

"You're talking about your time in Haiti?"

"I still haven't figured out what called my mom and dad to go there when they did. I was top of my class in high school, getting letters from

MIT, Stanford, Cal. All of the big schools. And still I wasn't close to prepared to learn what Haiti had to teach me. Taught me how science isn't about profit but life. Inclusion. Harmony."

"I'm not sure I'm following you."

"My mother told you that little island fought and won its freedom, right? Helped make America what it is? But she didn't tell you how all those ships bringing stolen African bodies across the Atlantic brought with them stories, science, even magic that would've otherwise been lost. You can feel the difference as soon as you land on the island. I ain't saying it's all good. They've drained the country of nearly everything. But what's sacred is sacred. We were invited in with the conjure women and houngans, we were told all the stories, the traditions, the ceremonies. We learned things I still have a hard time believing, but among them we learned resonance, consciousness, and harmony, in the old ways, were not separate. My father and I tinkered around trying to understand scientifically, and that's how we discovered an ultra-low-frequency version of the signal. You felt it in the prototype. We needed a lot more materials, more land, more power, to make a full version. So, we came back home to finish the work."

"And you knew what it was all along? What it could do?"

"Not entirely. I mean, you feel what it is. But I never imagined . . . I mean, when we turned it on, it wasn't even close to full power."

"But, it's not just about the power. You can't calibrate it, can you?"

Herald sighed and shook his head.

Charlie continued: "It can't be calibrated. That type of resonance, that frequency . . . it just is. It only knows how to operate at full power. But we turn it back on, and it could do to the whole world what it did here. Maybe worse."

Panic swelled in Charlie as he thought of Sidney. That machine could heal her but could equally feed into her worst impulses.

"I need to speak to Hosea."

"Word of advice, Uncle . . . you'd be better off going right to the source. My mother."

37

PHOTOS LINING THE hallway leading to the king and queen's bedroom made for Charlie a movie of their lives. He saw photos of Vivian, mouth mid-roar, fist in the air, delivering a speech to a crowd of hundreds. Photos of the children, Tau, Herald, Fela, and Nona, displayed the major stages of their lives, all smiling bright and free, the sun like gold on their skin. How different those images were from photos of the family back in the house Charlie tried to make a home. And yet, in resplendence, how alike. Awards lined the end of the hall, top school honors here, community achievement there. The most honored accomplishment had Hosea's name gilded above a master's in material science and engineering title from Tuskegee University. Charlie witnessed all the potential of his life fulfilled in another. Though, unexpectedly, the photos on the wall inspired a sense of pride. That while those beautiful black things did not happen to him, joy moved in his heart knowing they happened at all. He could imagine himself in those family photos, the vision of which distracted him all the way up to the moment Hosea answered his bedroom door.

"Charlie. What can I help you with?"

"Well," Charlie said, remembering why he'd come. "I was hoping to talk to Vivian."

"Coming to a man's bedroom door asking for his wife ain't peculiar to you?"

"It is. But it's important that I speak to her."

Hosea stepped aside, inviting Charlie into the room.

Daylight spread across the wood floors in the expansive space of their bedroom. Fresh flowers gave the clean, minimal room an earthy but sweet smell. On the far side, the queen stood on the balcony overlooking the courtyard. Charlie experienced a fright of anxiety as he neared. Anxiety that spiked even higher as she turned, made eye contact, and stepped into the room toward him.

"I'm blessed to have Charles Brunton at my door. Tell me something good, Charlie."

"I'm sad to say"—Charlie took a step back—"I come with bad news."

She gestured, and Charlie sat on a settee at the edge of her bed.

"It's the machine," he said.

"What about it?" The king leaned against the wall and folded his arms.

Charlie kept his eyes on the queen. "I can't work on the machine no more."

The king and the queen met eyes. "Go on. Explain," the queen asked.

"I've been working on the machine. I think what you've built is amazing. But it's too powerful, too wild. It can't be regulated. There's a good chance that if we turn it on again, it could hurt as much as help. Anybody who even thinks different could be at the bottom of the ocean. That's the walkers, that's people still out in rural towns and cities—my daughter. I can't do that. And I am here to recommend you don't do it either. I came here to ask you, beg you, to never turn that machine on again."

The queen's expression didn't change. "We knew it couldn't be calibrated," she said. "You know, when I met Hosea, I was going to school for social work. Back then I was walking right into people's homes in the projects and in the ghettos. All the welfare in the world couldn't help them from what they suffered. When I couldn't bear the social work anymore, I went into psychology, hoping maybe I could understand, deep down, the impact of their traumas—what it was that made their ascent nearly impossible. Psychology led to me studying history and seeing the real scope of how we got here. Do you really understand how long four hundred years of suffering is, Charlie? And that's just on these shores. What that does to the mind, it's hard to comprehend. Especially when it was still happening. So I started speaking, calling it out, doing everything I could to stop it so a collective healing could finally begin. But it was like trying to move a mountain. And so I learned quickly that the only way to move a mountain is to shake the earth. That don't have a thing to do with them. The mountain is us. The mountain is our minds. The mountain is our hope. That's how Haitians won their freedom against all odds. They found themselves together on the same frequency."

"But you've already done it. You have the land. You have the country. Why do it again?"

"I told you. It's not about them. Go to Haiti today. See how bad things have become. That frequency that connects us is a hard thing to achieve, even harder to maintain. You can give a man all the land and all the mules you want, but if his mind isn't on the level, he'll give it all right back. We have to turn it on again, because we have to be healed. We must. Or all that we've done won't change a thing. Just like Haiti."

"But, Vivian, the risk is just too great."

"The risk?" She again cut eyes at Hosea. "And what about the *worth*? Charlie, you went to prison for a crime you didn't commit, is that right?"

"Yes."

"You can't get back those years, nor what they did to your mind. But you still try."

"Maybe there are other ways . . ."

"What other ways?" Hosea's voice sparked with annoyance. "Aren't you angry about what happened to you?"

"Of course I am."

"Then how could you stop the chance to finally help our people?"

"Because anger isn't all that I feel." The warmth of Charlie's tears moved down his face. "Don't you understand my heart is broken? It's broken for them. It's broken for us. I'm hurt, Hosea. Anger by itself can't mend that for me. Anger by itself ain't gonna save my daughter."

"He's right." The energy in the room shifted as Nona stepped inside. "I'm sorry to eavesdrop, but I have something to say, if my word is welcome."

"Your word is always welcome." Vivian touched her daughter's shoulder.

Nona turned to Charlie. "Uncle Charlie, I think you are a special, special person. To have gone through so much, and you still have so much to give. You give to your students, I hear; you brought Sidney all the way across the country; and here you are giving so much to us. You're everybody's uncle, and we are all grateful. That's a healing in itself. So, whether my father's machine is repaired or not, the decision whether it ever comes on again should be yours to make. You decide, Uncle Charlie. It should be Charlie's decision."

"I can't . . . You can't expect me to make that kind of decision for so many people."

"And why not? When I look at you, I see all of us." She turned to her mother and father. "Uncle Charlie should decide. One way or another, Uncle Charlie should decide. That's my word."

Vivian, holding back a prideful smile, said only, "Then that's the word."

Hosea nodded, but said nothing as he walked out of the room.

"Then it's settled," Nona said, looking, suddenly, older in Charlie's eyes. "Uncle Charlie, whatever happens next you choose."

"Why would you put that decision on me?"

"Because we always rise when we need to."

The weight of the responsibility settled on Charlie. The worth. The risk. And, for him, the immensity of the decision circled around, of all the people who could be impacted, one person. The one human he could save, who just by living could also save him. Charlie's eyes flicked up to Nona.

"Have you seen Sidney?"

38

"ORANGE BEACH," HE mumbled absently. "She went to Orange Beach."

And when he looked back up at Nona, she nodded. "She didn't come back."

Charlie, activated by the fear of never seeing his child again, darted out of the bedroom, out of the house. On the street, Tau yelled for the young people to load up onto the school bus. Seeing Tau, his hulking form swollen with animosity, Charlie could think of no better person to go with him in search of his child.

"Tau." Charlie approached Tau as one might approach a bull. "My daughter, she went to Orange Beach—"

Tau growled a hot breath at Charlie. "Ain't that why she came in the first place? Because she think she's something she ain't? Like the rest of the wannabe rednecks down there."

"That may be so, but I need to find her and I need you to take me."

"I can't take you. We got shit to do—better things than changing a fool's mind. You can get one of those old heads to take you, can't you?"

"No, you will take us." Nona appeared beside Charlie, the solemnity in her face as stoic as her mother's. "You play too much. If you didn't run my sister off with your mouth, we wouldn't be here asking. Don't you realize Fela didn't come home either?"

Tau grunted again, then softened in the way a storm might ease without raining a drop. "All right, damn, calm down, li'l sis. You out here sounding like Momma with all that noise." He whipped his attention to the rest of the bus loaded with more than a dozen teenagers. "Y'all sit y'all's little asses down. We going on a field trip." He spun around, dropped his weight into the driver's seat, then fixed on to Charlie. "You sit down too, Uncle Charlie. And put a seat belt on. Safety first."

Tau energized the bus to life, and just before they took off, a face appeared at the window, banging on the bus. Tau switched open the door, and Zu swung their head inside.

"I'm coming. She's my sister too!"

Before they even left the city, all the people on the bus settled into the dully excited energy only a school bus could create, half the occupants invested in their own spirited conversations, the other half gazing with anticipation as the world rolled by outside. Charlie looked out along with the latter, anxious but intent to see his daughter and warn her about all of it. He'd no idea what good that warning would do, but she had to know. She had to be given the choice. By the time they reached the bridge that crossed over the bay, Charlie was out of his seat belt and standing.

"Uncle Charlie, you got to sit down, man."

"Why do you and everyone keep calling me 'uncle'?"

"Respect automatically makes you family, Unc. And I respect my elders. What you thinking you gonna find in Orange Beach anyway? Ain't nothing but a bunch a Toms dressed like fucking soccer moms and restaurant managers—Carltons and fake-ass Meg Ryans everywhere."

"I'm surprised you know who Meg Ryan is."

"You joking? *When Harry Met Sally* bops. That shit got me through high school."

Charlie realized he'd never imagined Tau as anything other than angry. Never imagined him as a child who passed notes to his crushes and said funny things.

"All right, nephew," Charlie said, aware of the great honor "uncle" was to receive. "What should I be expecting in Orange Beach?"

Tau looked at Charlie, his forehead wrinkled in creases. "Disappointment."

Tau focused back on the road. The bus rolled forward, and they seemed to hover in the vacancy of what Tau said for nearly an hour.

But then, slowly, the scenery changed from natural beach to man-made structures. As they arrived at the edge of town, Charlie saw the first functioning McDonald's he'd seen since he was a child and felt his mouth salivate at the thought of a Big Mac and fries. Out the window, he saw folks jogging along the beach with dogs on leashes, farmers markets packed with people filling straw bags with vegetables and fruits.

"Is that a farmers market?"

"Yeah, but we're the farmers," Nona answered. "We give it to them for free and they sell it back to each other."

Charlie saw surfers toting their boards under their arms and heard the growl of motorcycles carrying leather-clad people like a school of metal fish. American flags flew on every post and in every yard. And when Charlie saw police officers in full uniform, he sat down in his seat, dizzied with a terror he could not name. If the machine could not be calibrated, all these people would be gone.

"Don't worry, Unc. They hate it when we come, but they always glad we came. Who you think makes sure the Starbucks and McDonald's keep running? We have teams across the state clearing out freezers and making sure they have shit delivered here every month. Thinking of them like refugees helps me help them. They need us. They always have." Tau stood up to address the bus. "All right, you young motherfuckers, this ain't no sightseeing tour. We're here to find Sidney and Fela. If you get off the bus, that's what we doing. Otherwise stay ya ass here. Don't go sneaking off trying to get mocha lattes or some kinda shit. You hear me? Now, c'mon."

Charlie didn't wait to see how many people followed him off the bus before he charged down the well-manicured main drag looking for his daughter. He didn't stop when he passed the corn dog and snow cone booths that made the air smell like a carnival. He didn't stop when he passed the clothing stores or the beer garden with all the faces that turned to gawk at him. Charlie kept his head moving, searching, looking for his daughter, until he reached where the beach curved and could hear the familiar sound of stump preaching. Charlie saw the tents out on the sand: nothing like a revival to draw in every lost heart. Without hesitation, Charlie marched toward the tents. Those feelings consumed him such that he didn't become aware of himself again until he stood before a pulpit swarmed in shocked and staring eyes. He didn't realize he'd spoken—shouted—interrupting the service, until a voice shot down to him like a whip.

"Calm yourself. This is God's house, and your daughter is not in this place."

The speaker, Charlie saw, was a lean, well-dressed, preacher standing on a stage wreathed in flowers. He glared down, and the look he gave Charlie, more than anything else in Orange Beach, most resembled the world before.

Charlie glanced away from the preacher, around at the congregation's cold glares, and pleaded to their better judgment.

"Has anyone here seen my child? Her name is Sidney—"

"I've told you," the preacher said. "Leave now. She is not here. Leave or else I will have the police escort you—"

"Ain't nobody gonna be doing that!" Tau's voice shook the room. "We just here looking for our brother and sister. And this man is asking for your help."

Charlie spun around to find everyone from the bus, all those lovely black faces, standing with him. Among them, Tau exuded the most formidable power and strength Charlie had ever seen. All that rage shaped into a hammer and a spear.

"And I guess you'd bring all of Mobile down to stop us from our worship?"

"No, Padre," Tau answered. "We didn't come for trouble. But we ain't leavin' 'til my uncle gets a little hospitality. Otherwise trouble it'll be. And I'm the last motherfucker you want trouble with."

"I told you, your daughter is not here—"

"But she was." The woman's voice came from the front of the crowd, and when Charlie saw her face, her blond hair pulled tight and green eyes blazing, he knew she was the one who laid the path for Sidney. "Sidney was here."

"Agnes."

"Follow me," she said, turning quickly and disappearing out the side of the tent. Charlie glanced back at the others holding their ground, Tau never taking his eyes off the preacher, and Charlie followed where Agnes led.

When Charlie reached her, Agnes lounged in a nearby hospitality tent. He stepped in just as she lit a hand-rolled cigarette and closed her eyes to suck a deep drag. The sigh that followed filled the air with smoke.

"Damn, do I miss Virginia Slims," she said. "Haven't had a pack since I left Wisconsin. I miss a good steak too—surf and turf—I'd stab a man for that."

"You said my daughter was here?"

"That's right. Came proclaiming her father's innocence."

"She came to show you the letter."

"You know, I was there the night it happened. Thomas and I had just started dating. I saw them handcuff you in the back of the ambulance. Never seen Thomas so scared, not before or after. But I came to know his lying face. The face I saw that night and every time your name ever came up—well, that was something else. Like a dog cornered and wild. He would've defended himself until death. And I suppose that's just what he did." She thumbed her cigarette to the floor and stomped it out. "I was raised in Kenosha. There, you're either white or you're not. I knew what I really was and nobody had to tell me. I was passing already, of course, but I could feel it. In my mouth, you see? In how I learned to speak and not to speak. How to tilt it the right way—show disgust, or shock, or fear. It was all in the mouth. When I was young, there was only one black child in my school. He was the son of the janitor, Big Albert, who himself was the son of the janitor before him, Big Albert Sr. Their progeny didn't reach their size, so he never grew out of being Little Albert. We all just called him Little. The boys treated Little so badly. Truly terrible. All the time. Beat him. Spit on him. They would even kidnap him and pretend they were going to hang him. Put the noose around his neck and everything. I'd watch and keep my mouth shut. Our high school was the Screaming Eagles. Even had an actual eagle mascot that would fly over our games. 'Be Better Today Than Yesterday,' that was our motto . . . though I can't say anyone ever abided by it." Her eyes sparkled of tears when finally she looked at Charlie. "After the event, I saw Little. Seemed like he and I were the last people in the whole city. He had that eagle in his hands, holding it like a baby. He looked right at me and said, 'Be better than you were yesterday.'" Tears streamed down her face, but she never took her eyes off Charlie. "Sidney showed me Elizabeth's letter. Even if she hadn't, I wish I had the courage to tell you how sorry I am."

"The time for apologies done long passed. Where is my daughter?"

Her eyes looked shocked, but her mouth smiled. "She left with that Mobile boy."

"Fela."

"I don't know. But I know she was running from him."

"From him?"

"Somebody told her that his daddy—Alabama's self-proclaimed king—is the one who killed her family. Hit the switch on his little science experiment and killed everyone."

"Why the fuck would you tell her that?"

"Didn't say I told her. What you can't seem to understand is that this country was better the way it was. We feel the need to go back. Sidney can try and deny it, and she'll become just another Little too. Why do you think this city is growing every day with people who want things the way they used to be? You won't change that. You can't. Nobody can."

"You could've helped Little. See, you don't get it. The world has already changed—yanked right out of the hands of anybody trying to go backward—*be* backward. It changed. Period and forever. What you're scared of is the burden of changing yourself along with it. And that's your problem, not Sidney's."

Charlie started to leave, and Agnes stopped him with a few more words: "You loved her, didn't you? Elizabeth?"

Elizabeth. Her name was still a ghost on his skin, but he no longer feared ghosts. Regret gave phantoms all their power, and no more forgiveness languished in Charlie's body to be possessed.

"You can't turn the machine on again," she continued. "It broke the world before. It'll break it again."

"If healing our wounds breaks the world, then let it break."

When he returned to the main tent, the others waited where he'd left them, only there was another familiar face, young Fela.

With difficulty, Fela told Charlie the truth. He'd given Sidney the keys to his truck. He let her go. "She wanted to figure things out," Fela told him. "Who am I to try and stop someone from what they need?"

"At least she didn't start walking like the rest of those fools. Do you know which way she went?"

"I don't know. North? But once she gets to the interstate, she could go anywhere."

Charlie muscles tightened. "We have to follow her, Tau. We have to try."

"Uncle, you want us to take this bus all over Alabama with all these kids inside?"

"She may not even be in Alabama by now, Tau!"

"More to my point."

"I can't just leave my daughter out there by herself. I'm her father.

She has to know. I've got to protect her like no one ever protected me. You understand?"

"I do understand, Uncle. I really do. But we also have a bus full of kids. We can't just go hauling them around and you know it."

"Then what do you want me to do? Leave my daughter out there by herself?"

"Maybe that's the real decision, Uncle Charlie," Nona said. "Sidney needs space and time for her own sake. But you get my father's machine to work, and you'll be connected to her no matter where she is. Power the radio, and you'll find her."

Or I'll lose her, Charlie worried. *Or I'll lose her.*

39

OVER THE NEXT twenty-four hours, Charlie worked on the machine, digging up the thermal monitors at the bases of the obelisks and churning through stacks of articles, essays, and patents. He couldn't calibrate it, but if he didn't at least try, he might never see his daughter again. Over the course of the day dozens of people came to offer their services: strong arms to lift and dig, strong minds to test and offer insight, even some just to bring fresh juice and food. He worked and tinkered every possible way he knew and arrived at a singular conclusion: the machine was built as well as the radio could be built. Though old and rusting in some places, the machine was a sturdy fusion of ancient technologies and modern forms, so crafted as to not even feel to have been made as much as discovered, less *in* the world than *of* it. As far as Charlie could tell, the machine functioned as efficiently as trees. It did what it was there to do, and though the machine worked, the problem was unchanged: no power source he knew could activate it fully.

Charlie tried everything he knew about solar power. Nothing came close. Still, every time he wanted to give up, he remembered seeing Little with his hand gripped around Sidney and imagined her walking into the ocean to never return. The vulnerability of being a father revealed itself. As soon as Sidney fell into his arms, he was hers. Days blurred as he worked, time again seeming free flowing, Charlie unable to settle into sleep for fear he'd already lost his daughter.

"Force of will won't make it work. You need to take a break."

Charlie looked up to see Vivian, Nona, and Seraphin. Vivian stepped toward Charlie.

"I won't pretend to know how electricity works. But I know it's been here long before anybody thought to put it in a light bulb. It's all around us all the time. Not in a wire. Same goes for the answers you're looking for. You won't find them working without a break."

"I can't take a break. I have to find a way to power this thing."

"Take a walk, Charlie." Seraphin's expression left no space to debate.

Charlie sighed. He was tired. All the hours he'd given, and he had no results to show. A walk started to sound like medicine for mystification. Vivian winked at him on her way to the house as Nona followed, not before Seraphin tossed a nod back at him that arrived like confirmation.

Midmorning sun blazed as Charlie stepped out into the street, wandering through the king's neighborhood of colorful bungalows and cottages. Charlie peeked into window after window at families passing steaming breakfasts across the dining tables, through to backyards where kids played and drank from garden hoses, up on porches where fathers put clippers to their sons' heads, cleaning up fades and edges, teaching lessons in a soft voice with every stroke. He walked onto Dauphin Street, where readiness for Mardi Gras settled into a quieter, anticipatory tone. Still, everywhere and in everything, expressions of blackness shined. Shirtless boys, skin aglow under orange sun, tore up a basketball court in a full-court game. Back and forth they went, jumping, shouting, sprinting—moves as dynamic as they were graceful—shoulders shining, collarbones and chests superhuman. Fire raged nearby under a black pot, frying redfish and chicken; someone shucked oysters, left raw to be sucked out of a half shell. Charlie heard music everywhere. The day itself seemed to beat, the air humming, leaves whistling a song. And there was dancing in the bop of every step. Dancing in the smiles of people Charlie passed. Dancing even in the stillness of the old men playing chess on park benches—spirits in a two-step. Out in the park grass, four pairs of hands spun braids into the hair of a single girl's head, twisting out like roots but also like branches, and Charlie ached to sit among them and listen to their stories as his own. Sunglasses and leopard print, colors and compositions—Charlie observed how every person's style expressed the inside out, every decision in shoes and hair and jewels played out in the people he passed as if their very souls were on display. Kids zipped by him on bicycles, popping wheelies to prove they'd already tamed danger and wore it as gold necklaces on their necks. Black expressions, Charlie saw, spilled out as they did back in the Yard, covering the city in sublime dynamism. Sidney was never exposed to these wonders. She was taught to distance herself from its power. But what if he'd been there to teach her how to wear her soul? How different her life would have been to know the stories in the curls of her hair. Would she still carry his conflict? Would she come to see her darkness as elemental, magic woven into her essence? Would she accept herself completely? And, in teaching her, would he have learned to accept himself?

Charlie walked on, humbled that he'd not seen before the beauty of these black lives on full display. The creativity, love, and power intuitive with nature. Black bodies harboring all the magical qualities of soil.

Downtown, Charlie found a group of children, barefoot, sprinting up the side of a stone wall then kicking off, backflipping over and back down to the ground. A dozen of them, boys and girls, leaping, laughing, and running. The building, several stories tall, held a mural on one side painted nearly as tall as the building itself. The mural made up a collage of faces. Some faces Charlie recognized: Malcolm X, Duke Ellington, Lorraine Hansberry, Martin Luther King Jr., Nelson Mandela, Angela Davis, and others. But the painted wall contained twice as many faces he didn't know, all looking down at him with intense eyes. Written across the center of the mural were words, poetry, Charlie read but couldn't yet decode: IN THE END, BLACK IS THE SUN, AND SO WE RISE.

Charlie contemplated the mural, trying to sear every painted face in his mind. Then he took the fire escape on the side of the building up the ten stories to the roof. There, above the city, Charlie lay on his back. The sun was high, bright and hot, and the sky cloudless. He stared at the sun until his eyes hurt. He was thinking about Africa as he drifted off to sleep. He imagined his daughter washing her feet in the Nile. He dreamt that Africa was the great mother. Her body was made up of every woman he'd ever known, even Elizabeth. But Africa's face looked like his mother's. The sun made a halo behind her head, though could not silhouette her features. And it was the moon, glowing and visible, that was her heart. Celestial, that moon beamed love in every direction. *And in the end,* she said, *black is the sun, and so we rise.*

We are the feeling folk, Charlie thought, *who sparkle of magic and vigor. Who laugh like laughter is a gift to be given and sing like we have always been the chorus of angels. The feeling folk who allow the skin of the world to glide over us, rugged and tender, absorbed into the gospel of our empathies. The feeling folk who dance to songs in our heads because we know those songs source from a heart beating since the beginning. The feeling folk who heal right side in, wielding a power to make a history of horrors evaporate like steam from a stewpot. Power to make any place home.*

So, in his dream, Charlie thought only of *us*. The noble *We*. Not our dreams either, or even hopes. But the enormity. All the colors and energies and outcomes swallowed up to make a community of individuals never alone. No picket fences or pageantry, just open doors and all the space and time one needs to be oneself. *We are energies,* Charlie dreamt, *constantly exchanging and mixing and charging.*

When Charlie opened his eyes there was no longer one big sun in the sky but many faraway stars glittering above him. Day to night. And suddenly, everything he'd questioned made sense.

He'd been seeing the answer all wrong. They all had.

He looked up at that night sky, twinkling with life, and he felt the answer with confidence that jumped him to his feet. He knew precisely how to power the machine.

The euphoria he felt was equaled only by the terrifying reality of knowing, if he turned it on, he'd no way to stop the signal from taking his daughter.

40

CONFLICT.

As she drove, conflict knotted Sidney's world in irreducible complexities. Knots she was much too tired to attempt to unravel.

Every radio station, both AM and FM, returned the fuzz of static, and the best she could do to cut the density of silence was let the windows down, humid, sour air flowing loudly in and out of the cab. Sidney drove north until she saw signs for Interstate 10. Sailor had called the interstate an artery, she remembered, laying a navigable strip from one side of the country to the other. When she reached the interchange, she recalled all the times in school when she heard about the American frontier. Manifest Destiny. She'd heard the story of how Americans braved the west, cutting through the stone of the world to shape their dreams into reality. Even then she imagined great mountains and herds of bison, wild horses sprinting over stiff terrain, rivers of gold and all possibility—all the effort of the American dream, in the end, peaking to a house in someplace like Malibu overlooking the Pacific with its back to the nation.

Sidney sped past Mobile's glittering skyline, careful not to think of the warmth of her father's chest or the ease with which Nona called her "sister." She maintained her speed through Biloxi, where the sky took on the colors of the casino lights painting the air above the shore just south. Not until she saw signs for Louisiana did she ease gently off the gas just as her father taught her. There, in the middle of the road, finally, she wept.

Her tears grieved all the holes in her history. Up until then, her life was all black and white, leaving her unprepared for so much gray. Had not her mother loved her unconditionally? Had not her family always been kind and gentle? Since the day her mother's ancestors arrived selling bundles of lavender to make their way, did they not fulfill a dream through hard work over generations? But what of her father's ancestors, who did not arrive at all but were stolen, who bled, burned, and hanged to have their dreams deferred? Had they not suffered? Had they not endured? Did the crimes against their humanity not deserve atonement? If not by their own hands, then by the command of the very earth itself? In Sidney's mind, all these things were true and false at the same time. So she wept, caught in trying to add up the ludicrous arithmetic of broken knowledge. She wept knowing upon that flawed complication the framework of her life was built. Her life and, indeed, the framework uniting all the land rolling before her. *It's all wrong,* she felt. Wrong without counterarguments, or mysticism, or blurred edges.

So she drove, past Slidell and New Orleans, past Baton Rouge, stopping finally just outside Lafayette in a place called Iota. Not a soul occupied the town, the doors of cars and homes still open, anticipant. She found charging stations in the lot of a Walmart that looked untouched since before the event. She pulled the truck in and set it to charge as she'd seen her father do. She had no supplies, and because she'd no plan aside from driving until it felt right to stop, she braved the Walmart.

The automatic doors surprised her when they slid open at her arrival.

Inside, easy listening music played throughout the store. Most of the fluorescent lights burned, though whole sections where the dead lights had not been replaced, and would never be, created pockets of shadow. Still, the dull music and the eerie electric hum made the cavernous store as intimate as a haunting. Sidney checked three different carts for the quietest, careful not to disturb the serenity with noise, then crept the aisles checking prepackaged food for expiration dates. Rancid smells plumed from the frozen food and drinks, but she found all the bottled water still untouched and took a few gallons, but no more than she needed.

From the pharmacy, she gathered enough medicine and first aid pieces to make a kit. She found nothing in cosmetics that resembled what the women in Mobile used to keep her hair from matting, nor anything that could maintain the glow in her skin.

Sidney moved quietly over to sporting goods in search of a tent, lights, batteries, and sleeping bags. She stopped when she found a wall of rifles.

She hadn't imagined she'd ever hold a rifle again or have a desire to do so. But there they were, hung up above her like monuments. She did miss the power and the protection extended through the length of their barrels. She climbed over the counter and took down a bolt action. All that Rick taught her about the function of the weapon returned to her hands the second she felt the trigger.

Then something shifted not far from her, and her gun snapped up, aimed by the memory in her muscles. She wasn't alone in the store. But as she glimpsed the frightened eyes staring up at her, she saw that she was the only one holding a gun.

A woman not much older than Sidney lounged back in a tent, holding a book in her hand. "I'd put my hands up," the woman said, "but I thought we were done with all that."

The rifle felt as hot as shame in Sidney's grip. She dropped the weapon on the counter, stung by the memory of her father's words the last time she pulled a gun on someone: *We gotta be better than this.*

"You scared me," Sidney said resolutely. "What are you doing down there?"

"Reading poetry," the young woman answered. "And minding my own business."

"I'm sorry about the gun. I just . . . didn't think anyone else was in the store."

"*You* came here, didn't you? Shouldn't surprise you that someone else might've had the same idea." The woman sat up in the tent where Sidney could see her. A shade lighter than Sidney's, the girl's skin was peppered in freckles. "Besides, these stores are the sanctuaries for people passing through. Food, supplies, and most of 'em still have power. Better than staying in some dead person's house. You should expect to see people, y'know. This is as good a place as any to stop along the way."

"Along the way to where?"

"Mobile, of course. Ain't that where we're all headed? Mardi Gras is in two days, and it's in the air. Something's happening. Been feeling it for days."

"I don't feel anything."

"You sure felt the need to point a rifle at a stranger."

"That's . . . different."

"Huh." Her tone forced Sidney to look at the rifle on the counter. Sidney knew she'd pointed the barrel without thinking, a reaction at the edge of instinctive. Except that reaction wasn't her instinct. That level of defense was something learned, trained—believed. She stood on the counter and placed the gun back up on the wall rack.

The girl, still shrouded in the shadows of the tent, watched Sidney until the gun was latched, nodded her agreement, then turned casually back to her book. In the subtlest of ways, the girl reminded Sidney of Nona. Something gravitational to the point of enchanting, Sidney *wanted* to be near the girl. Connected to her even, just like she felt with Nona. Sisters.

"You said you were reading poetry?" Sidney asked. "Would you read one to me?"

The only part of the girl to move was her eyes, flicking up to Sidney for an instant then back to the page. She read, then, with a lilting voice:

I sailed in my dreams to the Land of Night
Where you were the dusk-eyed queen,
And there in the pallor of moon-veiled light
The loveliest things were seen . . .
A slim-necked peacock sauntered there
In a garden of lavender hues,
And you were strange with your purple hair
As you sat in your amethyst chair
With your feet in your hyacinth shoes.
Oh, the moon gave a bluish light
Through the trees in the land of dreams and night.
I stood behind a bush of yellow-green
And whistled a song to the dark-haired queen.

She turned to Sidney. "That's Gwendolyn Bennett. It's called 'Fantasy.'"

"It's beautiful."

"Enough to make anybody feel something."

"That it is. More than enough."

After saying goodbye, Sidney went on getting beef jerky, matches, and air fresheners that smelled like lavender. With her car filled with the supplies she needed, she winced passing the empty checkout lanes without paying, then stepped back out into the afternoon sun, ready to drive until she reached the water.

41

SERAPHIN'S DOOR OPENED as Charlie approached. Her silhouette, revealed in the doorway, created as angelic a shape as Charlie had ever seen, as if heaven was not made of light but the infinite canvas of space and she was an entrance.

"You bless me this evening, Charlie. Come in."

A somber Charlie stepped inside, and the warm smell of frankincense, candle flames stirring shadow and gold, welcomed him. Seraphin pulled him close and held him until he sank into the heat of her body, her hand stroking the top of his head. Whispers filled the house. Whispers from every dark corner, the walls, brushing up against Charlie's ears.

"Your ancestors are here," Seraphin said. "They've been waiting for you to talk to them."

She gestured toward the coffee table, where candles illuminated a deck of cards next to a handful of what looked like teeth and small bones. *Sit at the feet of feminine energy,* Charlie remembered Hosea say. "This is all for me?"

"Are you ready?"

"I can't say for sure that I believe in magic."

"You say that like belief is a requisite." As she shuffled the cards, a honeyed spice smell rose up like an enchantment in Charlie's nose. "The cards are not magic, Charlie, they're just totems for the magic inside you. Magic that's always been there. The teeth and bones are from a possum. I use them for divination. See, everything's energy. Our whole lives are made up of sharing energy between each other. Something lingers when energy transforms out of this living state to another state. These bones are fresh enough to still influence the transformed energy that left this three-dimensional world."

"You're talking about death?"

"More like moving between dimensions. I have possum bones because their consciousness isn't particularly fussy about what it'll show you. Also have some of the possum's teeth here, because they are the nearest imprint left of its identity. Like a fingerprint, all a possum does is eat, so that's all it knows, and that's all we need."

"Need to do what?"

"To listen to what all these souls watching you have to say," she said, closing her eyes. Then the energy in the room changed, tightened and warmed, pressurized. "*Papa Legba, Marasa, Èzili Freda—*" She stopped and sucked in her breath. Charlie had not even realized she'd already pulled a card, one that lay before him facing up. "That's unusual. An ancestors spread is typically five cards. But tonight, the ancestors saw fit to send you one message." She touched the card. "The hierophant card."

The card, Charlie saw, depicted a man carrying runes and books while, at the hierophant's back, a crowned priestess watched over him, her face gentle and pleased. Charlie took the card and studied its art and stock. "What does it mean?"

"My mother used to say the hierophant is the knower. But the card is more complex than that. It's about choice. The hierophant is the student and the teacher. A translator, a conduit between the ancestors and those who'll receive the message the hierophant brings. The hierophant knows shared traditions, heritage, history, values, and holds the choice to give that message to those who need to hear it or not."

Again, the energy shifted in the room. The pressure pulsed out and back before settling twice as intensely as before. Charlie looked up at Seraphin and saw the whites of her eyes were shrouded in shadow. When she spoke, Charlie nearly startled out of his seat to hear his own mother's voice coming out of her mouth. Layered in the sound, he heard his grandmother's voice. And other voices, of all the women of his line all at once.

"Come out, Charlie. Come out. Not all those other Charlies. Not the scared Charlie, the Charlie that don't think he's worth much. Not the Charlie that only see himself through other people's eyes. Charlie, Charlie. My Charlie. Come out."

"How is this possible?"

"You know."

"This isn't real."

"Where's my Charlie? Come out, Charlie."

Charlie righted himself, sat in his chair and watched Seraphin's body sway while her eyes stayed still. He felt the signal in the air around him, like he'd been placed back under the power of the king's machine. "Momma?"

"There he is. My Charlie. What's troubling you, son?"

Charlie had no real words to answer the question. What troubled him at the precipice of changing the world was the same thing that had troubled him all his life. The conflict. She asked to see the real Charlie, and he wasn't sure that Charlie even existed anymore, swallowed up in the darkness of that conflict. Back across the bulk of his life, no one ever really saw that Charlie.

As if she could hear his thoughts, she said, "Charlie's not gone. Our stories are written in your skin. When they see Charlie, they see us, and they have to turn away. When they see Charlie, they see a truth they can't accept. But just because they can't look at Charlie don't mean Charlie ain't there. Charlie has to see Charlie."

Charlie closed his eyes. For once, and as deeply as he could, he investigated the heart of that conflict, a darkness so powerful it inspired an entirely different kind of seeing. And Charlie saw. It was not conflict, but a beauty of his spirit buried in conflict. Like a great treasure of the world, hoarded and entombed so as to never know its worth. Down deep, in the heart of that darkness, Charlie found himself. Darkness vibrant. Joy. Creativity. Dynamism. Brilliance. And more love than could ever be buried. That's what Charlie saw. Darkness that generated a special kind of light. Saw the world with a perspective that made life truer. Made its every measure magnificent. Led him with empathy and compassion. He saw blackness not monolithic but wide, deep, offering all the space required to be included. All the space to imagine, experience, and become. Charlie had given that up, all because someone else refused to see him. What he thought was conflict, he understood, was not the problem but the answer. And it had been the answer all along.

In the darkness behind his eyes, his thoughts went to Elizabeth and her brother. What Charlie would do next was not about forgiving them. They didn't deserve forgiveness. He'd found himself, and he would not allow that Charlie to be lost again.

The machine could not be calibrated. Shouldn't be. But Charlie accepted that he could find his own frequency within the signal's power. Through him, the signal could be channeled by its capacity to love without condition, harmonized through culture and community, and reminded that it was deserving of more than retribution, but a full existence prismatic with color. The machine healed Charlie. Charlie could heal the machine.

He knew then exactly how he'd do it. Under the twinkling watch of ancestors, the black energy of Mardi Gras would power the machine. The machine would give blackness back to itself. And Charlie would deliver the message. Because while Agnes said the machine would break the world again, it would be in Charlie's hands. And Charlie only knew how to fix things.

He opened his eyes to find Seraphin back to herself, holding the hierophant card.

"Are you ready, Charlie?"

"I think we all are."

42

SIDNEY DROVE ON through the blaze of Texas, the heat and the dryness forcing her windows down. Vast emptiness stretched out in every direction. No cars shared the road with her. Empty barns stuck out against the horizon, and even the windmills barely turned, cows grazing in the distance the only movement at all. To her surprise, in that expanse she picked up a radio station playing classic hits, the lyrics of which lived in her psyche, having heard most of them in jingles and commercials all her life. Marvin Gaye sang about what he heard through grapevine, the O'Jays invited her to a love train, Bill Withers begged to be used. She was grateful for the company and distraction of their blues.

She drove until the night became so dark it revealed more stars than she'd ever seen at once. Big stars, small ones, even the dust of space, bluish against the black, making art of the sky. Onto the dry dirt shoulder she pulled over, got out, and lay back in the bed of the truck to watch the celestial display, the act of being outside becoming a habit. More lights in the sky sparkled than she could ever hope to count. Her father had called the stars messages. Signals, he said, moving through time. As she looked up at the theater of constellations before her, she wondered what all these messages were saying. She imagined her father back in Mobile, looking up at those same stars. She tried her best to create a new message to sparkle among them, a message to her father wedged in the cup of the Big Dipper.

"I'm okay, don't worry," she said into the darkness. "I just need time and space."

She left a message for her mother in the bow of Orion's weapon.

"I wish you'd protected him the way you loved me."

She fell asleep trying to burn those thoughts into lights in the sky. When she woke, all the stars consolidated into the lone, hot Texas sun at her feet. The magic of night became the consequences of day. So, she kept driving west.

The width of Texas took nearly all the power from Fela's truck. For unremarkable hours Texas whizzed by, all orange dirt and distant farms.

She kept her speed, slowing only once near El Paso, where the sky bruised with a flaming storm, and beneath the storm a cluster of Indigenous people in brightly colored dresses and tasseled robes danced. Her chest fluttered when she saw them. All of the spirit of Texas prevailed in their movements.

She stopped several times in the Texas glare, pulling over to sleep when the desert light burned. By the time she arrived in New Mexico, she could no longer feel water in the air. On that dry road, Sidney fought herself from questioning just how far the event forced so many to walk to find a body of water. She imagined bloody feet and blistered faces crossing the border into Arizona, where the land transformed Martian red.

An hour into that alien terrain, what she saw next pulled her off to the side of the road and out of the truck. Hundreds of them, maybe thousands, all dressed in white, striding silent through the red-orange landscape. Walkers. Seeking redemption by walking themselves into death.

"We are called home to our father's house." Through a bullhorn, a voice carried over the crowd of walkers. "We walk in the path of those who went before us. We walk until we stand in the house of our father."

Sidney could see their faces fighting the pain in their bodies to look serene, mimicking the same placid listening she'd seen in her mother's eyes.

"We are called home," the voice repeated, "to sit at the feet of our father."

Sidney climbed up on the top of the truck bed and watched them, aware just how easily she could have been among them. They'd walk all the way to the edge of death and judge themselves on the strength to cross. She wondered if they'd feel shame when they couldn't. Like her, all they knew, because all they'd been trained, was how well to suffer. And perhaps be rewarded by the consolation of endurance. How does anyone begin to free themselves from the cycle of that type of conflict? Such struggle assumes an enemy one cannot punch or kick or kill. One that ravages memory and future alike. One no amount of apologies could satisfy. Conflict one lives with and tries, mightily, to live better than it demands. Her mother had tried to give her a better life. Her father had tried to give her a wider perspective. But that enemy and its conflict remained. Like the walkers, she too had conformed her life to the shape of its negative space, defined in the contrast of a bright white background.

Sidney softened. Where her mother was blind, she understood she'd have to train her eyes to see. Where her father raged, she would have to convince herself to love. The enemy would always remain, but her life could wrap its ragged edges with her softness one day, protecting her children from it, and their children and theirs, until no one left in the world could feel the pain the conflict sought to inflict. But they would never forget. They *could* never forget.

Again, she wondered if some part of *us* died with *them* and, through *us*, a part of *them* lived on.

She watched the walkers until they became a caravan of ghosts in the daylight, wishing, all the while, that she had the power to turn their march east, to lead them to a farm outside Mobile where someone with a good heart could sit in front of them and help them feel the enormity of their value. Of their lives. Of their futures.

She drove on, as fast and as far as she could. The sun set in the distance. When she reached the end of the road, the moon hung full and high, stars jeweled the sky, and, finally, the Pacific Ocean extended immense before her.

Not a single person shared the shore. Not a single cross stood in memorial. The shore offered neither sandcastle nor footstep. Moonlight alone illuminated otherwise black ocean and black sky. Last shore of this land, but not the last shore of the world. Water before her reached out and out, and everywhere else reached back. Sidney had never imagined Kenya or India or Brazil. She'd never considered how their flower fields smelled on dewy mornings. Never pondered the favor of constellations at the tips of their mountains. And the people? Did the event change their world as it changed hers? Did their skies sag with the same burden as the skies above America? Did they ever doubt the *us* in their differences? All the shores of all the world and through all time, connected in the night by the same dark water and the same dark sky. She smiled at the thought.

Fully clothed, Sidney waded out into the water. First her feet, allowing them to sink into the pull of the undertow. Then her knees and thighs, the night chill settling through her. She walked out until her body began to float. Water in her ears dulled the sound of wind and waves, and slowed the world. There, afloat, she didn't feel confused or angry or lonely. The ocean was *us*. The sky was *us*. The vast and ever-changing *us*. Connecting continents. Speaking the language of the stars. Black water. Black sky.

Sidney closed her eyes, drifting gently between two forevers.

Free.

In Mobile, they'd just be starting Mardi Gras. She took her mother's letter from her pocket and let the paper catch the current of the sea. Drift away. Yes, Mardi Gras would be wrapping them all in a celebration of life. They'd be floating up in dance and sound and color. Floating just like her.

And then, in her heart, in her spirit, like a note played on the strings of her nervous system, Sidney felt the music of trumpets.

43

IN THE DEAD of night, and at Charlie's command, the king gathered nearly a hundred strong-bodied craftspeople to his driveway. Charlie tried his best to explain what he'd discovered.

"It's as simple as it is complex," he told them. "The sun ain't the only source of power."

He explained how they'd only ever looked to the daylight for the power they needed. But he discovered that they could find all the power they ever needed at night. Charging the machine would take more than one sun; it would require many. *Tomorrow night*, Charlie emphasized, the machine had to be ready for Mardi Gras. In Charlie's head, the plan all made sense even when he couldn't explain with clarity. The first step was to get the machine out of being hidden away in the king's garage.

"Most of Mobile is already under sea level," Charlie pointed out. "We have to get higher. Above the tree line. Above the city."

"The highest point is Forest Hill, but it's outside of the city a good ways," a woman among the craftspeople responded. "There's a tall hillside there. We can put the machine at the top of it."

"It'll take a while to ground it as deep as it is now," another craftsman added.

"We don't have a while. We have a day." Charlie stressed that the machine had to be ready for Mardi Gras. Ready for full power. "You have to understand, the machine is a transmitter and receiver at the same time." It was black people themselves, Charlie expressed, being happy, activated, and together that created one of the primary elements of the machine's power. Receive *and* transmit. Heads were scratched and eyes blinked, confused, all around Charlie. In the end, Charlie stopped trying to explain.

"Dig it out. Get it to the highest point. And have it ready for tomorrow night." The clarity and force of Charlie's voice got legs moving and the power of the people put into action.

As the craftspeople went to work, Charlie and Herald toiled through the night running tests and calculations. Charlie's theory arrived at a simple conclusion: we, all of us, had been blinded by the light. All power on Earth was built around what it could exploit. It leveraged, burned, absorbed, stored, and monetized every ounce of what the natural world could produce. Even solar power tapped the one sun in the sky, all systems and studies based on the measurements of monetization. One way, one sun. And we were all blinded. But then Charlie woke up on the roof and saw a night sky so full of stars he couldn't count them if he tried every night for the rest of his life. We'd been looking to the daylight to save us, when all it did was hide and diffuse the power. Night waited for our eyes to come home. Charlie understood the stars didn't just twinkle and burn—they sang, just like us. Across the dark distance of space every star vibrated, a song belted through time—the music of life—offering more power than ever produced. All our ancestors looked up at the same night sky. In the dark, under ancient, cosmic sparkle, they found their gifts. In the dark they evolved math and poetry and song, found the language of themselves. In the dark, they discovered infinite power, black power, a heritage of and beyond the world. With that in mind,

Charlie and Herald worked to develop a new system of energy that was neither thermal nor photovoltaic, but musical. Drawing power from the very vibration of the stars and the dynamism of our lives.

"It's still a theory," Charlie said to Herald. "But if we can get this to work, the machine will get all the power it needs to heal all of us, just like your father believes. Just like Vivian says. No matter where we are in this country, we'll look up at the sky and feel something. Connection. Hope. Heritage too."

"What about the calibration?"

"It has to be grounded, channeled through a source—tuned, in a way. See, we are connected, but our experiences are singular. Going to prison the way I did was about the worst kind of existence a person could have. But now, I'm seeing things differently."

"You said it needed to be channeled. What's the source?"

"I am."

Herald crossed over wires, realizing the logic in Charlie's theories of a focused tune and an unlimited power source. "It's like poetry, what you've discovered here, Uncle Charlie," Herald said. "All this power hiding in the dark all this time."

"It wasn't hiding. The world conditioned us not to see it."

"See what, Uncle?"

"The marvelous condition of being black. And that's the most important thing I'll ever give my daughter."

"Well, it's ready, Uncle Charlie. I've run all the tests. I've calculated all the numbers. Everything's ready up on Forest Hill too. When the stars come out tonight, Unc, it's time."

Charlie nodded, aware of the weight of what lay before him, feeling very much like a hero. "My mother used to say I was the villain in somebody else's story." Charlie tilted his head high. In the story of his own life, now he held the pen. "Not anymore. Come on. Let's go find my daughter."

The sun dipped down to the base of the horizon as they drove out to Forest Hill. The drive wasn't long but moved slow enough to give Charlie space and time with his thoughts. Outside the window, he watched the damp landscape pass before him, the swoop of herons and hawks against the pink-purple sunset. When his mind reached out to Sidney, he did not imagine her in a place but in a state of mind. He saw her as untethered, floating, liberated to go where and when she wanted toward realizing herself. Able to hear the tolls of her own heart. Able to unearth the roots of her instinct. His only daughter, finally free.

The craftspeople had hauled the king's machine, setting its bulk at the peak of a hillside that surged up from the ground like the beginnings of a mountain.

"It's grounded deep," Herald said. "They know how to get things done. They rooted it all the way to bedrock."

Charlie took the crude steps up to the top, where a makeshift platform had been built around the base. Dozens of craftspeople waited and broke out into applause as Charlie arrived. Fela, Sailor, and Zu stood among them, even Tau, for once smiling, happy to see Charlie.

"You get this thing working," Sailor said, slapping a hand on Charlie's shoulder, "and we're square."

"So I take it you got the gas you wanted?"

"Seems to me that it's about time for all of us to fly." His smirk spilled into a raggedy laugh. "Besides, the queen went on and gave me enough gas to get up in that sky and never come down. So, like I said, we square. Now go on, do what you're here to do."

What I'm here to do, Charlie pondered.

There was nothing special about him or unique. Nothing that suggested he should be the one who could decide for many. But, as he stepped up to the base of the machine, he stood there not to decide for many, but to decide for one. Freedom, connection, heritage, spirit, and a universe of ancestors were his to claim. Better still, his to bequeath. He wielded no power to change the world, but he could change himself.

A man, a maker, an idealist, and a father. Charlie Brunton fixed things. And he put his hand on the radio switch, at last, to fix himself.

From the height of the hillside, Charlie observed the city. The magic of Mardi Gras saturated the streets with the color and energy of our people. The colors seemed to grow brighter, the floats bigger, and the streets more and more crowded. Best of all were the smells wafting up. The flavors of seasoned crawfish boiled into the breeze. Rice and beans, curries, and meats grilled over flames, sweet, savory, earthy, and extravagant. Charlie's mouth wet with hunger.

Different music swam over Charlie with every turn of the wind. Drums, horns, violin, piano, and choir songs flowing as effortlessly as the songs of birds. Charlie watched from above as the growing crowd danced toward downtown. There, the party plumed, filling up with thousands, a great mass of people. From that height he could see the procession of the royal krewes. Their decorated floats barreled down the street, activating the crowd in a wave.

The first float came into view and sent the crowd into a frenzy. Drums boomed in powerful thrusts, preceding a vision Charlie had never seen before. A buffalo float standing two stories tall towered over the people. The beast's horns, its fur, its astonishing muscles, its every detail, meticulously crafted such that Charlie half expected the fabricated animal to huff and stomp into life. All around the float's base, embellished in colorful leather patterns, Choctaw and Cherokee tribe members danced their dance. In circles, to the crack of the drum, they danced a step that kicked up the dirt in the asphalt. In unison, they chanted words that sprinkled a coolness over Charlie's ears. He experienced familiarity in their movements, in their energy. As the great buffalo paraded down Dauphin Street, Charlie cheered, leaning forward to celebrate the gift of their dance.

Then came the Mexican krewe, their dance and their dress, perfectly patterned and symmetrical, until the prismatic colors of their dresses flung into the air like peacock feathers. The men in their embroidered jackets glided as fluidly as water within the pattern of their dance. They stomped and kicked and twirled. Behind them, the float to follow was made into a Mayan pyramid three stories high, atop which their chosen king and queen waved to the crowd. The great pyramid reached out to the edges of the narrow road, wide enough for streetwalkers to touch its base like a prayer.

Dozens of other floats followed, representing in multitudes the partnered nations of the world: Cuba, Haiti, the Dominican Republic, and Mexico. Charlie, so enmeshed in the American experience of his darkness, realized then how much that entanglement influenced his view of the world. He hadn't truly allowed himself to see the similarities in culture, history, and color. Mardi Gras, just like his life, was no singular experience, but the beginnings of the carnival of the world, connecting lands and people. And then a hush dropped over the city.

He felt them long before he saw them.

The king and queen of Mardi Gras. Hosea and Vivian.

The first of their floats was not adorned in jewels or fabrics. Flat and only a few feet above the road, the base of the float was made to mimic the raw red clay of the earth. Upon that raised ground, the queen's coterie stood powerfully in formation, Seraphin and Nona among them. They each wore simple dresses of a single color: red, purple, yellow. Strong stances, chin up, chest out, and unmoved. The coterie stared down the crowd. Charlie held his breath, wishing Sidney could be there, standing in that formation while the drum pounded a heartbeat to vibrate the ground.

Finally, when the coterie broke into dance, the Mobile crowd erupted, as resounding as thunder. The ground shook. Every move the coterie made sent more rumbles through the land, the earth itself trembling with delight. Rhythm, power, grace—their arms swung, legs kicked, backs and shoulders wrenched, both enchanting the crowd and holding their admiration at once.

The music increased and the dance sped, seeming to root into the earth and ascend up among the clouds. To witness so much beauty and ebullience blurred Charlie's vision with tears. And he shouted for them as loud as he could. Roared. All the tension of his darkness exploded out. Roared and roared. Tears unwilling to be held back. Joy like a combustion.

That was the moment Charlie flipped the switch on the receiver, tapping into that astounding black power. The machine hummed to life. Above him, the stars raged, their twinkle seeming almost gleeful. Messages, he thought, the celestial math and mythical music of our culture. He put his hand on the transmitter.

"They feared the night and how the darkness welcomed me. I absorb soil and shadow, the pulse of trees and the hummings of stone. And they feared it. How I absorb even the sun into a power that shines within me. And love without. No matter how deeply they feared the darkness within me. Love without."

"It broke the world," Agnes had told him about the machine. "It'll break it again."

But Charlie only knew how to fix things.

He closed his eyes. He saw Sidney in his mind. She floated somewhere in the sea of her own thoughts, staring up at the very same constellations. He tried to pin a message among the stars just for her.

"No, darling, they're not all gone," he said. "Everything will be okay. You are and have always been all of us."

Charlie switched on the transmitter. *Let them inherit the earth by inheriting themselves.* Connection washed over him as he gazed up at the stars, the energy of the signal flowing through his every experience. A life, even in its limitations, full enough to include all of us. Charlie let his conflict, his darkness, flow out across the world.

The sky has never been empty. History has never been silent. Finally everyone, everywhere, tilted their heads to the sky and heard our trumpets.

Everyone. Everywhere.

Finally heard our trumpets.

Acknowledgments

THEY SAY WRITING is toil in solitude. What they don't tell you is that a village of people stand guard so solitude is possible. And some have been vigilant in keeping space since before the solitude was even necessary. Special thank you to Byrd Leavell. I am so grateful you took a chance with me and that you always honor the work and message. Thank you. Another special thank you to Olivia Taylor Smith. I told you as soon as we met that I felt safe with you editing my work and I meant it. What a fun and rewarding partnership it has been.

I owe huge debts of gratitude to my mother, Mary. I love you, Mom. Thank you for always letting me work at your kitchen table.

My children, Eden, Cayman, Margaux, and Juniper, each one of you uniquely made me a better human and writer. Eden, you'll be next to put your stamp on the world and I for one am thrilled to see what you accomplish. Cayman, in my eyes, son, you are already GOATED.

To my brothers and sisters, my big, big family, thank you for not just believing but *knowing* you'd see yourself in these acknowledgments one day.

Barbara Steele, Sue Ann Tretter, Michelle Giessman, Jim Scroggins, thank you for being more than teachers and coaches, but mentors.

There are too many writers who have given dimension to my life and art to name them all, but one in particular has meant a great deal to me: Toni Morrison. I used to dream that one day I would write something Toni Morrison would enjoy. Something that would inspire her to pat a friend on the shoulder and with a smile say, "Let me tell you about this book I just read. . . ." I didn't get to do that, but I thank you, Mrs. Morrison, for changing the way I saw the world.

Thank you for showing me how to claim where I stand as the center.

And Riann. Well. You know. The answer is and always will be: *every day.*

About the Author

CEBO CAMPBELL is an award-winning, multi-hyphenate creative based in New York and London. He is a winner of the Stories Award for Poetry, and his writings are featured in numerous publications. As cofounder and CCO of the renowned NYC creative agency Spherical, Cebo leads teams of creatives in shaping the best hotel brands in the world. His range of talents as a creative director have sent him all over the globe infusing creativity, from working with the Shakespeare Birthplace Trust in the UK, to concepting the Million Miracles humanitarian campaign throughout Africa and India, to writing and directing the VR short film *Refuge: Triumph in Tulsa*, based on the famed Black Wall Street in Oklahoma. Cebo's expansive work as a writer, designer, and director are powered by a singular mindset: *contribute meaningfully to the culture*. And he does. With everything he touches.

At present, Cebo is likely somewhere in Europe enjoying good whiskey and better conversation.

About the Author